The Doctor

The
Doctor

TOM CONTI

ROBSON BOOKS

First published in Great Britain in 2004 by Robson Books, The Chrysalis Building, Bramley Road, London, W10 6SP

An imprint of Chrysalis Books Group plc

British Library Cataloguing in Publication Data
A catalogue record for this title is available from the British Library.

ISBN 1 86105 795 4

Typeset by SX Composing DTP, Rayleigh, Essex
Printed by Creative Print & Design (Wales), Ebbw Vale

For Kara, Nina, and my new grandson Arthur

Acknowledgements

Embarking on this saga, little did I imagine how many people would be vital to the completion of the voyage. It would never have got out of harbour were it not for my brother-in-law and dear friend, Gordon MacBain FRCS, who generously shared his experiences as a young doctor in the African bush and his subsequent great learning and wisdom as a consultant surgeon. These, and his contribution of some fine story points, cannot be over-valued.

My thanks also to the consultant gynaecologist Anthony Silverstone for introducing me to Kira Phillips, who, prima gravida, kindly shared her thoughts and sensations as she headed towards the Big Ouch. A boy, Rex. Both well.

Dr Adrian Naftalin ran his expert eye over a late draft and corrected some of my inexpert medical terminology.

Sir Anthony Hooper arranged access to the darker recesses of the Old Bailey, and threw me a 'Get Out of Jail' card when I'd boxed myself into a story corner within its walls. Bob Moxon-Browne was extremely helpful with points of law.

My cousin's husband, Wing Commander Ellis Artus, kept me right on Air Force matters and the older fast jets. Dr Ashley Pain corrected my errors in the handling and engineering of light aircraft and supplied me with recently historic aeronautical charts. Isobel McAllister kindly shared her memories of being an air traffic controller on Islay airstrip in the late sixties.

Farquharson's *Textbook of Operative Surgery* and Sir Stanley Davidson's *The Principles and Practice of Medicine* have been constantly by my side.

Lynsey de Paul, told of the existence of the manuscript, was kind enough to mention it to Jeremy Robson, the publisher. His great enthusiasm for the book, his encouragement and support have not only been of great help, but, to this first-timer, rather touching.

I have quoted from 'The Glittering Prizes'. Still in my memory, even after almost thirty years, are many of the wonderful lines of dialogue. I will forever be grateful for Frederic Raphael's brilliance, which gave me a career.

My gratitude also to those who cannot be named.

Hal

Will I be conscious after the impact? Will my brain still function for a few moments even though I'm in bits? Don't think, drive. It'll soon be over. I drive carefully, I've hurt enough people. I imagine what I'll look like. Bone splintered into the frontal lobes, cerebral tissue oozing through the cracked skull, thoracic cavity agape, revealing the heart, convulsing like the wounded animal it is. Fibulas and femurs stabbed through the flesh. I deserve it.

The sun was low. Low like in Africa, on that day of yet another catastrophic decision.

Francesca. Francesca the bold. Francesca the lost. Francesca the most beautiful thing I had ever seen. Francesca the greatest fuck. Francesca the greatest pain in the arse. Francesca, my only love. In another life.

That other life began in the mid sixties, with a lumbering Argosy, a military transport aircraft otherwise known as 'the whistling tit' because of its breast-shaped nose and twin tail boom which whistled, landed in lashing rain and a heavy crosswind. I admired the blokes who drove these winged elephants in often hair-raising conditions. The pilot of this one, like me, had seen service in Aden so knew what it was like to have his hair raised. He was a natural flier, sensing which way the aircraft was going to buck and starting the correction before it did. These were aircraft so different from the Kestrel, now known as the Harrier, the new jet fighter which I could make duck and dive in almost any situation and which, if I had to, I could land on the back of a truck. Not any more. Would I miss it? The excitement, yes. The rest of it? Oh God. Oh God, how could I have done it?

I drove into Cambridge on the bike. It was hell on a night like this but that was part of the attraction. I went into the pub, I've forgotten its name, across from Kings and there she was. A smile with the sun in it, sparkling eyes, the loveliest hair, and energy around her like a rainbow. You know who she is. You make her up. Blonde, brunette, big breasts, small breasts. If you're a man, she's all you ever dreamed of. If you're a woman, she's all you ever wanted to be – or perhaps all you ever dreamed of too – and who could blame you?

Our eyes tagged as I walked in. I took a half pint of ale and sat with my book away from the student crowd but my mind wouldn't settle to reading; it couldn't tear itself away from her. What age was she, eighteen, nineteen? Out of bounds for a madman of 36 with a questionable past and no particular future. Anyway, I looked like hell, in a sodden old flying jacket and baggy pants tucked into boots, my hair sweaty from the helmet.

'Hello.' And there she was. I stood.

'Hello.' *She needs a light. She thinks I'm someone else.* She sat. I sat.

'What kind of bike do you have? I'm Francesca Trestrail, by the way.' She offered her hand on a straight arm, her head to one side, smiling.

'How do you do. Hal Sinclair. It's a Sunbeam.'

'A Sunbeam?' A chuckle. ' "Jesus wants me for a sunbeam".'

'Is that the best he can offer?'

'Well, I didn't say I would do it. Jesus is probably boring, don't you think?'

'I don't know, but actually I think he's dead.'

'Cripes! Should we send a card or something?'

I snorted some beer down my nose.

'Oh, sorry, I didn't mean to make you laugh at the wrong moment.'

'And "Cripes"? Did you really say Cripes?'

'Yes. Would it have been funnier if I'd said "Christ", considering the context?'

That was it. A *coup de foudre*. I'd heard of it but I'd never believed in it. I had to get out of there. This wasn't in the plan. A plan? I had a plan? Whatever, it wasn't this.

'Tell me about your bike?'

'It's a Sunbeam.'

'Yes, you said. Sweet.'

'I'd never really thought of her as sweet.'

'Oh, of course she's a girl. Sweet Sunbeam. Are you good to her?'

'Fairly, but I'll be even nicer to her now that I know her name.' I took a final mouthful of my beer and rose.

'Do you have to go?'

'Yes.'

'You haven't finished your beer.'

'Sweet Sunbeam doesn't like it if I drink. It was a pleasure to meet you Francesca.'

'Someone waiting for you?'

'No. Bye.'

'Oh.' She froze for the blink of an eye then smiled brightly. 'Okay bye.'

I headed for the door but before going through it I had to look round. She was sitting with my beer mug cupped in her hands, staring into it. She didn't look up.

Sunbeam was parked under cover in the square. The streets were deserted, my footsteps a forlorn sound in the dark and the deluge. *What an extraordinary, wonderful girl. But there had to be something amiss, her coming on to me so directly. Then maybe that's what teenagers are like now, how the hell would I know? But she felt so familiar . . . so familiar, as though I'd known her all my life.*

I climbed on and kicked the starter. As the engine fired I heard another noise. A voice? I looked in the mirror and saw Francesca running towards me, waving. I kicked into gear and moved off. I could see her waving and calling but I drove on. Better like this. Another glance in the mirror saw her standing, her arms down by her sides . . . in the rain. *Oh . . . hell bloody . . . bugger*! I turned the bike around. What? You'd have been the big strong one and driven on, would you? Oh, sure. But then you didn't love her. I did. I loved her. Just like that.

'Sorry.' Her fingers curled over her cuff, she lifted her sleeve and wiped a drip of rain off her nose. It made me giddy how much I wanted to hold her.

'Are you angry?' she said.

'Why should I be angry?'

'Because I came after you.'

'It's not yet a capital offence.'

'Then the defence rests.'

'Are you reading law?'

'No, I'm getting wet.'

I laughed and she smiled her gorgeous smile.

'I'm sorry. You can go if you like.'

Fat chance and she knew it.

'Are you all right, Francesca?'

'Of course.' Then, laying her fingers on the handlebars, 'So this is Sweet Sunbeam.'

'This is she. Isn't she beautiful? Though she's a bit wet at the moment.'

'Like me. Yes, she's lovely. Can I buy you a coffee or something? Or . . . or not.' She made a face as though she had committed a transgression.

'Are you hungry?'

'Not really.'

'You are, aren't you? You're hungry.'

She crinkled her nose. 'Well, a bit.'

'Will Italian do?'

'My favourite. I haven't got much money though.'

'My treat.'

'Really?' Her eyebrows shot up.

'Really.'

She started to climb on the bike behind me.

'No, we can't go on the bike. You don't have a helmet.'

'That's all right.'

'No, it's too dangerous in the wet.' The thought took me by surprise. I *liked* danger.

'You don't have to go fast.'

'You don't have to be going fast on a bike to break your head. Anyway, it's only across the square. C'mon.'

During the next hour and a half in an Italian restaurant, I learned, among other things, that she was reading French and Italian. I learned about Boccaccio, about Cesare Pavese and Italo Calvino, that she liked classical music, as did I, and that her parents were heading towards divorce but that they had never paid much attention to her anyway. She didn't tell me that. Perhaps she didn't even realise it. Her early years and school holidays were spent in East Africa where her father had been in the Diplomatic Service. I also learned that of course this wasn't a sexual attraction for her, she was too young. *I was too old.* She wanted a chum – or the dad who never was one. She was just a precocious youngster who either didn't know or didn't care that she was living dangerously. And I loved her. What a shame.

She learned that I didn't go to university but to the Royal Air Force flying school at Cranwell and had, until today, flown jet fighters.

'Until today?'

She could unexpectedly look very serious and concerned. For a brief moment it was as though she knew of the horror I'd recently experienced. My guts fell as the image again ripped into my mind, but mercifully she dispelled it with her next question.

'Is that the end of your, whatever you call it, your National Service?'

I smiled at her slender grasp of recent history.

'No, we don't have national service any more.' I was a career officer.

'Oh. I hope you weren't cashiered or something. My uncle was.'

'Really? Why?'

'He was caught doing it to the sergeant's wife. Apparently you're more likely to get away with fucking up than fucking down. He was a major.'

She said 'fucking'. Well, it was the sixties, we just didn't quite know it then.

'Yes, I suppose that's true. What does he do now?'

'He's at the Home Office.'

'Doing the charladies?'

'Yes, I imagine so. So what happened to you?'

'Nothing so exciting. I quit.'

'Really? Why?'

'I'd had enough, I suppose. It's time for a change.'

'Did you ever have to drop bombs on people or shoot them down or anything?'

'No', I lied.

'Do they mind that you've left?'

'I'm sure that they're heartbroken.'

'Well, I would be.'

What did she mean by that? *Nothing, fool. It was a joke.*

'So what will you do now?'

Smiling and shaking my head, 'Oh God.'

'Sorry, I didn't mean to be nosy.'

'No, no, you weren't. I was just laughing because I haven't a clue. No, that's silly. I have. I'll probably find another flying job somewhere.'

I'd lied again. I did have another job, actually in Kenya, as a pilot to the flying doctor service, based in Nairobi. But I wasn't telling anyone because I was trying to escape.

Swilling the dregs of her espresso, Italian style, she asked, 'Where do you live?'

'For the moment, on the station.'

'The railway station?'

I smothered another laugh to spare her from feeling silly. 'No, that's what we call the airfield, the airbase.'

'Oh, sorry,' she chuckled, 'I was worried for a minute that you might be a train spotter or something.'

The ridiculously large bill was paid and we left.

'Which college are you at?'

'Newnham. Do I seem like a Girton girl?'

'I don't know. How do you tell Girton girls from Newnham girls?'

'They have more teeth.'

'I'll walk you back.'

The rain had stopped and the cloud had broken from nimbostratus to cumulus, allowing moonlight. We walked down King's Parade and crossed the Cam on Silver Street. As we were approaching Newnham she asked, 'Would you like to see my room?'

This was asked with the bright, excited smile of a youngster proud of being a Cambridge student who wanted to show off her college billet. I got the impression that her parents had never been here.

'Do your parents bring you down at term time?'

'No, Hopkinson does. He's my father's driver – well general factotum really.'

'I see. Yes, I'd love to see your room.'

'Then follow me.'

We cut off Sidgwick Street and headed around the back of the college.

'Francesca, where are we going?'

'We can't go through the porter's lodge. Chaps aren't allowed in at night.'

'Oh no, wait a minute — '

'No, it's fine, really. There's a bent railing behind the lab. We can squeeze through.'

'No, Francesca, this is bloody crazy. We'll be in the *News of the World*. "Diplomat's daughter sent down in Cambridge scandal. Group Captain sought." '

'No, silly, we all do it. If they cared all that much, they would have fixed the fence.'

Why was I doing this? I had no sexual intentions, so why take risks? I supposed because I knew that I would never see her again, therefore wanted to be with her a little longer.

We were in. As we walked along the path, hidden by trees and shrubs, she linked her arm to mine. So familiar. I'd known her forever.

'See? It was fine.'

'Yes, but we're not in yet.'

The next move was alarming and laughable. It resembled a commando assault. Our objective was Sidgwick, in the middle block. Francesca was legitimately in the grounds but I was an alien. When we broke cover from the trees, she would walk forward, check for the enemy, then beckon me. I would dash for the nearest cover. Fortunately there were lots of little hedges and bushes. By this means we reached the door, which, as Francesca knew, was locked.

'Now what?'

She raised an eyebrow and, holding my eyes with hers, brought her hands to her mouth – and made the sound of an owl. Oh God, how I loved her.

'What's the response,' I asked, 'A cuckoo?'

'At this time of night? Hardly.'

The response came a few moments later when the crash bar was pushed and the door opened. We scuttled in.

'Thanks Jill. This is Hal.'

We how d'you doed. Jill was holding a towel around her.

'Sorry. Are you with Tom?'

'Yes. No, it's OK. Bye.'

As she sped back along the corridor, the towel slipped and we were treated to her bottom.

'Oops!' said Francesca, 'Rather nice, actually.'

We climbed the stairs and tiptoed along the corridor to Room 224. It must have been one of the best rooms in college, small, in the eaves, but with a beautiful window and little balcony. It was tidy, despite piles of books, photographs and posters on the walls – one of which read 'College girls do it standing up'. I didn't comment.

'This is lovely. I envy you being here.'

'It's all right. It's a bit boring really. Well, no, it's not. That was silly, it's not boring at all, it's wonderful but you're not supposed to admit that. Would you like a coffee?'

'No thanks.'

There was a picture of her by the Pitti Palace, on the hill overlooking Florence. She was sitting on a wall, a boy in front of her, her legs over his shoulders.

'When were you in Florence?'

'I was there for the summer.'

'Is that your boyfriend?'

'No. Well . . . he was sort of my boyfriend there.'

'I see.' *A breath.* 'Francesca, it was a delight to meet you.'

'Oh. Thank you. You too. And thank you for supper'

'A pleasure. Good luck. Enjoy your time here.'

'Are you around tomorrow?'

Tomorrow. Was I around tomorrow? No, I was going down to London tomorrow. *Get out the door.*

'Tomorrow? Yes, I suppose so. Why?' *Wimp!*

'Well, I just thought maybe we could go to a recital or something. I mean if you like.'

'Yes, I like. What time?'

'They usually start about seven-thirty'

'See you at seven, where I parked Sunbeam?'

'Great.'

'Goodnight Francesca.'

'Goodnight, Hal.'

It was the first time she'd addressed me by name. I was surprised she'd even remembered it. Again she offered her straight arm, firm handshake and I left, praying that I wouldn't hear 'Oi, you there!' on my way across the gardens.

I mounted Sweet Sunbeam. Sweet Sunbeam. Once I had a motor cycle, now I had Sweet Sunbeam. It was all I could do not to say hello.

Despite so many years in the RAF, it remained a thrill driving past the guard and under the red and white pole on to an aerodrome. Second World War movies and David Niven were to blame for that. The reality of what I'd been doing these last few years no longer fitted the romance though, so these were my final two nights as a serving officer. Then off to London and real life, one I'd never known, having been sheltered by the Air Force – and Cadell's outfit.

Cadell. The voice which once caused my senses to thrill and tighten was now the voice which I dreaded hearing, from which I was now running.

'Hello Hal, Cadell here. How about coffee tomorrow at about eleven at Robert's?' This translated as 'Be in London tomorrow for a briefing at the safe house in the unlikely named "Fifth Avenue", off the Harrow Road.' It didn't matter where I was, I'd have to be in London the following day.

Again, the nightmares. Not even the image of Francesca as I dropped off, could frustrate them.

The recital the following evening was hysterical. A student piano trio. The piano and the cello were fine, but the girl who played the fiddle had wild hair, wild enthusiasm and a wild, anarchic notion of tonal accuracy. The first few clinkers we ignored, then during a presto passage when she accurately hit only one in every seven notes, I felt Francesca turn. I looked at her. She was smiling at me with her eyes crossed and we got the giggles. Well controlled though, so as not to upset those around us who were surely deficient in either hearing or humour, or both. We suffered until the interval then scarpered.

'We could have omelette and salad in my room if you like?'

'Fine, if you can be bothered. Shall we get a bottle of wine?'

'Oh yes, shall we?'

Again, we successfully ran the gauntlet through the gardens. There was even something about the way Francesca ate that was attractive, an enthusiasm, a concentration. I suppose she ate like an Italian. Again, the evening passed in easy conversation. A few probes – 'was I ever married?' Enthusiastic questions about my girlfriend which confirmed to me that this was, in her eyes, a platonic friendship – as it should be. I didn't have a girlfriend, well, not a steady one.

As I made signs of leaving—

'You should stay some night and we could have breakfast in hall. It's lovely.'

Stay some night?' *She's so innocent, it doesn't occur to her that someone of my age might make a pass at her.* And I didn't – and me a hopeless cuntaholic. Cripes! A social kiss on the cheek and I drove home on Sweet Sunbeam. We felt virtuous, Sunbeam and I.

The next night, her knickers were off.

It was absolutely not my intention. Even though we had now spent three consecutive evenings in each other's company, I still refused to see it as anything other than platonic. As I moved to give her another social goodnight kiss, she slid inside my arms and offered her mouth. Well, Your Honour, I didn't want to seem rude, so . . .

I shouldn't joke, it wasn't one bit funny. It wasn't amazing sex, either – then. She was very eager and energetic, probably to indicate how sexually experienced and emancipated she was. What *was* amazing was how I felt as I held her, how I felt knowing that she wanted me. She was so soft, so smooth and when she wasn't being energetic, so tender. And there was a fragrance from her upper lip which was, well . . . it was a 'fuck me' smell. We fell asleep entwined.

And so dawned the day I became a civilian. The squadron lent me a Land Rover in which to move my modest goods to London. Some books, some clothes, hi fi, that was it. Until I left for Africa, I would stay with a chum, Harry, one of my crew when I flew Canberras in the early days. Now a captain of the Queen's Flight, he lived with his wife Gwen and their children in a gigantic flat in Chiswick. Not too convenient for Northolt, where the Flight was based but Gwen taught painting for bugger-all money at a local arts centre and couldn't bear to give it up. Quite right.

London was a mystery to me. Apart from a few days now and again and the briefings by Cadell, I'd spent no time there and knew no one.

I didn't see Francesca for the next few days. When I did see her, I got my first warning sign. It was a Saturday afternoon. I was an hour late and there was no way to contact her. When I arrived, the girl from the next room was with her and the floor was covered in tiny pieces of torn paper.

'Hello, I'm so sorry I'm late.'

'This is Meg.'

'Hello Meg.'

'Hello. I'd better get back. Nice to meet you. Bye Francesca.'

'Bye,' says Francesca, smiling.

'Bye,' say I, also smiling. She left. Francesca picked up a book, plonked herself heavily into the armchair and started reading. Or pretended to. I was astonished.

'What happened here?' Indicating the paper on the floor.

Without looking up, 'Nothing.'

'Nothing? What, no wedding?'

'What are you talking about?'

'The confetti on the floor.'

'That's not confetti.'

'No, I know that, so . . .'

She was chewing her lip. 'I was angry, all right?'

'Looks like you still are.'

'Yes, well . . . ?'

'Because I was late?'

'So there was someone much more important than me.'

Get out now. This is bad news. If she's this unreasonable when she hardly knows you, what's it going to be like in a month? Just say, 'yes, much more important' and go.

14

But I said, 'They were important. Two children.'

Her eyes came up from pretending to read. She no longer looked aggressive, but defensive and frightened.

'You've got children?'

I remained friendly and reasoning. 'No, not mine. Harry and Gwen's, the people I'm staying with. Harry was working and I agreed to stay with them until Gwen got back from her doctor. There was some drama in the surgery and she was kept waiting.'

Francesca couldn't just leave it but she was simmering down.

'Didn't she phone you or anything?'

'Yes, but I couldn't very well say that I had to leave the children alone because I had a date. If you had a phone, I'd have phoned you, Francesca.'

She rose and rushed at me, hugging me. 'I'm sorry. I'm sorry. Please don't be angry. Of course you had to stay with the children.'

I wasn't just angry, I was furious – and troubled . . . The girl I so loved was damaged.

'It's all right. I'm not angry, Francesca.'

Her mouth broke into a wide smile and she kissed all over my face. Then she pulled up her top exposing her breasts and pressing them against me. I wondered was it just me she wanted or would anyone do?

'I've made a pasta sauce, is that all right?'

'Very all right. Thank you. How was today?'

It was okay. I had an Italian tutorial. I think he's a bit of a lech.'

'You mean like me?'

''Yes, just like you except I don't fancy him. You're a nice lech.'

A vision of my tombstone 'Hal Sinclair, A Nice Lech'.

She's unbuttoning my shirt and rubbing her breasts against my chest.

'Some of the students let him fuck them.'

'No, really?'

'Yes, a lot of the tutors do it.'

'Do the girls do it for higher marks or just for the kudos of pulling the prof?'

'Both, probably. You know, until recently, if you had a male visitor in your room, the bed had to be moved into the corridor.'

'What, they were so academic that they didn't know you could use the floor? Have you ever done it?'

'Not here, no.'

'Not here?' I laugh. 'So where?'

'At school.'

'No.'

'Yes.'

'You did it with a teacher?'

'Yes, the French master.'

'My God. Did you want him to?'

Her brow furrowed. 'Of course. I wouldn't have let him if I hadn't.'

'Where did you do it?

'In the chemistry lab. On the floor, naturally.'

'How old were you?'

'Fourteen.'

My expectation was to be in Nairobi within a few weeks of leaving the RAF but the pilot I was going to replace had stayed on because the job he was moving to had fallen through. It was like being caught in a property chain.

I had to get out of Harry's flat. Apart from imposing upon them, I could easily have been found by Cadell if he'd needed me.

Harry had been ribbing me about where I was going on the nights I was in Cambridge, so I told him. He said that I was a lucky bastard and that I should feel free to bring her to London for the occasional weekend, so I did. Francesca was sweetly delighted to be included. Harry and Gwen liked her on sight. She was wonderful with the children. She was always wonderful with children, she didn't ever consider them a nuisance, she gave them her full attention and they loved her. I remembered the night of the torn paper and how her anger had dissipated when I mentioned the children. Anyway, the evening was a great success, then . . . there was a problem.

When we got into the bedroom, her mood changed. From being good company all evening, with everyone obviously liking her, the moment we were alone she fell silent. We'd had a few 'scenes' over the last weeks so I recognised when one was coming. Sometimes, in fact usually, I knew what it was going to be about and could avert it. There were times though when it seemed that she needed to expel her rage and on those occasions there was nothing that you or I or the Great Psychotic in the Sky could do about it. I tried but this time I had no idea what it was about.

'You're a hit, Francesca, everyone instantly liked you.'

'Not everyone.'

'Well, no, I don't like you because you've got buck teeth and a moustache.'

She didn't laugh. 'Are you fucking her?'

I could never have guessed that this would be it. 'You know me fairly well now Francesca, so do you honestly think that?'

'She wants you to fuck her.'

'Is this women's intuition?'

'She didn't take her eyes off you all evening.'

'You know, when I was in the kitchen with Gwen, she said of you "she never takes her eyes off you". Now, if you were watching me all evening, how could you have seen that *she* was watching me all evening?'

'Oh, you're so clever, aren't you?' She pulled her shoes off and threw them on the floor.

I let rip. 'Yes, and so are you Francesca –' her eyes flared in alarm for an instant at my raised voice but it had to be said '– so why don't you engage your fine mind and understand that even if Gwen did want me to fuck her – and people are entitled to want, perhaps not always to get, but certainly to want – that's no reason to take it out on me. And since there's no chance that I am going to fuck her, why don't you feel a little sisterly sympathy instead of upsetting yourself over nothing. Now will you please get on your knees, take your knickers down and lean your elbows on the bed so that I can fuck *you*.'

She did and I did, though we didn't stay that way for long. Well, lovemaking needs eyes, doesn't it? We fell asleep at peace.

My happiness, though, was adumbrated by the knowledge that one of my generation had no right to Francesca, that she had only been lent to me and that it was incumbent upon me to give her back, re-attach her to her true life and watch it spin her away, knowing that I would never love or know her like again.

Francesca didn't see the age difference as a problem. She would when I was fifty and she not yet thirty. Still hungry for everything and realising how many of her child-bearing years she had wasted on me. It had to end – soon, before she became too dependent and it hurt her more. That was why I didn't ever tell her that I loved her.

I had to find something to do until I went to Nairobi. What I knew best, obviously, was flying. I could have been contracted back to the RAF as an instructor, but then Cadell would easily have found me, so I phoned round the flight schools looking for a post. The only one available was in Scotland. Well, that would precipitate the break with Francesca.

Telling her was awful. This was her greatest fear, being abandoned. We were in bed, in Cambridge. She didn't rage, or protest. There was a long silence then she said, 'But I love you, didn't you know that?'

And she turned her back and curled into a ball. I tried to hold her but she pulled away.

'No, it's all right,' she said.

The next week was grim. I went to Cambridge a couple of times, but each time I regretted it. It was too sore. Francesca wasn't unpleasant, just distant. On the second visit, her bed was unmade and the room had an odd odour. Sex. The smell of sex. There was a tingling at the sides of my throat and a rush of saliva as though I was going to vomit. I said nothing, it wasn't my right. I couldn't tell her that all I wanted was her, that there could be nothing in my life, now or ever, as important or beautiful in every way, as she.

The flight school was based at the new Abbotsinch Airport which served Glasgow. Its principal feature was weather – lots of it – and none of it good. Wind, rain and a cloud base about ten feet off the ground. The information most frequently given to the students was, 'Sorry, your lesson's cancelled.' It was so boring that I even envied the airline jockeys who flew Glasgow to London. Actually, in one respect, that was one of the less dull routes to fly. It's so short that as soon as you reach your given altitude, you begin your descent, so there's always something to do.

The lack of action made the pit in my stomach even deeper from the loss of Francesca. I had one photograph of her. We'd been on a punt on The Backs in Cambridge and she was in shorts and a top, no bra. She'd stood up, taken her top off and said 'Quick!' and I took the picture. It was a beaut. It stood on my bedside table at Mrs McLafferty's house, on the Paisley end of the Glasgow Road. Mrs McLafferty was a cheery Catholic, which is a damned sight more tolerable than the other kind. Her house was festooned with items all too familiar to me: pictures of gods and their mothers, all in different outfits, martyrs gushing blood, and bits of dried palm fronds twisted into the shape of the cross. I had Francesca with her tits out. Mrs McLafferty said nothing, but on my wall was a reproduction of a famous picture of the boss's son, the one where, if you look long enough, the eyes open and follow you around the room. Well, they didn't follow me because once they were open, he couldn't tear them off Francesca's tits.

Commercial flying can be described as years of boredom punctuated by moments of stark terror. In military flying I had experienced my fair share of stark terror but that was to be expected. Now, as a private flying tutor, I didn't foresee such problems with Lorna Fleming.

Lorna had taken up flying at twenty-eight, after the birth of her first child. She had suffered post-natal depression and her husband, Duncan, knowing that Lorna had always been interested, pushed her to take flying lessons as a diversion. She had taken to it easily and had learned quickly. When I became her instructor she could already fly. She'd had another child and was now working to get her night rating. She didn't chat much, just seemed quiet and concentrated. Nice looking, with a lovely bum. I thought that maybe sometime we'd . . . Anyway, no one knew anything about her depression. It's not that she had purposely withheld the information, it just hadn't occurred to her to give it. If she had, it would have been an impediment to her being accepted for instruction.

I found out because one day Duncan drove her to the airfield and he and I chatted while she changed her clothes. He said how grateful he was to the school for 'helping her over this'.

'Over what?' I asked

And he told me. He said that she had really got over it but then when they had the second child it had returned.

'Why did you have the second child?'

'French letter failure.'

'God! How is she? She doesn't say much.'

'That's how it manifests, she just goes quiet.'

This was a worry. She was *always* quiet.

'I see. I'm sorry, but I have to ask this because being in charge of an aircraft is a pretty responsible position. Has she ever talked about suicide?'

'She did the first time but not since.'

I said nothing but didn't take my eyes off his. If someone is being less than truthful, they always buckle under this look. The next movement of the body will always give them away, a scratch of the nose, some physical attempt to be casual or to divert. He did drop his eyes but that was merely social embarrassment.

'No, I'm sure she wouldn't do that now.'

'Okay. I'm glad.'

I looked out of the window. Lorna was already at the aircraft, doing the walk around with her flashlight, checking the surfaces. She hadn't come to pick me up or say cheerio to the husband. I thanked him and walked out to her. I tried to dismiss the idea that hers was odd behaviour. Maybe she'd already said 'cheerio' as she went to change.

Professional pilots are by nature, watchful. It's what you've missed that kills you. At the same time I had to be reasonable. This woman seemed extremely competent and diligent. Anyway, why would she wait for me? If she wanted to end it she could have the engine started and be taxiing before anyone could stop her – and why should she choose today, she could have done it three days ago – or last month. The hell with it. I was sorry that Duncan had ever mentioned it.

We climbed in, she in the left hand seat, which is customary. Normally, the senior pilot sits on the left but during training, the instructor relinquishes that position.

The plan was to fly south west, leaving the mainland at Ardrossan, then west to Arran over Goatfell which, at 2,800 feet, she would try not to hit. A slight turn to north would take us across Kintyre to Gigha where she would execute a U-turn to take us back to base. The first cloud layer had a base of 1,100 feet and a ceiling of 2,300. There was a further, patchy layer around 5,400 feet. She took off and requested a height of 3,000 feet which would keep us in clear air.

The two most important tasks for a pilot are, to avoid colliding with other aircraft and, hitting the ground unexpectedly. I know it sounds funny but it's easier than you might imagine. Air navigation is three dimensional, and one of those dimensions, the vertical, changes constantly. The altimeter, which indicates your height, works like a barometer, it measures air pressure, but air pressure is far from static, changing according to weather, among many other things, so if Lorna was to clear Goatfell summit at night, she'd have to make sure that her adjustments were correct. In addition, wind does its best to blow you off course at all times. There's a lot to know, and there's lot to do.

All seemed to be going well, though Lorna was silent except to answer my questions. As we cleared Kintyre, over Kilbrannan Sound, we were alerted by Air Traffic Control to the presence of another light aircraft above and to the north east. This is standard procedure, not an emergency by any means but we should find him in the sky and keep him in view until our paths diverged. Similarly, he would have been alerted to our presence.

I was looking for his lights when everything went haywire. The engine note rose and the nose dropped dramatically. As I looked to Lorna the aircraft inverted. She had the yoke fully forward, full right aileron and rudder and the engine at full power. Her eyes were closed. As I grabbed the yoke and got my feet in my pedals to pull us round, I yelled, 'Lorna!'

She said nothing, she just kept her eyes tight shut and held the controls against me. She was trying to die. I couldn't get control from her to correct the aircraft. We were plummeting. Pulse pounding terror, the dials all showing impending doom. We were spinning, so the artificial horizon indicator was spinning. The altimeter was moving anti-clockwise at a terrifying rate and the airspeed was rising. From 3,000 feet it doesn't take many seconds to get down to hell.

She wasn't holding the throttle, so with one hand I pulled it closed and with the other I grabbed her thigh above the knee and squeezed my fingers and thumb together hard. Remember when people did that to you at school? The reflex kicked in. Her hands flew off the yoke to grab mine and her knee jerked up, removing her foot from the rudder pedal. The next manoeuvre was less fun, but standard procedure. A short, sharp punch to the jaw which rendered her unconscious and knocked her headset off.

This had taken maybe four seconds. I had no idea what my height was. In fact, knowing would make no difference to my action or the outcome – except to increase the terror. I did what was necessary to stop the tumbling and brought the engine speed up a bit to try to get a grip on the air. While scanning the instruments to determine where the sky was, they went dark. Vanished. Everything was black, the cockpit, the water below, the sky above – or the water above, the sky below. I was probably in cloud by now anyway. When things go wrong in an aircraft, they tend to do so exponentially. You can survive if you have time but alone in the cockpit, there's too much to do.

Disorientated by spinning, I had no reference point, I couldn't automatically feel which way was 'up' so the only information I could get was from the instruments. Mine were out. I grabbed the little flashlight which hung around my neck and switched it on. Nothing. It must have been whacked against something during the aerobatics. There was no time to try to reach Lorna's, so I unplugged my headset, and let the cable dangle. Without much hope, I threw the switch for the landing lights. Miracle! They came on and, because I was in cloud, some light was reflected into the cockpit. The cable hung about 45 degrees upwards of my eyes which meant I was headed down, at an angle, on my back. If I was in cloud, I still had some air below me. I flipped her round until the position of the plug told me that I could start to bring the nose up. Everything went dark again. I was out of the cloud.

A few seconds remaining . . . I took a chance, closed the throttle again and gave myself a quarter flap. That would reduce my speed and give more lift. Though if the airspeed was too high, it would start to rip the flaps. I didn't think it could be since I had shut down the revs pretty quickly on mad Lorna. It wasn't. As the flaps bit the air I felt comforting pressure on my arse as the plane started to pull out of the dive.

But now I could see the water in the landing lights. Too close! Oh God, oh God, oh God, oh God, oh God . . . Another quarter flap, Oh God, oh God, oh God, oh God . . . Not going to make it. Fuck it! Fuck it! Fuck it! The water's here. Fuck it! I felt a tiny tug, as if a giant thumb and forefinger had pinched the aircraft and slowed it for half a second then released it. I felt pressure now on my chest. We were climbing. I had no idea what the climb rate was but if it was too high we'd stall, and I knew for certain that we wouldn't have enough height to recover from the stall. I eased the stick forward and there ahead was the best thing I'd seen – other than Francesca. Some lights. The shore. I was so happy, I almost punched Lorna again just for the sheer joy. Instead, I re-plugged my headset. Mercifully, the radios were still functioning so I called Air Traffic Control which, no doubt, having watched with alarm my erratic progress through the sky was rather keen to know what the fuck. I didn't go into details; I wanted to know a bit more about Lorna before the law was involved. I simply said that my student had taken ill and that I'd had a systems failure.

Lorna regained consciousness and looked at me. I got ready to sock her again but I could see her say something. I couldn't hear because she wasn't wearing her headset and mic. So I shouted. 'Put your headset back on.'

She did and said, 'What happened?'

'I'll tell you later.' There was other business to take care of first. 'Give me your flashlight.' She did and I directed it around the instruments. The pressure-driven instruments, altimeter, airspeed and vertical speed indicator were giving readings. Phew! Also the magnetic compass which, as I'm sure you know, is plugged into the north pole. It doesn't like trauma, however, so couldn't be trusted to give an accurate reading.

'Prestwick, this is Private Golf Echo Six Tango Romeo.' I told him what instruments I had and requested guidance to the nearest airfield.

'Tango Romeo, that's understood. Please increase your speed to 100 knots and climb to two thousand. Try to hold your present course. Stand by.'

I know what you're thinking. That since I was teaching navigation, why wasn't I using that to find my way home. Are you crazy? When you're lost in the sky and there's help, you take it, you don't bugger about being Amelia Erhardt who, incidentally, died probably because she didn't listen to her navigator. I looked over at Lorna. In the dim light, I could see it coming back to her. She tried to put her head in her hands but couldn't because of the microphone. Sort of funny really, in a black kind of way. I took her hand for a moment and she cried.

Air Traffic Control was back on the radio. 'Tango Romeo, there is another light aircraft in your vicinity. He will guide you to the nearest airstrip which is on the island of Islay. Approach will be from the south east on Runway 31.'

I was relieved to see Lorna reach for the Jeppeson charts which give details of all airfields, height, terrain etc; all the information required to safely approach and land. She was functioning properly, so I had some help. I handed her the flashlight.

Air Traffic Control continued. 'The airfield is closed but they're trying to scramble a controller. Goosenecks will be lit. Tune to 118.3 for your escort. Call sign Eight Foxtrot Mexico.'

'Tango Romeo, confirm re-tune to 118.3. Levelling off at 2,000 feet.'

'I will position Foxtrot Mexico zero two miles ahead and 500 feet above you. Please advise when you have him in sight.'

'Understood.'

'When you have the runway in sight, retune to 123.15 for the local tower. Hopefully there will be someone there.'

'123.15. Thank you.'

'We'll keep our eye on you. Good luck.'

'Thank you Prestwick. Goodnight.'

Lorna was already tuning the second VFR radio.

'Foxtrot Mexico this is Tango Romeo. My name is Hal.'

Back he came. 'Hal, this is Archie, you should see me at any moment.'

And as he spoke, Lorna said, 'Got him. Slightly high, ten o'clock.'

And there he was, our guide, just like in that wonderful Frederick Forsyth story *The Shepherd* about a De Havilland Vampire pilot who was lost in the night and led home by the ghost of a Second World War Mosquito night fighter.

'Archie, we have you.'

'Good. What control do you have?'

'I told him, then flicked to the other channel and advised Prestwick that we had a visual on him.

'Archie, I'm going to close up on you.'

'Fine. How many hours do you have?' He was worrying that I'd fly straight up his arse.

'About 4,000.'

'Bloody hell! I won't worry about you flying up my backside then. Sorry.'

Lorna said, 'Runway is three one. Asphalt. Elevation zero-five-four. Watch out for deer and large flocks of geese. With luck, they'll all be asleep. The grass is soft and unsafe.'

'Thanks, Lorna.'

We were now slightly above and about 500 feet behind Archie. When he turned, we turned. He told us when he was descending and we followed.

He said, 'There's the airfield, at ten o'clock.'

And there it was, a strip and a half of blazing flares and a chap lighting the last stretch. Archie asked did I want to make a pass or go straight in. We chose to make the pass, so followed him and flew down the runway at about 100 feet Archie said he would circle north of the strip at 1,000 feet till we were safely down. We called the tower but silence told us that they hadn't raised a controller.

We passed the strip, parallel to it on our left, made two 90-degree left turns, which brought us in line with the runway, dropped the landing gear and the flaps. Archie peeled off, we landed, bade him thanks and goodbye and taxied towards a lit hangar. A mechanic waved and we headed for him and parked. As we climbed out, 'I could get the runway lit for yous but I canny operate the tower.'

'That was great, thanks. Lucky you were here.'

'Aye, just finishin' aff an engine. Whit wiz yer problem?

'The instrument cluster failed.'

'Aye, well thirs nuthin' we can dae fur ye the night, but Duggie'll be here in the mornin'. He does the electric. Hiv yis got someplace tae stay? Yis'll have missed the last ferry.'

Lorna and I looked at each other and I knew. I didn't know if she did. 'No, but we'll find somewhere.'

We made the necessary phone calls, me to my office and she to her Duncan. Instrument failure and the diversion to Islay was all that was mentioned.

A taxi took us into Port Ellen.

'Drink?'

'Oh. Oh yes, I think so.' She shook her head in self-awareness as she said it.

The pub was functional. We each had a whisky.

'My face is quite sore.'

'I'm very sorry.'

'You hit me, didn't you.'

'Yes I did. I'm sorry. It was punch or perish, I'm afraid.' I smiled at her. 'Perish in your own time.'

Again the shake of the head. 'I don't know what to say to you Hal. To say I'm sorry seems a wee bit inadequate. How *do* you apologise for trying to kill someone? Or, rather, not caring whether or not you do kill someone?'

'It's all right. I know all about it.'

'About what?' She knew what.

'About the post-natal depression. Your husband told me while we waited for you. It hadn't occurred to him that we wouldn't know.'

'I try not to bore people with it.'

I sort of laughed, 'Well, when you did decide to tell me that something was wrong, it wasn't boring at all. Far from it.'

She smiled and her eyes filled. I took her hand again. She covered mine with her other hand and fought her quivering lip.

We downed our drinks and departed the pub.

'I'm quite hungry, what about you?' I said.

Yes, I am. And cold, isn't it?'

I put my arm around her and we searched for the only available food. The chip shop. Over delicious fish and chips, bread and butter and a pot of tea, we talked about flying. She wanted to know about different aircraft and how they handled; heavies, fast jets, stunt planes, what it's like operating from a carrier. She clearly loved flying. It wasn't going to be easy to tell her that in all probability she'd never fly again. I was sad for her.

Back in the street, I said, 'We'd better find a hotel.'

'Yes. We passed one on the way here.'

'Yes. Do you think it'll do?'

'I can't imagine there'll be a huge choice.'

'No.'

We walked on in silence. Half a block from the hotel, I stopped. She stopped and looked at me.

'Do you want to talk, Lorna?'

A pause. 'Yes.'

'Do you want your own room?'

'Oh.'

She looked at her feet. She looked out to the black sea, then to me. 'No.'

We took up a bottle of wine. The choice was an Italian dental solvent or the ubiquitous Beaujolais Villages. No contest, we took the solvent. Only kidding.

The room was warm, thank God. The first few minutes were taken in opening the wine with my Swiss Army thing and finding that the only glasses were small tumblers from the bathroom. We agreed that wine out of tumblers was just fine.

At the same moment, standing before the mirror, we saw that we were dressed alike. I was in the school instructors' uniform, navy blue trousers, white shirt and navy sweater with silly epaulettes, she was in navy blue trousers, blue shirt and navy sweater with not-so-silly poitrines.

As we laughed, our arms naturally found each other. As we hugged, she tightened her arms around me and seemed to freeze. I held her for maybe a minute before she released and broke down. She lay on the bed and wept.

'I'm sorry. I'm so sorry, I'm sure you could do without this.'

'No, if you want to cry, you should cry. Just let go.'

She cried. I massaged her scalp. After four or five minutes her sobbing ceased and she lay still as I continued to massage her head. Another couple of minutes then a hoarse whisper. 'That's so nice. Thank you.

She pulled herself up, looking like shit. Her hair was a mess which was admittedly my doing, her face was blotchy, her eyes swollen and leaking mascara. The bruise was upsetting.

'Oh God, I must look awful.'

'That, is indisputable. The great thing though, is that it's not permanent. But if you want a laugh, have a look.'

She looked – and thank God – she laughed.

'That's going to be a corker of a bruise in the morning,' I said. 'Sorry.'

'Oh well. Can I just . . .? She picked up her handbag and headed for the bathroom.

I thought of Francesca and nearly cried myself. Where was she? What was she doing? Who was she about to receive between her open legs? Don't. Don't think. Lorna was nice, the right age but she had a husband and children. Mustn't mess with that. Tonight she needs a stranger's arms and the stranger sure needs hers.

She came out of the bathroom and tossed her sweater on the chair. Three buttons of her shirt were undone. I smiled and said, 'My turn.'

As I passed her our hands met and held. We turned to each other and looked. Looked in the eyes. Her eyes dropped to my mouth, mine to hers, then down to her cleavage. As I looked, I drew my hands from her back to cup the sides of her breasts. I saw her nipples harden under her shirt. 'Lovely,' I said, and we kissed. I feared that it might, because of her state of mind, be a bit frantic with clashing teeth and everything but it wasn't at all. And she smelled nice. We pulled apart and she said, 'That's the hard bit over.'

'God, I hope not.'

She snorted. 'Oh, right. Yes, I hope not too.'

I went to the loo. When I came out, she was standing in exactly the spot and attitude in which I'd left her, but wearing just the shirt, white bra and small, white, lacy knickers. The girl had a sense of humour.

'Your turn,' she said. 'Although I see you've already started too.' I had. I'd removed my shoes and socks, that's always the awkward bit.

'Are you going to help or just watch?'

She unbuttoned my shirt as I unbuttoned hers. She put her hand in the waistband of my trousers.

'You do the top bit, it's too difficult.' I undid the top fastenings and she pulled down the zip and then the trousers. I sat on the bed and pulled them off. She still stood beside me so I put my hands round her bum, pulled her to me and laid my cheek on her tummy, soft and warm. We got on to the bed and settled, our arms around each other.

'You know . . . Is it my imagination – and I'm not saying this because I'm lying here with my hands on your bare arse but, after we landed – I mean – are you feeling a bit better since our adventure?' I saw her eyes instantly fill again but she held it.

She nodded, not quite able to speak, then, 'Mmm. Yes.' She laughed. 'Yes, I think I am. No, I am. Why do you think that?'

'Because as the evening wore on, for the first time since we met, you weren't distant. You'd always been perfectly proper and I knew that you listened carefully to everything I said and you assimilated information well. But if one day I'd turned up dressed as an ostrich, I doubt you'd have noticed.'

Another laugh then quiet. 'Depression is awful. I mean, it's more awful than you can ever imagine. It takes all your strength to do the simplest thing, there's nothing left over for what isn't vital. And you in the ostrich suit, well, I would have thought it odd but not vital, so you're right. I would have appeared not to notice. If you'd got into the aircraft wearing it, I would probably have thought about it a bit more seriously. Those big three-toed feet in the rudder pedals . . .'

We laughed and kissed, and kissed, and kissed, and her pants were off and her tits were out of her bra and she couldn't wait, not another second.

Her orgasms fell into the category Negative/Pleading/Devout. 'Oh no! No! Please, No! Oh God no, God. Please! Please! No, no, no noooooohhhhGodddddddd!' She wanted everything. She came and came. She wanted it all out. Catharsis. Over the next two or so hours she purged herself – and I buried myself in her passion. It was lovely. Finally, 'Where's the wine?' She picked up the bottle. Her glass was on the other side of the bed.

'Do you mind if I use your glass?'

'I've just been licking your fanny, why should I mind if you use my glass?'

As we lay quiet in the dark, 'Why do I feel so much better?'

'I've been wondering about that.'

'Have you?' she said. 'You can fuck and wonder at the same time?'

'Only if I'm filled with wonder at the fuck.'

Her eyes came up to mine as she asked, 'Was it okay?'

'Are you serious? It was wonderful. You're delicious.'

'Really? I don't really know what you're supposed to do.'

I gave her a mock serious look, 'Well, in that case, Lorna, I think we have to acknowledge that you have an innate talent for sexual dalliance.'

She returned the look. 'That's the nicest thing anyone's ever said to me.' Then she slapped me hard on the rump and added, 'But you've got to trust. I trust you.'

Should she have? Wasn't it her distress that had led us to bed?

'You trust a man who punched you?' I teased.

'Maybe it was being punched that made me feel better.'

'Yeah, wew, 'at's wot every bird needs, innit? A fuckin' good frashin'.'

She kissed me, then in broad Scots, 'Oh, yir a right broote.'

'I don't know why you feel better, Lorna. Maybe you just came to an extremity. To the end of the pain. Maybe making the decision to die, and you did make it, there's no doubt about that, and the consequent trauma – although you did sleep through the best bit – did something to change your body chemistry. That's what caused your depression in the first place, chemical imbalance.'

She gave me a long look. 'How do you know that? You're right, it is, but how do you know?'

'It can hardly be anything else, can it? You're fine, you have a baby, and it starts a kind of hormone war which is ended by a kamikaze attack.'

'That could be part of it but there was something else.'

'What?'

'You.'

'It wasn't the punch, Lorna. Really. I don't think hitting people makes them better.'

I took a mouthful of wine and offered her the glass.

'Want some?'

She looked at the glass, my mouth, her crotch, shrugged and drank. I laughed and kissed her.

35

She went on: 'You know, I tried not to go on about the depression to people. I wasn't much fun, but I tried not to be a pain. If you have a leg in plaster everyone rushes to help but if it's your brain that's broken they're less sympathetic because they can't see the wound. Duncan's wonderful, he's a really good, decent man. But even so, I always felt that he thought I should be able to pull myself together, that somehow, I was to blame. I'm sure there were times that he would gladly have punched me, but he didn't.'

'And I did.'

'Yes, but you're right, that's not what helped.'

I looked at her.

'You took my hand. When I expected to be screamed at, maybe even hit again and threatened with God knows what, you took my hand. I had almost robbed you of your life and in that one gesture of taking my hand, you said you understood and forgave me. Even after we landed, you didn't say or ask anything. No recriminations, just a warm presence. You just created the right atmosphere and waited – and out it all came.'

'It's easier to talk to strangers.'

'True, but it's not that. It's you, you have a gift.

'A gift?'

'Intimacy. You have the gift of intimacy.'

I didn't know how to reply, so I kissed her left tit and said, 'Do you want a cup of tea?'

'Good idea. I'll make it.'

'No, it's okay I will.'

'Listen, I tried to kill you, so I'll make the tea, okay'

I watched as she filled the kettle and clattered the cups. She had a lovely body. Voluptuous. The image of Francesca popped

36

round the door of my mind. Francesca. My love. *Don't betray Lorna by looking at her and thinking of Francesca.*

Lorna turned, saw me looking and had a wee attack of shyness.

'What?'

'You look great.'

'No, I don't.'

'Yes, you do. You look lovely.'

'Thanks. I'd forgotten.'

She turned away for a moment, then, 'Do you want a Glengarry biscuit?'

'Is that some wondrous mode of sexual congress?'

'No, it's just a Glengarry biscuit.'

So we drank the tea and ate the Glengarry biscuits which, as we took them out of their stupid Cellophane wrappers, broke and covered the bed in crumbs.

When all was cleared away and we were close and comfy, Lorna said, 'Tell me what happened, after I pushed the stick forward.'

I told her. In the telling, I remembered that little tug I'd felt and realised what caused it. The rear end of the fuselage, under the tail, had touched the water.

'Oh my God. I'm so, so sorry.'

'It wasn't your fault. When did you decide to do it?'

'I don't think I actually made a decision. The possibility is always with you and the opportunities are always there. The razor blade, the aspirin bottle, the big truck as you cross the road. Death becomes your constant companion, the friend you know you can always count on if it gets too bad. And when the moment came it had no drama. I just thought, this is what I do now.'

'So there was no particular trigger?'

She sat up and hugged her knees. 'Well, it had been really bad. I don't think I'd spoken to anyone for two days. Like you said, distanced, as though looking at the world through the wrong end of the binoculars.'

'Why did you come for your lesson?'

'Because Duncan said it was time to go, and not going would have meant answering questions. Then I would have had to call you, and . . . Easier just to go.' Then she laughed.

'What?'

'No, it's funny.' She laid a hand on my chest. 'I didn't like my previous instructor very much. He was always making lame jokes and couldn't resist sexual innuendo. There were days I could cheerfully have dunked him in the sea.'

How easy it would be just to let the night go, say goodbye in the morning, make my report and let her receive a letter from the Federal Aviation Authority, but . . .

'There is something we have to talk about, Lorna.'

'No, don't worry, I won't be a problem to you. I know what tonight is.'

'No, it's not that. In any case you're the one married with children. I should be assuring you that *I* won't be a problem to *you*.'

'What, then?'

'Do you know anything about the regulations covering an event like this?'

Silence. Then she switched on the light. 'My God. Attempted murder. No, It would be manslaughter, wouldn't it? I could plead temporary insanity.'

I was astonished that she could think that, though there was a logic to it.

'No, no. Jesus, Lorna. Anyway, the only one who could bring charges like that is me and I couldn't do that to anyone who gave me a Glengarry biscuit.'

'It's not your decision. In Scotland it's the procurator fiscal who brings charges.'

I thought, she could be charged with endangering an aircraft, but . . . 'I'd do anything to protect you from that.'

She hugged me.

'It's the FAA I'm concerned about. The kamikaze dive was recorded by Air Traffic Control and a report will already have been made. I'll also have to make a report.'

She ran her hands along the sides of her head, gathering her hair into a bunch. 'They'll suspend my licence for a while?'

'They'll suspend it for life.' She turned to me, her mouth open.

It's a most singular experience, flying. Flight is something which, literally, we dream about. Within the confines of the planet, being a pilot is the nearest we can safely come to that reverie. Being a passenger in a airliner is not remotely similar to being in charge of the smallest, slowest aircraft. I would probably never fly a jet fighter again and that was a huge sorrow. To be alone, flying at astonishing speed at 65,000 thousand feet where you can see the curve of the earth and above you the sky is turning black because it's not sky for much longer, but outer space, is an addiction enjoyed by so few. Lorna's addiction, though she might never ever fly above 5,000 feet, would be just as fierce – and for her, not only was it the magic victory over gravity, it was sanctuary from distress.

'What do I do? By law, I'm required to make a truthful report . . .'

'Then you have to make it.'

'No, wait, let's just look at it all. If I do that, you'll be grounded for life. It would be considered a manic episode and that would be that.'

'But if I can prove a period of stability, if I'm given a clean bill of health . . .'

'It would make no difference. That's the rule. Also, the Aviation Authority will be delighted to ground a private pilot. They don't like amateur flying and make it as difficult as they can.'

'Amateur flying. I'd never thought of it like that but I suppose it is. What do you feel about it?' She got up and pulled on her sweater.

'Amateur flying? I actually don't think it's all that safe.'

'Why?'

'Because if things go wrong, you're on your own. Even if you've got chums in the aircraft, if you're the only pilot, you're on your own.'

She was now sitting facing me, cross-legged on the bed. I continued, 'Tonight, if the weather had changed and you hadn't come to your senses and been able to help, I might not have made it, just because of the workload.'

'I didn't do much.'

'Just shining the torch on the instruments and reading the charts was enough. If I'd had to do that, *and* cope with wind, rain and no visibility at low altitude . . .'

'You'd have coped all right.'

'*Maybe*, but that's because I'm RAF trained with thousands of hours behind me.' A smile. 'I'm a professional.'

'Touché!'

'How much better do you feel?'

'I feel normal. I can't believe it. It's as if I've clicked back on.'
She pulled one knee up and rested her chin on it. Involuntarily,
my eyes dropped to her crotch. She caught the glance and
flashed for me.

'That was nice. Has this ever happened before, that you get a
day of feeling better?'

'Like this? No.'

'Do you think it'll last?'

'To tell you the truth, I'm frightened to leave this room in case
it comes back.'

We talked for a long time. She knew a great deal about the
condition and said that such illnesses could, though rarely do,
suddenly remit. She expected to get better anyway, as she had
once before. We struck a deal. Providing she remained as she
was now, with no regression, she would fly but only with me. I
would make a report that she had suffered seafood poisoning
and had gone into spasm, locking the controls. I exacted a
promise from her that until she had enjoyed a two-year period
free from depression, she would never, ever fly. And if she got
pregnant again, she would never, ever fly. She said she would
never get pregnant again. Well, there are only two ways to
ensure that. Hysterectomy or abstinence, and I couldn't see
Lorna taking a vow of celibacy.

'I promise, Hal. I absolutely promise.'

'Okay. Now, to cover myself, because flying is my livelihood,
I'm going to do something else.'

I became very grave. 'Something that you must also
solemnly promise that you will never, never mention to
anyone. Husbands, lovers, absolutely trustworthy bestest
friend. No one.'

'What? I promise. Of course I promise.'

'I'm going to put a military Blue Notice on you. This means that you'll be watched. Your photograph and details will be circulated to agents everywhere and if you go near an aircraft it'll all be over. For good. This is a secret system.'

'My God, they can do things like that?'

'They can do anything.'

'How do you know about this.'

'Because I'm one of them.'

'Jesus.'

This was total baloney. There's no such thing as a Blue Notice. I wanted to give her a chance but failing to make a truthful report was, well . . . it was criminal. And I had to make sure that both she and the public were protected. I felt secure that they were.

It was now ten past four in the morning.

'Do you have to get back early for the children?'

'No, my mother's there. Duncan said to call if I needed him to come and meet the boat.' A pause. 'But I'll wait with you if you like.'

'I like.'

She took her sweater off. We got under the covers and lay like spoons, my arm around her, hand cupping a luscious, heavy breast, and fell asleep. I woke around seven and we were, inevitably, turned away from each other. Isn't it odd? We all love the idea of sleeping curled up together but the body can't abide it. It's the heat, I suppose. And the arm on which you're lying becomes a problem because there's really nowhere for it to go. The whole design is a disaster in many ways; it's a bloody miracle we manage as well as we do.

As usual on waking, I was aroused, so I turned and slid into her. I know, I know. You can do that only in fiction. How could she have been ready. Of course she wasn't but I don't want to go into the details of preparation, okay? Anyway, she made nice noises and was soon awash all on her own.

If I hadn't met Francesca, would I have fallen for Lorna? Of course that relationship too would have been unsatisfactory because of her family. There was no *coup de foudre* here but, my goodness, I felt such affection for this girl. It was love in its way. We'd been through something extraordinary together. Extreme trauma and great intimacy; stirred *and* shaken. A heady cocktail.

The instrument module was repaired in no time. Careless assembly by the artificer at Glasgow had caused disconnections during the aerial acrobatics. I wouldn't be so forgiving of him as I was of Lorna.

Lorna had control all the way back. Textbook flying. Not an error or hesitation. Well, hesitation only in her speech when she asked, 'Have you . . . have you . . .' She laughed. 'Have you ever done it up here?'

'Not when I was in the driving seat, no. But I have done it.'

'Tell me.'

'No, you'll get horny and crash.'

'No, I won't.'

'Yes, you will. Look, you've already dropped ninety feet.'

'What?'

Her eyes shot to the altimeter. She hadn't.

'You bugger!'

'I'll tell you on the ground.'

And I did, in the back room of a small empty hangar as we said our goodbyes. She sitting on a table, knickers pulled aside, her legs open and around my waist. She cried, but from joy at being, for the moment anyway, out of the black pit.

When she had settled, she said, 'I'm going to have to stay away for a bit, Hal, because . . . you know.' And she kissed me in the softest, loveliest way.

'I know. I'll miss you, dearest Lorna. And what we went through together, all of it – I wouldn't trade for anything.'

'Thanks. You know, you're in the wrong job, Hal.'

'Really? What should I be?

'You're a natural healer.'

A drip of disappointment fell on me. I hadn't put Lorna down for a fey fruitcake.

'What do you mean, a faith healer?'

'Oh, God, no. You should have been in medicine.'

Relief. 'Well, that's something I've never thought of. And a bit late now.'

'Yes. Pity.'

I had no idea what to say. Though there was something in what she said that I sort of recognised. I said, 'Do you have a job? I mean before.'

'Yes'

'What did you do?'

'Don't laugh.'

'No. What?'

'I'm a psychiatrist.'

I laughed. And so did she.

I never saw her again.

Hal

The following weeks were dull – how could they have been otherwise – and lonely because now I missed both Francesca *and* Lorna. Christmas was particular hell, as invariably it is for the unattached – and frequently for the attached. Francesca would be at the family home in Sussex, trying to get on with her parents. It was so hard not to lift the phone. She knew where I was but she too, resisted calling.

Mrs McLafferty's little house was now festooned in coloured paper and there was an addition to the religious artefacts. A crib, a model manger containing little figures of Mary, Joseph, her geriatric and highly frustrated husband, the baby, shepherds, wise men and asses.

One of the instructors kindly asked me to Christmas lunch. I would have preferred to check into a hotel somewhere and be on my own with a book but I graciously accepted his invitation. A mistake. He had two boys who loathed each other. It was Bedlam. Bedlam, Bethlehem. How appropriate.

Ordinarily, my days were spent with earnest young men who were praying for a letter from an airline accepting them for training. One morning the letter *I'd* been praying for arrived. Sod's law dictated that it arrived with the one that I had been praying would never arrive – one from 'Uncle Humphrey', scolding me for being neglectful of him and asking me please to get in touch. This was actually Humphries, Cadell's junior and dogsbody, a rather sad man who, due to an insufficiency of old school yeast had risen as far as he would. These were the last of the days when such things mattered. I had always liked Humphries and we'd talked a few times over the years. I had the feeling that he was really less committed to the service than he might be but was grateful for its protection. Also, he was probably too frightened of Cadell to resign.

Humphries's letter was addressed directly to me, not at the flying school but care of Mrs McLafferty. My Blue Notice story to Lorna wasn't really so far fetched. Harry, the chum I stayed with in London, was the only person who knew where I was and he would never have betrayed me. The other letter, the one I had been praying for, forwarded by Harry, was from Africa. Escape!

Cadell was obviously miffed that I hadn't given him a contact when I quit the RAF, so if I didn't get in touch now, then someone, probably Humphries, would come calling. I'd have to plan with care my exit from the UK. It's not easy, when you're dealing with people of the dark, to keep paranoia at bay.

I haven't really told you about Cadell, have I?

Cadell is Military Intelligence. He comes under the umbrella of MI6, though his is an occult unit within it. He is, as it were, the business end of yet another covert unit within the Foreign Office; put simply, they are advocates of the 'divide and rule' policy. Cadell supplies the wedge.

Whatever happens on the surface, governments tumbling, ideologies crumbling, has no effect on those conduits of communication that exist between countries by means of such shrouded bodies established over decades, indeed centuries. They don't exist but they are funded. How? Fear. It's a great inducement to pay up. 'Oh, you have men on the battlements, watching? They won't save you. They may even turn on you. We'll save you – by keeping the enemy busy. We'll turn one of his friends into his new enemy. We'll sell him swords to help him fight his new enemy. Then by skilful legerdemain, we'll have someone else supply his new enemy with even bigger swords and a couple of trebuchets. Just pop the royal seal on this parchment and get back to fucking the pageboy, Your Majesty.'

I delivered swords, I delivered gunpowder, I turned friend into foe. I could drop down in a Harrier – which, if you don't know, can take off and land vertically – hide it, yes, hide it, drive twenty miles on a light motor bike, which was clipped to pylons under the fuselage, set a charge with someone else's signature on it, drive back and be gone in under an hour.

'Oh look! A fight has broken out between the Frosnians and the Klerbs. How did that happen?'

'Well, in 1323, apparently some Frosnian rogered the king of Klerbia's fattest tart and someone's just remembered.'

For the first thirteen years in the RAF, I'd been a regular and a test pilot. There was no better time to be a flyer. This was the Golden Age. It was the beginning of jet propulsion and there was still public excitement about any new aircraft. Not only that, but the solution to that great mystery, Mach 1, *The Sound Barrier* was coming tantalisingly close. I flew everything, Spitfires – Fairey Gannets, de Havilland Vampires, Gloucester

Meteors, Hawker Hunters, the massive Vulcan bomber, which patrolled the globe carrying a nuclear weapon just in case Ivan got frisky. Jets flew faster and faster, what every mad boy wants. The thrill is phenomenal, but the edge wears off everything even though you're still happy doing it.

Then Cadell came calling. It was just as you've read it in fiction, lunch at the club, an occasional drive to the country to play golf with a couple of chaps. Cadell was delightful. He was old school, old guard, tall and slim with silver hair at the sides and a trim David Niven, albeit white, moustache. Come to think of it he *was* sort of David Niven. Cadell was one of the last great Whitehall eminences, but only the spooks knew what he actually did. He was a great wit and knew art, music, theatre and literature. He was also the most ruthless man I'd ever met. Whatever had to be done, he'd do it – whatever the cost in blood or silver – and happily go off to the ballet afterwards.

During the 'romancing' period he never inquired as to my views on anything, he simply chatted, thus with ease acquiring all relevant information. Occasionally he would tell the story of an operation then go back and alter an event and ask, 'So what then would your course of action be?' He wasn't looking for courage, if you could call it that – mild insanity would be nearer the mark – but the safest, original solution, safe not for oneself necessarily, but for the mission. Outcome and concealment were everything.

I was removed from my squadron and assigned to one that existed only on scraps of paper and given an aircraft that didn't exist in any squadron; the kestrel, which could take off and land vertically. My use of it would be part of its test programme. I was given no reasons for the missions on which

I was sent. I'd joined for the excitement and was not disappointed. As the years wore on, however, I began to change. 'Growing up' some might call it. And with this maturing came awareness and the realisation that I'd been brainwashed. I, the son of an aircraft designer and a non-working mother, was brought up in the Lake District and educated in a Roman Catholic boarding school where religion was knocked out of me for ever, thank God. The other indoctrination was more insidious. It led to profound faith that the Establishment practised what it preached: loyalty, decency and justice. This preaching was done from neither the pulpit nor the Dispatch Box but from the pages of the *Rover* and the *Hotspur*, boys' papers, which purveyed to youngsters hungry for adventure and heroism, the fortitude of track ace Alf Tupper and the gallantry of Squadron Leader Matt Braddock. Further sermons came wrapped in celluloid from Ealing and Pinewood and we, the faithful, were permanently immersed in the medium waves of the BBC Home Service.

For girls, the same applied, but for *Rover* and *Hotspur*, substitute *School Friend* and *Ballet Shoes*. I read those too, by the way, because I *always* liked playing with girls.

My mind never suffered invasion by such thoughts as, 'What kind of person am I?' Had it done so, the response would have been that I was a decent bloke like most I knew. I did favours, I wasn't stingy, I didn't hurt anyone. When Cadell told me to do something, I did it. He was one of the secret rulers of The Realm. He knew what was right. Look at his suits, for God's sake. Listen to him talk. The man knows what's what.

But the world was changing. There were youngsters who had escaped the boys' papers and the BBC. There were those who had seen Hiroshima, there were serviceman who were telling unflattering stories about the British Army in Palestine and Aden. I had flown Venoms and Hawker Hunters giving air support in Aden, then Rhadfan, so had seen a few things myself; seen and erased.

Now that we had come a distance from the Reich and the Rising Sun, enemies were no longer so readily identifiable, no longer so easy to hate. So, questions began to form in my mind and the few answers that came were less than satisfactory. I soldiered on – or flew on – until there occurred an event so appalling that I cannot bear to think of it.

I helped out? I didn't hurt anyone? Me? Smiling, I flew the skies and on my wings, bore Death.

Francesca

Did I know? Did I feel my foot kick the phone off? Did I, in the ensuing horror blot it from my mind in my desperation not to be blamed? So many years and still haunted. And now yet another fatality, the third from that day. Not corporal this time, but spiritual. I'm sitting in a Lloyd Loom chair staring out beyond the veranda. The view is abruptly blurred as, with a loud hissing thump, African rain falls in a lump from the sky. From nothing to a million gallons a second, in a second. And all rain brings the same memory.

Cambridge. The pub door opens and in walks a man, absolutely drenched, in a sort of Spitfire outfit, carrying a crash helmet. Completely delicious. We tagged eyes as he walked to the bar to ask for a *half* pint. A continental to boot! He glanced at me again then vanished round the corner. Infuriating beyond measure. He was far too good to miss.

'Just a sec,' I said to the others.

As I walked away, Willie said, 'Francesca's found her fuck for tonight.'

A bit bloody previous, but not unfounded.

The Spitfire man was reading a book, crime or spies or something, but at least it was a book and not some stupid sports page.

'Hello, I'm Francesca Trestrail.'

'Hello, Hal Sinclair.'

Hal Sinclair. H.S. Heaven Sent. I felt something happen to me in his presence. A sort of tremor and a sensation of my insides metamorphosing into a viscous substance. Not just my bits; everywhere. But we talked for only a few seconds then he left. Shit and derision! How could he? I couldn't understand it? He'd laughed at my jokes. He'd just laughed and hadn't tried to top them. Why leave me just like that?

I ran after him and found him just as he was riding off. I called and waved but he couldn't hear me. Désolé! Then the bike turned around and he came back. I was trembling, ready for his anger at my delaying him, but there was none. He was smiling and there was something, I don't know . . . something. He took me to supper, bliss, and listened while I blathered about Italian literature. He was an 'older man'. Exciting. Why? Made me feel more grown up? I'm not sure. It's historical, isn't it? A jet pilot, he seemed at once both wild and sad – and frightening. I don't know what it was. He didn't say or do anything remotely frightening, but he was the most frightening man I'd ever met. And he wouldn't sleep with me, not even kiss. The following night, the same and I had the same tremors, the same oily insides and was so juicy for him. On the third night he was about to leave *again*. It occurred to me with complete horror that he must be queer. A queer pilot who rides a motor bike? How completely peculiar. I had to find out because I couldn't bear it, so I kissed him. He wasn't queer, not one bit.

As we loved, I felt enveloped in such . . . tenderness. And once again, I felt that . . . something which so warmed me but which eluded definition. When the revelation came, it heaved at my stomach and roared in my head. It came as he said my name. Out of nothing he said, 'Francesca.'

And I realised that he *cared*. For the first time in my life, someone truly cared for me, and I truly cared for him and knew that I would be with him until death and love him for ever beyond it. What I couldn't know was that it was I who would lead him to Death's outstretched hand.

Oh Hal, my darling, my only love. How could you die and leave me here alone?

Hal

Now to leave Britain without being seen. I couldn't use public transport because of passport control. I needed only some clothes and a few books for the journey. Harry was willing to keep my other bits.

My biggest problem was what to do with Sweet Sunbeam. Reluctantly, I drove her to Norfolk to the dealer from whom I'd bought her. This was Dennis, a man who, like me, was excited by fine engineering. The Sunbeam motor cycle was something of an exotic. It had twin overhead cams and a shaft, rather than a chain drive. The Sunbeam Company, in its great racing days before the war, built the Rolls-Royce of motor bikes. It had subsequently been taken over by BSA from which time this bike dated. You're fascinated, I can tell. It was also a rather unusual green, by the way.

Dennis had lost his right leg – odd phrase, that, as though one might have carelessly mislaid it – on HMS *Hood* but was determined never to let the bloody Bosch deny him his greatest thrill, which was driving a motor cycle; so any bike he bought he cleverly adapted to enable him to change gear with his left foot. As Dennis was about to write the cheque I looked at Sweet

Sunbeam and into my mind dropped the image of Francesca sitting saucily astride her, her dress pulled up and no knickers. She'd made me start the engine and when I did, and the vibration hit her spread fanny, her eyes had opened as wide as both her smiling mouths.

'Cripes!' she shouted, 'these machines are for girls, not boys.' That memory brought the knowledge that I could never sell Sweet Sunbeam.

Consequently, I had a ridiculous but thrilling idea. I'd take her to Africa. Dennis thought the notion was 'bloody cracking, actually'.

What I really wanted was the impossible. To take Francesca to Africa. There was not a moment of the day when she was not in my mind. One might imagine that being apart was being apart, but the fact of being separated by continents illogically increased the distress. It would have been so easy to jump on Sunbeam and drive to Cambridge, say 'I'm sorry Francesca, I was wrong. We'll make it work somehow.' *What a nerve, what a bloody nerve to imagine that she'd welcome me with open arms and feel she could trust me for ever.*

The following day I drove to a truckers' caf on the A2 to Dover, where I met Teddy from Barnsley who, totally toothless and with the thickest glasses I had ever seen, was driving his twelve-wheeled Foden to Lyons. What was he carrying? Nails mostly. Yes, nails. Well, someone has to do it and the task fell to Teddy from Barnsley in his Royal Navy greatcoat.

I put a bit of Lancashire in my voice. Barnsley is of course in Yorkshire and a Lancs man in the wrong circumstances could have been treated as hostile. These though, were the perfect circumstances. We were united against the common enemy – the South. After tribal markings had been displayed and approved, 'So where ye headed?' asked Teddy, his lips flapping.

'Anywhere out of 'ere.'

'What, have ye had a spot of bother 'ave ye?'

'Fookin' right. Gorra gerr out.'

'What were it?'

'Ringin' cars.'

This means cutting up stolen or damaged cars and welding the good bits together, making what appears to be a proper vehicle which is then hawked to the unwary. So called perhaps because it is a dead ringer for a real motor.

'Have you been inside?'

'Not yet. I will for this, though. That's why I've gorra gerr out. You?'

'Yeah, wunce. Fookin' shite, that.'

'Yeah. I don't fancy it.'

'I'll help you out.'

'What?'

'I'll take you across.'

The enemy common to all, Northern or Southern, Red Rose or White, is Old Bill, Plod, the Rozzers, and if you're a Nancy, Mavis, otherwise known as the Police. No ordinary bloke will ever rat on you. He may not necessarily help, but he'll never grass you. Teddy from Barnsley with his pebble glasses, bless 'im, was going to help me out.

'In the back? Can I ride in the back?'

'Ye want to ride int' back with bike?'

'Aye, got no passport. Ye know?'

It wasn't that. I didn't just want to show my passport. At that time, due to the financial crises in the UK, each person was permitted to take no more than fifty pounds sterling out of the country. I had a great deal more than that strapped around my waist.

'Aye right. Ye can get in behind t' crates.'

'Ye'r awright you, Teddy. Thanks.'

He smiled. When he closed his mouth, his chin met his nose. His toothlessness was an impediment both to his speech and the mastication of his bacon. He blamed the bacon.

'What 'appened to yer teeth?'

'They was goin' rotten so I 'ad them all took out years back.'

''Avn't ye got false ones?'

'No, I tried those. They were fookin' shite an 'all.''

''Ow d'ye mean?'

'Fookin' agony, they was.'

'Why didn't ye take 'em back?'

'Take 'em back, where? I bought 'em off t' bosun's mate.'

So, I followed Teddy until we found a place to turn off the main road where, unseen, I could ride Sweet Sunbeam up into the back of the truck and hide myself among the nails. The ride was like the cakewalk at the fair but more violent. I hoped that Teddy's choice of specs was made with more care than his teeth because, if there was to be a pile up, these crates would succeed where Lorna's kamikaze dive had failed.

Passing customs at Dover was plain sailing. The sailing itself, was not so plain. There was a hefty roll with a pitch to match. Locked in the dark of the airless truck, I fought and was victorious in one of my greatest battles, a triumph of mind over a bacon sandwich which had a grim determination to return to the open air. I don't normally suffer from motion sickness but under those conditions . . . Some wise wag defined sea sickness as 'The terror that you'll die, followed by the even greater terror that you won't.'

After a voyage of about ten months, I heard the engine note change and knew we had reached Calais. Even when the boat is docked you feel sick. You fantasise movement. On stepping ashore, the sickness is instantly gone.

I felt the truck move down the ramp and off the ferry, drive for half a minute, then stop. Voices. This must be customs. Teddy had said that in the 70 crossings he'd made, they'd looked in the back only once. But the engine died and I heard the cabin door slam shut. Then the sound I really didn't want to hear, the back of the truck being opened. I crouched, hidden at the far end but Sweet Sunbeam was lashed just inside the doors. Light flooded in. A French voice, in very good English, said, 'What's this motor cycle? It's not on your manifest.' *Fuck, bugger!*

Then, Teddy from Barnsley, hero that he was, 'No, that's mine.'

'You brought it to sell?'

'To sell? Bloody hell, I wouldn't sell that, that's a special bike, that is. I saved for five years to buy that bike.'

'So why did you bring it here?'

'When I come to France I like to see a bit of the real country, ye know, not just drive through it on t'lorry. See the villages, ye know, 'ave' a glass of wine.'

I heard this being translated, then another voice, '*Aimez vous La France?*'

'Wot?'

'Do you like France?'

'Yeah, I luve it. I were 'ere int' war, like.'

God, Teddy, I thought, don't overdo it. I hoped he wasn't wearing his Navy coat.

'You were in the British Army?'

'Yeah.'

'But this is a coat of the British Navy.'

Shit, fuck, bugger!

'Yeah, this is me brother's. He were int' Navy. He were killed.'

'Your brother was killed?'

'Yeah, a Gerry plane strafed the ship and got 'im. They sent 'is coat back.'

He was so good *I* was believing him.

'I'm sorry,' said the Frenchman.

'Yeah, thanks.'

'All right. You can go. Enjoy France.'

'Yeah, I will, right. Thanks.'

And we were off. Soon he stopped and I got back in the cab.

'Fookin' listen to you,' I said. 'You were fookin' great, you.'

Teddy was quiet.

'Was that true, about your brother in the Navy?'

'No, I were int' Navy, he were int' Army, young Len. But 'e were killed all right, just along t' road, in Caen. But 'e wouldn't mind, ye know, helpin' us out, not young Len.'

Teddy and Len from Barnsley, the boys who helped out.

We parted company just outside Lyons.

The following morning brought soft, uniquely French light. I changed some money and started towards the port of Marseilles. There was a long way to go so I didn't push Sunbeam. I arrived about ten in the evening, booked into a cheap hotel and the patron let me put Sunbeam in his garage.

Wanting neither to eat nor sleep alone, I picked up a girl. They stood in a group and I felt awkward because I didn't want those not selected to feel insulted. Ridiculous. I chose one who had proud tits and slim hips and no, you're wrong, it was not those attributes that encouraged my decision, it was her face. She had sad, dark eyes and a mouth with a delicate curve. She agreed to dinner and the night. Her name was Françoise, can you believe it? Dinner was pretty good, with a decent Provençal red. She thought it *très, très exotique* to be *un aviateur*. I said that lots of people probably thought it *très, très exotique* to be *une pute*.

'*Ah, c'est drôle.*' she said, clicking her tongue. She continually glanced towards the door. I was uneasy that she might be expecting trouble. No doubt in her business it was permanently close by, so I asked. The pute pouted. *Pas du tout.* But her eyes continued to flick to the door. I supposed that she did it to every door, constant in the hope that one day, something good might walk through one of them.

On the way back to the hotel, she stopped abruptly, said, '*Attendez,*' hiked up what little there was of her skirt, pulled down her pants, bent forward and peed backwards into the gutter. '*Exotique!*'

We didn't do it, my heart somehow wasn't in it, to her relief I'm sure. What I wanted was the company and the warmth of her body – and that, she gladly gave. Maybe that's what she wanted too. I hoped that Teddy from Barnsley had found someone to cuddle him.

In the morning, she wouldn't be roused.

'*Oh, non. Je dors, je dors. Mmmmmmmmm.*' She turned and covered her head. I went for coffee and brought some for her but it was no enticement from the horizontal. I told her that I had to leave but she could sleep until midday. She waved a limp hand and drifted off again. How many of her days began like this and in circumstances considerably more seedy? How long before that lovely curve of her mouth became a snarl?

Francesca

Poor, dear Reg. A large rock to hide under but which became too heavy. We married an indecently short time after Hal's death. I imagined that Hal, from the other side had sent me to Reg, knowing that Reg would look after me. He was right. Reg Fraser, a surgeon, was from Glasgow and it took me some time to understand what he was saying, most of which was either fuck or cunt or fucking or cunting or bastarding. He was huge, with red hair, the angriest man I had ever met when dealing with either medical incompetence or failing to find something in the kitchen. Underneath, he was pure gold.

Hal

Sweet Sunbeam rose high in the air and swung away from the dock on the end of the jib arm, which then lowered her into the small aft hold of the *San Vittore del Lazio*, an Italian merchantman bound for Mombasa with a cargo of power generators. There were two passenger cabins, modest but clean, in which I was the sole occupant. The whole ship was pretty clean, crewed entirely by Italians. Some spoke a little English, some a little French, so with my schoolboy French, communication was entirely possible if often hilarious. These were surely the cheeriest seamen in the history of water. Why?

The ship's master, Captain Arcangeli, had a simple philosophy and one which made perfect sense. Men who are underpaid and forced to live in confined, disciplined circumstances with their fundamental appetites unsatisfied, become resentful, then angry, then careless. Consequently he employed, from the manual, *How to be a Successful Italian Wife*, rule one: 'Keep his stomach full and his balls empty'. So the boat was full of women, wives, girlfriends and tarts. One big happy family. This is highly unusual. Seafarers are devoutly superstitious and legend has it that a woman on board brings bad luck. There were no children though. The ship was considered too dangerous for them, so young parents were never signed on.

There was no official cook. Everyone mucked in, including the men, but they were assigned the donkey work such as preparing the vegetables – apart from two of them who were great cooks – but the art was, on the whole, left to the women. And what art. I'd never in my life eaten so well or in such irrepressibly jolly company. Every mealtime was a party and because the day was divided into watches, one meal dovetailed into the next. The men and their partners took the same watches so that they bedded together and ate together. I offered my help in the galley but they wouldn't hear of it, my being a paying passenger.

Being surrounded by Italians made me ache for Francesca all the more – if it were possible to increase the ache.

We set out across the Mediterranean. When news came from the bridge that the Italian coast was on our port side, although beyond our visibility, there were loud cheers and everyone sang 'Bandiera Rossa', the anthem of the Italian Communist party. This was surprising because during the meal 'parties' there had been no indication of a particular political leaning. But then they all sang 'Giovinezza', the anthem of Mussolini's Fascist party. Then, to a man, they shouted, '*Va fa'n culo tutti!*' 'Fuck the lot of you!' Then, to cover all the bases, '*Il Papa e un cazzo anche lui!*' 'and the Pope's a prick too.'

Captain Arcangeli, who thankfully spoke excellent English, and with a movie-star accent, was a unique being. He had in his vessel created a fine world within a foul one. True anarchy. There was no rank except for his, and that, he had no need to exercise. He did his job, which was to command the ship. The men – and women – did theirs and each was considered as important as the other. If there was ever a misdeed it would be brought up at the weekly crew meeting. They would discuss it, elucidate what provoked it, and measures would be taken to reconcile the transgressor(s) with the victim(s). This was done without castigation, the understanding being that everyone is prey to moments of rancour and the surest way to provoke further ire is public rebuke.

This understanding did not of course come naturally. It was explained by Arcangeli to new crew members when they signed on, which wasn't often because vacancies were rare, but the difference between life on board and anything they had ever experienced was so startling that they became acclimatised in short order. Some of the crew had done time for serious crimes, and these were Arcangeli's greatest success stories. At first they had been suspicious and belligerent, testing everyone at every opportunity but, when instead of anger or fear, they were constantly countered by good humour, and their arguments at subsequent meetings treated with respect, their anger quickly abated.

The most serious incident had occurred one month into a voyage. A few months after completing a six-year jail sentence, Aldo, a new crewman, during an argument about football, of all pointless things, had gone berserk. Ducking into the galley to find something he could use as a weapon, he grabbed the first handle he saw on the work surface. He turned back into the mess with it, intent on serious damage, but it was an egg whisk. This brought a gale of laughter. Ridiculed then, he attacked with feet and fists and kicked one man in the head with such force that it knocked him unconscious. Although they had found, through the captain's guidance, a different way to live, these guys, were far from soft, so they leaped on him, tied him up and put him in what they used as a 'cooler'. He screamed medieval revenge for ten minutes or so, until Pasqualina, the wife to Mauro, the guy he'd knocked out, came along with a smile, a bowl of pasta and a glass of red wine. Then Arcangeli came along and asked if he was feeling better and would he like to come and eat in the mess with the others.

Aldo naturally imagined that this was a ruse to get him in the open and no doubt chuck him over the side. Arcangeli had then done the most amazing thing. He had gone to the galley and brought back a long, sharp kitchen knife which he gave to Aldo, telling him that although he wouldn't need it, he did have the right to defend his life. Pasqualina lamented that the pasta was getting cold and would he please make up his fucking mind. Aldo, now somewhat bewildered had, clutching the knife, followed them back to the mess, where he was greeted with applause and an outstretched hand from Pasqualina's now black-eyed husband, Mauro. In no time, egg-whisk jokes were flying, Aldo laughing as loudly as anyone else.

Captain Arcangeli and this story changed my life. He was the first person I'd met who not only knew that hitting people doesn't make them better but who had positive proof that the opposite was true. A 'difficult' child, he had been sent by his aristocratic Italian parents to a school in England called Summerhill, run by a crusty Scotsman called A S Neill who had a reputation for sorting out unruly kids. He did this by such unorthodox means as being nice to them, respecting them, and surprising them. For example, if he knew that a child had stolen a shilling, then at an appropriate moment he would say casually, 'I hear you're a bit short of money, maybe this'll be of help,' and give the kid a shilling. If the kid stole again, another shilling would be handed over. Neill would patiently wait for the kid to approach him. They'd have a few friendly chats, absent of any reproach, and the kid would rarely steal again. The weekly meetings on the ship originated at the school. Arcangeli had resolved as a young man that one day he would have his own ship and that's how it would be run. It had taken 38 years for these incandescently obvious realities to invade my blinkered vision.

The justice that I was taught, and which I more or less accepted, was based on vindictiveness. This sprang from the pronouncement of the Great Psychotic in the Sky – 'If you, my children, don't love me, then I'll burn your arses in hell.' This is the bloke who allowed the Crusades, the Plague, Auschwitz, the Burma railroad and Hiroshima; the bloke who saw young Len from Barnsley so carelessly abandoned. 'Our Father in heaven . . .' What happened to our *mother* in heaven? He probably killed her.

We steamed down the Med, squeezing between Corsica and Sardinia then between Sicily and the toe of Italy, turned south east past North Africa and through the Suez Canal. We navigated the canal on 1 June, and not a moment too soon. Four days later, Israel, the Gulf of Aqaba having been closed to her, and anticipating an attack from Egypt and other Arab nations, made a pre-emptive strike now known as the Six Day War. In a total rout, the Egyptian Air Force was destroyed before it left the ground and Israel's borders were extended. In rage against everyone, Gamal Abdel Nasser, President of Egypt, closed the Canal.

The Red Sea and into the Gulf of Aden was familiar territory to me but only from the air. First in a Venom, then, in the early sixties, in a Hawker Hunter, a Christmas tree of rockets and cannon. We were based at Kormaksar and, briefed by intelligence who sniffed out terrorist hideouts in populated areas, Shackletons would then drop leaflets, giving a fifteen-minute warning of a strike and exactly where it would occur, so that civilians could scarper. We would then come in and bomb a specific target. We spent a great deal of time practising precision bombing so that we were able to demolish a building without damaging the adjacent structures.

A few more days down through the Indian Ocean, and we tied up at Mombasa docks. I disembarked the *San Vittore del Lazio* a man much richer than the one who boarded at Marseilles.

8

Imagine the most vivid colours ever to have startled your eyes. Imagine both a jabbering cacophony which seems physically to invade your brain – and utter tranquillity. Bring to mind the most verdant, exuberant growth, and the most arid, barren dirt. The most intoxicating fragrance, and the most putrid, emetic stench. Envisage men seven feet tall, elegant, proud and powerful, surrounded by hideous disease and grotesque deformity. Multiply those visions and senses by a hundred.

You're now in Africa.

So am I and oh God, it's so far from Francesca. Why can't I leave Francesca behind? She was trouble. She'll always be trouble – and so will I. Love can be such a bastard.

The Air Rescue office was in a small building on the grounds of Wilson Airport.

'Hello,' I announced myself.

'Are you Hal Sinclair?' This from the administrator, good looking, in her late thirties, the sort who could have won the war on her own.

'Yes.'

'Joan Ashplant-Beer.' I didn't catch it but resisted asking for a repetition. She walked towards me, 'Dr Koston's on his way. You'll have to leave immediately. How do you do?' A firm grip offered, soft skin and a smile.

'Where are we going?' She handed me a typewritten sheet with names and map co-ordinates.

'It's all there. The aircraft's being fuelled. Could you start your check now please so that you're ready to go when he arrives.'

I had imagined that I would have at least the morning to look over the three aircraft, two single-engined Cessnas and a twin-engined Piper, but obviously there was a flap on.

'What's the flap?'

Before she could reply – 'That bloody car has got to go.' A tall, slightly stooped man of forty was heading for me, hand outstretched. 'John Koston, how are you?'

'Hello. Hal Sinclair.'

'Can I trust you with my life.'

'You can trust me with *mine.*'

He smiled. 'That'll do fine.'

I headed out to do the walk around. You can immediately tell whether or not an aircraft is being properly looked after. The air surfaces will be clean. Cables and linkages will be lubricated, the engine will be spotless and the oil a good colour. No wiring will show signs of fraying. Engine noise is also a clue – as is the look of the mechanic. This was Daniel, a Kikuyu, himself spotless in white overalls, who called me *Bwana*. This simply means 'Mister' but the first time you hear it, it makes you want to laugh because you think you've turned into Clark Gable.

I was in the cockpit completing the pre-flight check when John hurried out with Joan. He climbed in.

'Can we go?'

'Yes. What's the flap?'

'A hyena got a kid. They beat it off but she's badly hurt.'

We shook as a Pan Am Boeing 707 with a mean look taxied past. I fell in well behind him as instructed.

'Was this on a safari?

'No, in a village.'

'Is that unusual, an animal attack?'

'No. You only have to be careless for a minute out there and something'll get you. Have you read the rule book?'

The 707 opened its throttles and the engines blazed.

'I've glanced at it.'

'Learn it. We white alien townies are out of our depth here. This is another planet, with diverse and highly inventive means at its disposal to dispatch us.'

The Boeing was still on the ground and going like hell. Jet engines love cold air and wings love fat air. Nairobi is a mile above sea level and close to the Equator, so the air is hot and thin. V2, or lift off, therefore took a lot longer to achieve than it would in London. After what seemed an amazing length of time, we saw the tops of the wings appear as she pushed herself into the sky.

I was cleared by the tower to take off but waited until I was sure that the vortices caused by the Boeing's wingtips had settled. These could pick up a small aircraft, throw it around and dash it to earth.

After a long run, we were airborne and heading north west toward the Kedong Valley. The villagers had done as requested and laid a cross of white cloth at the point of touchdown. We did a low pass to check the ground we were going to land on. Landing at high altitudes is even more interesting than taking off because, in the thin air, it's more difficult to slow the aircraft down. I dropped the flaps and undercarriage well in advance to increase drag, and made a steep, dropping, nose-up descent to avoid speed increase – while at the same time trying to avoid a stall in the thin air.

The child, a girl of four, was in terrible shape. A burst of machine-gun fire down one side of her body could not have done more damage. It might have done even less. Bullet wounds, unless they're dumdum or something equally horrific, are fairly clean – at least on the way in. Animal teeth incise and tear. The medicine man was in attendance and had covered the girl's wounds in some sort of moss.

I expected trouble at the intervention of white medicine but my fear was groundless. John was very courteous, very deferential. Like one specialist to another. This demeanour was returned by the medicine man who evidently appreciated that in some areas we might have an advantage.

Antibiotic was pumped into her and her wounds cleaned and examined. The greatest danger to her life was a ruptured artery in her leg, the bleeding from which had been stemmed by the packing used by the medicine man. What was really wonderful to watch was Koston in action.

John Koston was the sort of doctor we all want; kind, sympathetic and strong. He could have been wealthy, practising in any of the world's Harley Streets, but came to Africa because he thought it was right. He was born and brought up in New Zealand. Jewish on his father's side, instilled was the principle of giving back to society some of the good fortune with which he had been blessed. I wished that my motives for coming to Africa had been so laudable but, having met John and been briefed about the job, I tried to convince myself that perhaps through this, I could atone in some small way for my trespasses.

The flying doctor service allowed me the kind of flying I had missed, being bound by the strict disciplines of the service. This was old-fashioned, seat-of-the-pants stuff through mostly empty skies. There were small clinics established here and there throughout Kenya and small hospitals mostly run by missionaries. During the Mau Mau wars, many had been abandoned but were slowly, under Jomo's so far sensible rule, being re-established.

As the months became a year I felt a change occurring. A lightening, not of the pain in my heart for my lost Francesca – Captain Arcangeli had once quoted to me an Italian proverb, *L'amore fa passare il tempo, il tempo fa passare l'amore,*' 'Love makes time pass, time makes love pass.' Not true, in my experience – but a lightening of my spirit. It manifested itself in the return of a kind of recklessness which I'd had to bury in my latter years in the service. I enjoyed riding Sweet Sunbeam at speed along the treacherous, pitted murram roads – and riding other sweet things too.

I had also learned, under John's tutelage, to do simple bandaging and, when he was pressed for time, give injections. We were now firm friends and spent much time discussing medicine, which fascinated me more and more. He was interested in the physics of flying and loved stories of my exploits but wild buffalo couldn't drag him to the controls of an aircraft.

9

Precisely thirteen months after arriving in Kenya, I sat with a beer at the Norfolk Hotel and heard a chuckle. *So like her.* It sounded so like Francesca but I didn't turn around. Better to sit and dream. No, not dream, dreaming makes distress. There was the sound of a glass going over, then, 'Shit and derision!' My heartbeat shot to about 150. Still I didn't turn. I couldn't bear the disappointment of it not being her. But what if it was her? So what? What would she want with me? I ditched her and she was young, she'd be well over it by now.

Curiosity was too great though not to turn, so I did. And of course it wasn't her. A young woman who did actually have a slight physical resemblance to Francesca, something about the shape of her head and the way she stood, was dabbing her dress with a napkin. A man and another woman fussed around, looking for a waiter and mopping the table. From beside me, 'Hello.'

I turned. Looking at me was Francesca. My mind short-circuited. It was an unearthly sensation, as if I wasn't really there. The acoustic of the room changed as a high, whistling noise was generated in my brain.

I whispered, 'Good God!'

'How are you?' She smiled, calm.

I couldn't get my brain to work. 'Em . . . I don't know. Em . . . Fine, thank you. You?'

'Yes, fine. What are you doing here?'

'I have a job as a pilot with the flying doctor service.'

'Oh good. Is that interesting?'

What the fuck was this? A conversation between two people who had once met briefly at a party? Whatever romantic notions I had harboured were dashed on jagged rocks. It was over. For her, it meant nothing. Well, that's what I wanted. I loved her and I didn't want her wounded. So that was fine.

'Yes, very interesting. It's funny, because I thought I heard your voice . . . but it was that lady over there . . . then . . . suddenly you were here. So peculiar.'

'That's my sister.'

'Ah! Good heavens.'

'Come and meet them.'

'Ah! Right. Yes, of course.'

I don't want to meet them, I want to go away and fucking weep.

'Angela, this is Hal that I told you about.'

As Angela extended her hand in exactly the way Francesca does, 'Hal?'

'How do you do?' I said.

Her handshake was less firm though.

'Hal and I met in Cambridge, remember?' said Francesca.

'Oh yes, your older man. How do you do?'

Jesus, this is some piece of work, the sister. Francesca had barely mentioned her.

To Francesca, 'What are you doing in Nairobi? You've finished Cambridge of course.'

74

'Yes, I'm visiting Angela. She lives here.'

'Oh, I see. What did you get?'

'A Two one.'

'Well done.'

Mind fizzing. How long would she be here? If for long, how would I bear it?

'I really wanted a First. He said I'd get one.'

Images of her presenting sexual favours to the prof in return for her First clatter in my mind.

I was introduced to Jeremy, Angela's husband, and Rita, both from the British Embassy. Rita had something of the soldier about her. Jeremy would almost certainly be a spy. Not much of one but a spy none the less. There was a pause, which Francesca filled with a gay smile.

'Can we meet up – or . . . or not? I mean coffee or something.'

'Yes, of course.' Jesus, this was almost a replay of our first ever meeting.

'Tomorrow? I've got a boring dinner thing tonight.'

'I'm on call so it'll have to be where there's a phone.'

'We're in Karen, why don't you come there?'

Karen was a residential suburb to the west, named for Karen Blixen, the coffee planter. Think Meryl Streep and 'Ahhfrikah'.

'Yes, fine. About eleven? If I'm not in the air.'

'Yes, okay.'

Addresses and numbers were exchanged and I left, an emotional wreck. I went back to Wilson in the hope that I'd have to fly somewhere. I couldn't stand the waiting with nothing to grab my mind. There wasn't even John to talk to; he was at the hospital and Joan was deep in paperwork. The sun headed toward the horizon and I headed home. In fact I lived on the way to Karen.

Did I want to have coffee with Francesca? Open the wound? The idea of polite small talk in the company of the waspy sister was short of enthralling. With any luck there would be an emergency call and that would be that. As the evening wore on and my heart sank lower and lower I knew that there was nothing to be gained for either of us by meeting. What was over, was over and it had been my doing. She had obviously moved on, so I resolved not to go.

I arrived at exactly eleven, on Sweet Sunbeam. I hung between dreading the polite, distant conversation and being hardly able to wait to see her face again. As I dismounted, Francesca ran from the door into my arms. She buried her face in my neck and held tight.

'Don't let me go Hal, pleasepleaseplease don't let me go.'

'Francesca.'

'Yes, Francesca. I'm your Francesca.'

We stood still, holding each other for I don't know how long. I could feel our hearts thumping.

'That's Sweet Sunbeam.'

'Yes.'

'You must love her a lot to bring her all this way.'

'You christened her, I couldn't sell her.'

She drew back and looked at me sideways. 'Is that true?'

'Yes, it's true.'

'Oh.' She pulled into me again. 'Come inside.'

'Couldn't we stay out here just for a bit?'

'There's no one here, just Gertrude, the aya.'

'The aya's called Gertrude?'

'Her mother was in service to a woman called Gertrude. There's a rumour that she was actually Gertrude's husband's child, which would make her the Honourable Gertrude Ripley-Grant.'

'I take it that's not reflected in her wages.'

Francesca raised an 'are you kidding' eyebrow at me.

We went in. As we did, that same hollow feeling, that I'd originally had with Francesca, returned. The notion that this wasn't right. Why? She loved me, I loved her more than life. Was I reluctant to accept responsibility for her? Such hunger and such nagging unease all at once.

Entering the house, Francesca's arms tight around my waist, we could have been anywhere in the south of England. Chintz heaven. Brass fire dogs, Staffordshire dogs, prints of dogs, a grandfather clock. The Brits just can't get over it. Francesca sensed my thoughts.

'It is a bit fucking Carshalton, isn't it?'

'A tad.'

She pulled us on to the sofa then became still and looked at me, her brow in that sudden, serious furrow which was so familiar. 'I'm sorry . . . Are you with someone else?'

It had taken her a while for this thought to occur. I was thrilled that she had presumed that I would still be hers.

'No, Francesca, I'm not.'

And then the smile, the adorable, wide smile.

The sofa wasn't comfortable. We couldn't get close. She got up. 'C'mon.'

I knew we were headed for the bedroom. 'What about the Honourable?'

'You've never been in the Diplomatic Corps, obviously. Domestic staff are either spies or they see and hear nothing. Gertrude's a little different, though.'

And with that, as we opened the bedroom door, Gertrude appeared. She was beautiful, about thirty and, it was perfectly reasonable to suppose, of mixed blood. In her hair she wore a yellow ribbon.

'Hello Gertrude. This is Hal Sinclair. We're just going into the bedroom for a bit.'

Jesus!

'Hello Gertrude.'

'How do you do, Mr Sinclair? Can I get you some tea or coffee?'

'No, thank you Gertrude.'

'No peeking through the window,' said Francesca, unbelievably. Gertrude put her hand over her mouth and giggling, ran off.

'You've got no shame.'

'No. Since I caught her being fucked over the kitchen table, it's been gloves off.'

'No!'

'Yes, by one of Jeremy's staff. You're now the only person who knows. Gertrude and I trust each other completely.'

'A blackmailer's bond. Who did she catch *you* with?'

A comedic, arch look. 'None of your business.' It wasn't and best that way.

Now that we were in the bedroom a sort of shyness took over which made it difficult to lie down, so we went to the window and looked out at frangipani, jacaranda and God knows what else; violent blasts of colour. The fragrance of frangipani was almost anaesthetic in its power. Our fingers interlaced. She spoke first.

'I'm sorry I leaped at you.'

'No, you're not, and nor am I.'

78

She looked sideways at me and, with her little finger, hooked away a strand of her hair lodged in the corner of her mouth.

'Do you still feel the same?' she asked, 'I mean, I know you didn't ever really say what you felt, but . . . I always knew it.'

'I still feel the same. You?'

'I'll never feel any other way. Ever. No matter if you stay or you go, *mia anima d'oro, la vita mia legate a te,*' my golden soul, my life is bound to you.

10

Francesca

So, here we were, Hal and Francesca, tied at the heart. Both damaged and he, could he but see it, more gravely than I. Having been deprived of love, I could ardently and gratefully embrace it. Hal, though having enjoyed an abundance of love, was unable to forgive himself his past and accept that he was worthy of me. In my youthful ignorance I interpreted this disposition as an incompleteness in his love, so, on occasion, to keep a part of me as only mine, I sought refuge from hurt by dallying with others. Hal knew this and, I suspect, though he would never admit to it, accepted it as penance.

John was perplexed by the relationship I had with Hal and our inability to reconcile whatever differences we might have and just enjoy our love – though any inability was Hal's, not mine – and irritated by what I'm sure he saw as my 'delinquent tantrums'. I sensed that Hal too was becoming increasingly impatient with them, but I had no power to stop them. That's bloody well what 'delinquent' means in this regard. An impairment of the ability to control oneself when wounded. I'd been like that for as long as I could remember. I reacted instantly upon feeling threatened. No matter that I could later analyse the situation, in the moment, I was overwhelmed and my intellect lost control of my emotions. Hal was the opposite, his intellect cracked down, grabbed any wayward emotion by the scruff of the neck and throttled it. It was the thing about him that drove me completely crazy. Perhaps out of envy.

The months passing without my having a job were undermining and made me even more lonely when Hal was away, which he was much of the time. I refrained from voicing this, lest his response was, 'Go back to England, Francesca, you're wasting your life here.' There were clinics all around the country which John attended, plus emergencies, of which there were many. It had always astonished me how often people were attacked by animals, particularly buffalo, which are miserable buggers.

I wanted to go with Hal and John and be of help but space in the aircraft had to be reserved in case they had to bring people back to Nairobi for treatment. Eventually, in desperation, I asked Jeremy if he could find me something to do at the embassy. This infuriated Angela, which was in itself rewarding. Angela's a complete bitch and I love her because she's my big sister but I'm not above putting the boot in now and again. She puts it in constantly and always has. She was Daddy's favourite because she was first and perhaps, although I haven't found anyone to verify my suspicions, because I bear a rather striking resemblance to Uncle Rupert who isn't an uncle but used to be around a lot. Anyway, everything in Angela's life was, she told me, good until I came along, then she was, she complained, forced to spend much of her valuable time tormenting me.

Jeremy was always sweet to me and given half a chance would have had my knickers down. He continued to live in hope and if ever Angela pushed me too far would have his constancy rewarded.

My first naughtiness was not with Jeremy but Sandy, a recent posting. It was in the embassy library which I had been assigned to re-catalogue. This hadn't been tackled since Kenya became a republic in 1964 so it was a Herculean task requiring the recruitment of any willing hands. Sandy's were willing and so, I discovered, were mine, so I let him.

I'd always been able to separate sex and love, perhaps because I'd had a lot more sex than I'd had love and could just enjoy the feeling. With Sandy though, it quickly became evident that there wasn't going to be much to enjoy. He was old enough to know more than he did, but then age has nothing to do with it, does it? He was clumsy. If I'd treated his in the ruffianly way he treated mine, he'd have run home in tears to Mummy. Instead of just doing it on the carpet, he felt he had to be inventive and have me against a bookcase. I was just getting bored and sore when the pounding caused one of the many stacks of books to fall and a large tome hit him on the head. The expression on his face was so comical at the moment of impact that I'm afraid I guffawed rather. In fact, every time I saw him after that I wanted to guffaw again. Poor Sandy. No man would ever get on a horse knowing so little, but they'll all gaily climb on to a girl. We should bolt more.

That night, when I went back to Hal, I felt wretched and empty. Mercifully, he was tired because I couldn't have done it; I felt unclean. Oh, Hal, why couldn't you accept that we were born for each other and let our hearts have rest.

Hal

We were at a clinic in Kalungu, well, John was. I was cleaning scrub and dust, which we'd collected on landing, out of the air intake and landing gear. When I'd finished, I jumped into an ancient Land Rover and headed for the clinic. The Land Rover must surely be about the best vehicle ever made. It's tough as all hell and, with little attention, just keeps going. This one, a Series I, was now well into its second decade. We bounced – or thudded might be a more appropriate verb – along the dirt track, the wheels sometimes leaving the ground altogether. The boy in me who wouldn't grow up, still loved to be reckless at times.

The clinic was a simple whitewashed structure with a corrugated iron roof. A long, ill-formed queue snaked from the door, maybe a hundred men, women, children, dogs, goats and God knows what. At its head, some people, including Mitra, the Indian administrator who ran the outfit, were trying to persuade a terrified man with an injured finger to go in.

'Hi Mitra.'

Mitra smiled. 'Hello Hal.'

I watched the tussle. The man looked mid fifties and was probably forty. Skinny as a stick. Mitra had him by one arm, a woman I took to be his wife had him by the other and they were pulling him. He was in a sideways 'v' shape, his feet dug in and his arse sticking out. He reminded me of a dog which had decided it wasn't going another inch and was being pulled along by its lead, its nails scraping the ground. The poor guy was terrified so I spoke to Mitra.

'Mitra, he's too scared, let him go, let me try.'

'You can bloody try,' she said in her Indian accent. Then she said something in Swahili to the other woman. They let him go and I gave him a smile and he came in with me.

John was finishing a plaster cast on the arm of a pretty Kikuyu child.

'This bugger was trying to escape.'

'What's wrong with him?'

'He's cut his finger.' John gave it a quick look. It was a deep gash. 'He'd better have a stitch in it.'

I gave the man another smile and sat him on a treatment couch.

'Just sit here and the doctor'll cut your finger off in a moment.'

John, now washing his hands, smiled. 'You can't bloody resist it, can you?'

'My nature favours bad taste. There's a helluva bunch of people out there.'

'We're giving away T-shirts.'

'We're getting a bit tight for time. Can I help?'

'You could put some anti-tet into your friend, there.' He gave me the key to the drugs cabinet.

'Pleasure.'

I found a phial of anti-tetanus and tried as best I could, in case
the man bolted, to hide the syringe and needle while I drew in
the liquid. But he sat, his finger pointing skywards, waiting, in
a rigor of fear.

'Now, you're not to worry. I'm a fully qualified pilot and
know nothing about medicine so you're going to be just fine.'

He didn't understand a word of course but he tried a smile.
At that moment a lot of screaming and yelling began outside.
This took his attention so I swabbed a patch of his arm with
surgical spirit then blew on it to make it cold as I darted the
needle in. He yelled. Well, why not?

As I pushed the plunger, I said, 'Yes, good, that's okay? Yes?
No lockjaw now, eh?'

He was holding on to his terror just fine. I pulled the needle
out and swabbed again. 'That's it.'

More yelling from a distressed, large, heavily pregnant
woman being carried in, surrounded by friends and family.
Everybody was yelling and Mitra was yelling at them to stop
yelling. By this time, my man was lying on the treatment couch
trying to get over his trauma.

'Can you get him off that?' said John while Mitra told the
bearers of the woman to put her on the couch. I touched the
man's arm and indicated that he should make way. He didn't
move but muttered something which I took to be a negative
response. I was about to ask Mitra to speak to him in Swahili,
when a woman beside me suddenly yelled so loudly at him that
I nearly lost my water. He was off the couch like a shot so I
imagine that she suggested something to the effect that 'If his
rickety arse was not off that bed in one second she was going to
remove his wedding tackle with her teeth'. The pregnant woman
was laid down, knees up, hands on crotch, yelling blue murder.

'What'll we do about the finger?' I asked John. The man stood apart, his finger still pointing skywards.

'It'll have to be a bandage – and give him some Elastoplast to take away. Mitra, tell him to keep the bandage on for four days and keep it clean, then Elastoplast for another four.'

Mitra translates as John starts to examine the woman. People are crowding in to see the action. John calls to me, 'Hal, can you shoot this lot or something?'

I pushed them back and pulled a curtain. 'That's it, the show's over. Thank you all for coming. Did you get a good look at her fanny, sir? That's fine then. And for free, too. Off you go now.'

But people were still trying to see around or under the curtain. The chatter was deafening.

'What have we got?' I asked.

'I'd say obstructed labour. Can we take her back?

'We're a bit edgy for weight.' I pointed to her huge belly. 'And that's not a her, it's a them.'

John gave me his measured look, to which my response could only be, 'Oh . . . okay.'

'I'll take her down to the strip,' said John, pulling a trolley to beside the couch. 'Mitra, ask her to move over.'

The woman, with much wailing, got herself on to the trolley. John would take the woman to the aircraft, accompanied by family members. I would clear up at the clinic and Mitra would radio to Nairobi to alert them to the arrival of the woman.

Mitra had gone to the radio shack, a six-by-six-feet corrugated-iron hut furnished with a chair, table and transmitter. No sooner had she gone in, than she ran out again, screaming, 'Hal! Hal!'

I ran to her. 'What the hell?'

'I've been bitten by a snake.' She held out her arm which was already turning red.

'Did you see what is was?'

'Bloody puff adder.'

'Are you sure?'

'Yes.' Fear tears swelled out of her eyes and with reason. The puff adder is a nasty snake. In fact, deadly if treatment isn't quick and proper. One encounters very few snakes in Africa because they bugger off as soon as they sense you coming. Not this bastard. It freezes, then if you come too near, it strikes. The faster your heart beats, the faster the venom spreads, so it's best to be still if bitten. I picked her up, carried her in to the clinic and put her on the couch.

'Lie still and try to relax. We need a tourniquet.'

There was nothing immediately evident that we could use, so I took my knife, cut a sleeve off my shirt and bound her arm above the wound.

'I shouldn't have run.'

'It's okay. This should be incised, you know that?'

She looked at me, her mouth open, sweat breaking on her face. She nodded. 'Yes.' I could feel my own sweat running down my back. It always happened when I had time to be frightened.

'Can you do it yourself, Mitra?'

'No, I don't think I could. Can you?'

'Probably. I've never done it though. Do you want me to?'

'Yes.'

I had watched John doing such procedures and knew that the fangs would have gone deeper than I could safely go without endangering muscle and nerve tissue. All I could really hope for was that the issue of blood would wash out some of the venom. When John made incisions, he did so without hesitation. I knew that if I was tentative, I'd bungle the first shot, hurt her, then have to hurt her again with the second – or indeed the third. I put an enamel dish under her arm, grabbed a scalpel from the steriliser, and swabbed the wound with spirit.

'Ready?'

A barely audible 'yes'.

Forefinger along the top of the blade as I had seen John hold it, I sliced into her arm. A cut of about three inches across the fang marks. It's a startling thing to do, to cut into a human being – and the surgical scalpel is an alarming instrument. It's hard to imagine something so viciously sharp. You have almost just to *look* at it and it cuts you. Blood poured over her arm. Some dripped into the dish and some down to cover her hand. I couldn't tell whether venom was mixed with it. The wound was supposed to be held open a little to facilitate a greater blood flow.

'This is going to hurt, Mitra.'

She knew what I was going to do.

'Just do it,' she said. But it wasn't so easy. Blood is slightly viscous so my fingers slipped on her arm as I tried to open the cut. Then she fainted. I took advantage of that for a moment or two to let her bleed. I had to make sure that her tongue wasn't blocking her airway and was about to feel into her mouth, but my hands were covered in blood. There was nothing on which to wipe them so I used my shirt. I opened her mouth but there was still blood on my hands so now it was on her face. It didn't feel as though her tongue was blocking her airway and she was breathing normally. She woke up with my fingers in her mouth, and made a noise. I pulled back and knocked the dish off the couch, covering my trousers in blood.

'Sorry, Mitra, you fainted, I had to make sure you were breathing.'

'Ok.' She looked dazed.

'Where's the anti-venom?'

'Left-hand cupboard.'

'You know this has to be given intravenously. Maybe we should get John.' I said

Her bottom lip quivered. 'That'll take ten minutes. Can't you do it?' Her brown skin was now becoming grey, and sweat was darkening her shirt beneath her breasts.

'I've never done it. How difficult is it?'

'If I tell you what to do will you do it?'

'Ok.'

At this point, my poor taste kicked in and the comic side of the situation hit me. It looked like there had been an axe murder. There was blood everywhere. On her shirt, on her face, on her trousers, on my shirt which of course had only one arm, all over my trousers and all over the couch and the floor. My hands were covered in it.

'Why are you smiling?' Mitra asked with a hint of concern.

'Sorry. It looks like a scene from *Blood of the Virgins*.

'Does it? I'm not a virgin.'

'I don't expect the actress in the movie was, either.' She looked at me as if I was speaking Norwegian. I don't think she had ever understood a joke in her entire life. Mitra was a nice woman, helpful and intelligent but humour was to her a secret code, unbreakable even if she'd had a warehouse full of Enigma machines. Mind you, she *was* dying of a snake bite which I suppose further taxed her poor jestation.

We now needed another tourniquet to bring up the vein in her good arm, so my remaining shirt sleeve was sacrificed.

'If you have a tourniquet on both arms won't your head explode or something?' as John always said, I couldn't resist black humour even though I knew Mitra wouldn't laugh. In fact, that made it irresistible.

'No, it won't.' she said. Having tied the second tourniquet, I took a syringe from the steriliser, fitted a fresh needle, read the dosage, drew the liquid from the phial and squirted some out to achieve the correct dose and expel the air. Just like they do in the movies. I did know, though, that if I injected air into her vein, I'd have a very bloody corpse to explain away.

The vein on the inside of her forearm was now sufficiently engorged. I swabbed it with spirit.

'Okay, what do I do?'

'Hold the body of the syringe between your thumb and forefinger and bring it parallel to my arm, with the point of the needle to the vein.'

I did.

'Now push down slightly on the front of the syringe so that it nestles into my arm and the needle is pressed directly against the vein.'

I did.

'Now, when you push, the needle should slide about three millimetres into and parallel with the vein. Do that, then stop.'

I pushed but the needle didn't as easily puncture the skin as had the scalpel.

'Give it a little controlled push.'

I did – and it was in. Mitra gasped and said –

'Now I'll hold the syringe and you undo the tourniquet.' I did. Then –

'Now support the body of the syringe with your left hand and push the plunger with your right. Slowly.' Her speech was breathy and halting.

I began to push the liquid into her.

'When it's all in, put the swab over the puncture and pull the needle out.'

I did.

'God! Are you okay Mitra? I'm sorry if I hurt you.'

'I'm fine Hal, thank you. What about you?'

'I'd quite like to go home to my mummy now, actually.' She didn't laugh.

As I write this, years later, the use of tourniquets and the incising of such injuries are procedures no longer considered advisable. Oh well . . .

I bandaged her arm and ran to the airstrip to get the Land Rover. When John saw me, in the remains of my shirt and covered in blood, his face said, 'Oh my God, some nutter's run amok with a machete.'

'It's all right,' I said, 'Mitra was bitten by a puff adder so I incised it.'

'You incised it? You look as if you bloody amputated it.'

'I know. It's not as bad as it looks.'

'That's good news. Where was she bitten?'

'In the radio shack.'

'No, where on her body, you daft bastard.'

'Oh. Her right arm. We'll have to take her with us. Do you want to get her while I load up?'

He drove off and I went to the aircraft. All around, people stood, nattering, watching. The pregnant woman was already in and wailing. Sitting beside her was, I supposed, a relative. On the ground was a gigantic suitcase which weighed a ton. They had obviously packed for a six-month trip. What they didn't know was that, since Mitra was now coming, the relative would have to be left behind.

John arrived with Mitra who, despite being by now really unwell, was able to explain to the pregnant woman that her relative could not now go with her. There was immediate remonstration with much yelling but when they heard it was a puff adder bite, the relative promptly relinquished her seat.

The next problem was weight. Fortunately we had, with the relative, lost some of the contents of the massive suitcase, but John was a big man, almost 200 pounds and the pregnant woman was even heavier. The far end of the grass strip had been allowed to grow over so we'd lost some distance. There was some clear ground behind where we would normally start our run but off at an obtuse angle of about 120 degrees.

'I think what we'll have to do is taxi back and start our run from down there.'

John looked at me as though I'd lost my mind. 'What, round a corner?'

'Where's your sense of fun?'

'Well, Mitra's sustained a snake bite, a stabbing and an intravenous injection by an amateur, so a plane crash would probably finish her off nicely.'

'That's exactly it.'

Before we started off, John released the tourniquet on Mitra's arm for a few seconds. This was to allow fresh blood to circulate and so prevent gangrene, an additional danger with certain snake bites.

I cleared bystanders away from what would be the outside of the turn just in case we went wide. I didn't feel I could cope with multiple decapitations that day.

It was a relief to get the headphones on and enjoy a slight respite from the wailing which was more or less continuous. We taxied back about three hundred feet and turned to start the run.

'Are you sure about this?' asked John.

'If we can be doing 40 knots when we turn on to the strip, we'll be fine. If we don't achieve that speed, I'll abort.'

'That's not a word I want to hear right now.'

'Sorry. Here we go.'

In the event of being short of hands at the crucial moment, I instructed John that when I said 'now' he would push the throttle fully open. I raised the revs and we bumped forward. The ground was very uneven which made acceleration slow. Resistance was greatest before air got under the wing and lifted some weight from the wheels. The corner approached alarmingly quickly despite our lack of speed. Thirty knots and about a 100 feet to go. I began to worry that if we were doing 40 knots we might not make the turn. I would have to use the ailerons to try to prevent going too wide. If I could get the left wing to lift a bit it would push against the corner. Forty knots. The corner was here. I turned the yoke to the right, put some pressure on the right wheel brake and gave a bit of right rudder. We skeetered into the turn. I said 'now' and John pushed the throttle to full. We went a bit wide but pulled back and settled on to the airstrip. Now all we could do was wait to become airborne. We waited – and waited. We should have lifted at about 80 knots. Eighty-five knots, nothing. Just under 90 – we were off. No. We settled back down. No fucking air! A few seconds later we lifted again but again came back to ground. The end of the strip was in sight. Just beyond it was a clump of bushes. I glanced at John. He was staring straight ahead, shoulders hunched, brow furrowed.

'Forget it,' he said.

'Too late,' I said. 'Don't worry.'

About 20 yards before the end of the strip we lifted, climbed to 30 feet clearing the bushes. I was about to bring the wheels up – when a very loud honking filled the cabin. John jumped, the wailing from behind was turned up to a series of yells.

'Jesus Christ! What the hell's that?'

'It's only the stall warning.'

'I'll get out here, thanks.'

I turned and made calming signs to the pregnant woman, who thankfully turned the yell back down to a wail.

A stall happens when an aircraft is climbing and the speed drops to the point where the wing loses its grip on the air. If the attitude is not corrected the aircraft will fall out of the sky like a leaf.

I dropped the nose slightly and the honking stopped but the aircraft suddenly lost height. Anxiety! The terrain was far too uneven and scrubby to land safely. A moment before the wheels would have touched the ground again, we lifted. I promptly raised the wheels to reduce drag and give us a bit more speed. Soon the flaps were up and we were flying. Relief!

'Sorry John.'

'Bugger.'

'It's these sick people, they drag you down.'

'You're a saint, you know that? A saint.'

'I know, but thanks.'

I got on to the radio to tell Joan that we were on our way back and to have an ambulance waiting but before I could, she asked if we could divert to Kamanga.

'Speak to John.' I looked for Kamanga on the map.

'Joan, what's up.'

'Someone's been mauled by a lion. Lost his arm.'

'What's at Kamanga? We've got an obstructed labour and a snake bite on board.'

'It's a mission hospital. They have a full theatre set-up but the condition of the airstrip may not be good.'

I broke in. 'Joan, do they have fuel at Kamanga?'

'Yes.'

'We have to know if there's somewhere we can land because if we don't, we haven't enough fuel to get back to Nairobi.'

'There's a Sister McTeague there. She says you'll find somewhere you can set down.'

'Does she know this isn't a hot air balloon?'

'Yes. This woman survived the Mau Mau. If she says there's somewhere to land, there's somewhere to land.'

'Is she a sister of Jesus or Hippocrates?' asked John.

'Wife to Jesus, sister to Hippocrates,' pronounced Joan.

John turned to me, 'What do you think?'

'She sounds a bit bloody old to me.'

'Be serious, what do you think?'

'I don't know. What do *you* think?'

'I don't know. Jesus!'

'Kamanga's less flying time than Nairobi so the Wailer would get help sooner,' I reasoned.

'What about the airstrip?' asked John

'I don't know. What do you think?'

'I don't know. You're the pilot.'

'Fuck!' I turned and headed for Kamanga.

The buildings of the Kamanga mission were small and white. I came in to make a low pass and look at the runway.

'What do you think, John?'

'Of what?'

'The runway.'

'What bloody runway?'

'See that sort of tractor track?'

'Yes.'

'That's it. I'll go around again.' We circled and passed over the tractor track. I asked, 'Do you see any boulders?'

'I can't see the boulders for the bushes.'

'Well, we've got no option now.'

We could see locals gathering at the sound of the aircraft. At the head of the crowd stood a couple of nuns in white. I remembered my school and those days when there were collections for the foreign missions. The White Fathers who, we were told, took the true faith to the savage, and who risked their lives among barbarous cannibals even, to bring the miracle of the resurrection and the joy of communion. 'Eat of my body and drink of my blood.' In other words, cannibalism. I wanted my sixpences back.

With Mitra and the Wailer as tightly strapped in as possible, I made the landing. It was fast and rough, in a huge cloud of red dust. Some of the bushes met the edges of the propeller blades and there was the most hellish, alarming noise as it chopped through them, throwing debris violently against the windshield.

As John attempted to help the Wailer out of the aircraft, she fell on him. He gasped, as well he might, for it was like being hit by a bungalow. Nuns and locals lifted her off and got her on to a trolley. The wailing, although now doubled in intensity, mercifully faded with distance. John was sitting on the ground clutching his arm. His face was white. 'God! I think my arm's broken.'

*

We stood, John's arm now splinted and slung, beside a bed whereon lay a lacerated, sweating, tearful, one-armed giant.

'That's a right shambles,' John muttered. He sat on the bed and laid his hand on the giant's shin.

'*Habari yako? Baridi?*' How are you? Cold?

'*Ndio.*' Yes.

As he pulled a blanket up over his legs, in swept Sister McTeague, an Irish nun in her sixties. Yes, of course she had blue twinkling eyes.

'You're wantin' of a little knowledge in the obstetrics department, Doctor. Obstructed labour is it? She's had a lovely baby girl and they're doing fine.'

John smiled. 'Thanks Sister, that's great. How's Mitra?'

'She's in a mild sweat but she'll live. You got the antidote into her good and early.'

John gave me a 'what a clever boy' look.

She brought us to the matter at hand.

'So what are you going to do about our bold lion tamer here?'

John shook his head and looked down at his own splinted arm. 'I don't think I can do anything with this arm. Could you do it Sister, if I talked you through it?'

'Not any more, I'm afraid.' She lifted her stethoscope, and her hand shook, displaying a considerable intention tremor. This is a condition which affects some older people. Their hands don't shake – until they try to use them.

I looked at the lightly bandaged stump and asked, 'What has to be done?'

'Why do you ask?'

I shrugged. 'I don't know. Is it very complicated?'

'The nerves and blood vessels have to be tied off. But the main thing is to get rid of any infected tissue. Lions carry some pretty horrible bacteria in their teeth and claws. If anything gets a hold, he's had it.'

'Do you think *I* could do it?'

John looked at me as if he hadn't understood. Sister McTeague looked at John, then at me, then back to John. The Giant looked at us all in turn, no doubt wondering why we were all looking at one another instead of speaking. Then John, 'Do *you* think you could do it, if I talked you through it?'

I immediately regretted having asked. What a ridiculous idea . . . and yet . . .

Fifteen minutes later we were in the little operating theatre, scrubbed and gowned. Scrubbing up, to the uninitiated, is quite a painful business. We laymen wash our hands and think they're clean. A surgeon washes his and they're clean from Cleanland. Sister Blue Eyes filed my nails. As she held my hand, I wondered if she had ever been 'de-consecrated'. I knew from my boyhood that there were priests who were anything but celibate – indeed, I had been propositioned a couple of times myself by a pink-faced Irish clown. Nuns, we supposed, were a different matter, wearing nighties in the bath so that they didn't see their own tits. A ruling no doubt made by a pope who knew that tits through a wet nightie were rather fetching. Anyway, five minutes with a scrubbing brush up to the elbows and I was red and raw but clean as buggery – well, probably a bit cleaner than that.

If you're squeamish, skip the next bit.

The limb had been severed not straight across, but at an angle. What we were required to do was remove anything infected and try to provide the stump of the bone with a reasonable covering of soft tissue then fold the remaining undamaged skin flap over it.

We'd had to strap the Giant to the table just in case his remaining three limbs flailed. Sister Blue Eyes was behind his head dropping ether on to a mask over his nose and mouth. This, though seeming primitive, was the normal method of anaesthesia in such circumstances. A second nun, whose face I had not seen, apart from her eyes, for she came in gowned and masked, would be in assistance with instruments and swabs. She was young. I sat by the now exposed stump of the Giant's left arm. Sister's voice made me jump.

'All right, you can start.'

John's finger indicated points on the wound. 'Cut that stuff away, here, here and here.'

A pair of scissors appeared in front of me, held by their closed blades. I took them. The first problem, exactly as John had forecast, was the gloves. Thin as they are, they're gloves and you can't believe that it's possible to do anything serious while wearing them. There is a huge urge to yank them off. Out of the question, though, so . . .

'Go ahead, just cut. The way you'd cut the rind off bacon. How are we off for breakfast, Sister, should we keep a bit of this?'

'No, we still have some from the last fella. We smoked it.' Even nuns, it seems, enjoy gallows humour.

Vowing that I would never again eat my favourite meal, I began to cut. It wasn't like cutting bacon because these were not kitchen scissors. These bastards were *sharp*.

Soon the nasty stuff was gone and we were into tidying the blood vessels, me fiddling incompetently with sutures and having to wash and change gloves because I'd sliced through one with a scalpel or stabbed myself with a needle; little moments of drama. As I was about to cut into a damaged artery, 'Be ready for it to spurt a bit.'

Spurt it did. With such force that blood hit me in the neck.

'Jesus! Sorry Sister.'

'Don't worry yourself. Anyroad, I think that would count as a prayer.'

The blood bursting forth under such pressure was a pointed reminder that we were dealing not with an inanimate object but a fabulous machine which, despite enduring huge trauma, unconsciousness and invasion, kept its own indescribably complex systems running on schedule. Then John delivered the bad news.

'The bone is too proud. We'll have to take a bit off.'

'How?'

'You'll have to saw it.'

'Saw!' Oh, don't speak. Can I stop for a minute?

'How's he looking, Sister?'

Sister Blue Eyes looked at me. 'He was fine till you mentioned the saw. Now he's a bit green looking.'

'No, the patient.'

A light bell of laughter broke from her, 'Oh he's doin' just fine, and as black as the day he was born.'

John put a stethoscope to the Giant's heart and chest.

'Okay Hal, straighten your back.'

'I'm shaking.'

'Oh, don't you start,' said Sister Blue Eyes, indicating her trembling hands, 'I think I'm putting more of this ether in the fellow's ear than ever I get on the mask.'

I looked at the clock. We'd been at it for a hour so far. Much longer, obviously than John would have taken. I asked, 'How much more is there to do?'

'You're more than halfway. You're doing great.'

The young nun offered me some water in a glass with a straw.

'Thank you.'

'Just move away from the table and I'll slip the straw under your mask.'

A Scottish voice. I remembered Lorna. I looked properly at the youngster for the first time. She had lovely dark eyes and, in her theatre garb, she had shape, a bosom. I pulled my mind back to the Giant.

'Right. Tell me about the bone.'

'It's not as awful as it sounds. Well, no, it does *sound* awful but you'll be through it in three strokes.'

Dark Eyes handed me a saw. A gleaming, stainless steel saw. John said, 'You've sawed wood, right?'

'Yes.'

'It's similar but actually, easier. Don't push into the bone, let the saw do the work, just gentle pressure and even strokes. Lay the blade . . . just there.' His rubber finger indicated the spot. 'Don't think about what it is you're doing. Just do it.'

Dark Eyes held the soft parts of the arm back clear of the blade. It took seven strokes. I think it was the longest period of my life. The sound, I will take to my grave and probably beyond.

Back in the tiny ward as we sat by the sleeping giant, a drip in his good arm, Sister Blue Eyes told us his story. He was a Masai desiring to become a warrior. One of the tests was to hunt and kill a lion – not with a gun, but a spear. As Sod's law decreed, the lion had jumped him rather than the other way round, therefore, although he had driven his spear through the unfortunate beast's heart, it didn't count as a pass. So here he now was, poor bugger, a mono-brachial with a C minus.

Sister Blue Eyes asked, 'When shall I change the dressing?' The odd thing was, that she addressed the question to me.

John caught it and smiled, 'We'll look at it in the morning Sister.'

We had supper with Blue Eyes and Dark Eyes. It was highly entertaining, primarily because of Sister McTeague, who had a rare wit and that delightful, inventive use of language peculiar to the Irish. I told them about the philosophy practised by Captain Arcangeli. She thought it remarkable but sadly couldn't overcome the indoctrination that had persuaded her that there was bad and there was good, and if you did something bad, it had to be paid for. I could see that Dark Eyes was thinking about it though. Perhaps she might yet see the light of reason and kick the habit.

On our camp beds for the night, John and I went over the events of the day. I think what I liked best about Africa was talking – or rather, listening, to John. I had many questions, such as, 'How long would it have taken you to tidy up the arm?'

'Twenty minutes or so.'

'No!'

'Yes. If you think what you actually did, it wasn't much and what there was, was very simple, wasn't it?'

'Well . . .'

'You cut off some tissue, tied off some vessels, cut through some bone and sewed the whole thing up. Mechanically, where's the mystery? It was only your inexperience that took the time.'

'What if something had gone wrong?'

'There's not much to go wrong with amputation. The repair and rehabilitation of damaged limbs is much more exacting because you're working with complicated nerve and muscle structure. But because amputation is the most horrendous thing you can imagine, you think it must be difficult. It's not.'

'So I needn't have worried about doing something that would have killed him?'

'No, Sister McTeague was the one who could have killed him.'

'How so?'

'Anaesthetic. Ether's very primitive but it's all we have out in the bush. It was actually the first proper anaesthetic. She had to give him enough to keep him under but giving too much would have paralysed the part of his brain that keeps him breathing. In surgery, anaesthesia is always the biggest risk, even in big western city hospitals. Never have a general anaesthetic unless you have to.'

'Or be operated on by a pilot.'

'That too.' He paused. 'I'm amazed you could do it.'

'Why? You just said it wasn't that difficult.'

'No, I mean that most people couldn't face the idea. They're squeamish, understandably. Medical students work up to it. No one's asked to saw through live human bone on the first day.'

I *hated* the bit with the saw. I really . . . *hated . . . the . . . bit with . . . the saw.'*

He laughed, 'Yes. I remember my first. It's the degree of brutality that's disturbing.'

'And the sound. Oh, the fucking sound!'

'What was your overriding emotion? Did you find it revolting? Terrifying? What?'

I was myself surprised at the recollection of how I'd found it and was hesitant to confess. John sensed my wariness. So? What?

'Thrilling. I found it thrilling. Is that perverted?'

He smiled. 'Perverted? No it's not perverted. In a doctor, I'd say it was probably essential.'

*

The following morning, all was well with our three patients. We were about to set off with The Wailer, who was now the Smiler, and her newborn. Mitra who'd had a sweaty, fairly painful night but was now safe, also wanted to go back. I asked about the Giant.

'How long will you keep him here, Sister?'

'Oh, there'll be no keeping him. Tomorrow morning I'll go into the ward and there'll be nothing to greet me but an empty bed. He'll just up and off back into the bush and we'll never see the sight of him again.'

'But he'll be in pain, won't he?'

'Yes,' said John, 'and he'll get pain from the limb which is no longer there. The phantom limb.'

'Aye, the phantom limb,' said Sister Blue Eyes. She looked at me. 'An' the phantom surgeon'll never get to know if his patient lived or died.'

Over the following months I worried about Francesca and me. There was nothing for her here and her mind was far too good to be lying idle. Unfortunately, there was nothing for me in England. Our relationship was deteriorating because we had no common goal. She wrote some poetry which I thought was terrific. In fact she presented me with a book of poems which she'd started writing after we met, in Cambridge. I encouraged her to send it to someone in London but she wouldn't. She began a new translation of Calvino's *The Baron in the Trees* but gave up, thinking there was no point. One evening, in bed, she said that what she wanted was a baby.

'Why do you want a baby?'

She chewed her lip. 'I'm a woman. I'm designed to want a baby. Anyway I don't just want *a* baby, I want *our* baby.'

I took her hand. 'Are you sure you want a baby? Or are you afraid that we're coming apart and think that a baby will glue us back together?'

'Are we coming apart?'

'I think I'm wasting your life.'

'But I think that life without you is a waste. Isn't life without me a waste?'

'Life without you was miserable.'

She smiled, 'Don't you want a child?' You'd be a lovely daddy.'

The vision, the memory that I sought more than any to keep at bay, blasted into my consciousness. My eyes filled and I gasped.

'Hal! Hal, what's the matter?'

This was the worst yet. I couldn't speak for fear of breaking down completely. I tried to pull other pictures into my head. Anything. Nuns, snakes, elephant.

'Tell me what's wrong, Hal.'

I dragged myself back to Francesca.

'Sorry, darling. It's just . . . I'm fine really. Sorry.'

'But what happened to you?'

'Please, just . . . I can't . . . It's something. Please don't ask. Let's go to the Norfolk for a beer or something.'

In seconds we were dressed and out the door, poor Francesca, utterly bewildered. That night we spent apart, at my insistence. I took her to her sister's house. I was afraid I'd break down again and if so, I wanted to be alone. Francesca wasn't a bit happy.

The following morning, as I was reading, the phone rang. It was Francesca.

'How are you?' I knew instantly from her voice that she was still smarting from last night.

'I'm fine, thanks. I'm sorry about last night.'

'Shall I come over?'

'I'm just going out.'

'Oh. Where are you going?'

'To meet John. He wants me to look at an old Merc for him.'

'Can't you do it another time? I really want to see you.'

'This is one of his few mornings off. You know he hasn't a lot of time.'

Silence from Francesca. I wait.

'I'm always second place, aren't I?'

'No, you're not, but on this occasion, you are, if you choose to look at it that way.'

'What about this afternoon?'

'I'm on standby.'

'So?'

'What do you mean, "so"?'

'You can stand by anywhere can't you? You could come here and they can call you.'

'Francesca, I really don't want to have this conversation now.'

I heard her voice catch in her throat.

'Please Francesca, don't get upset. I'll call you.'

Cold, 'Oh, will you?'

'Yes. If I say I will, I will. You know that.'

'Do I?'

'Yes, Francesca, you do. I'll talk to you later. Bye.'

No response from Francesca, so I hung up. I wanted to hurl a wardrobe through the window but instead, shook my head at my self-inflicted frustration and tried to get back into the book. Farquharson's *Operative Surgery*, the chapter, 'Amputative Surgery'. So? I was curious. The doorbell rang. It was John.

As we drove down Government Road, past the Emporium, we saw a boy who was sitting on a low, wheeled, wooden cart, withered legs folded beneath him, propelling himself with his arms. I said, 'What caused that?'

'Spina bifida probably'

'I've heard of it. What is it?'

'A congenital spinal defect. The spinal cord, which is part of the central nervous system, starts off as what's called the neural tube. At some point there's a defect and the tube fails to develop and close. Or sometimes the vertebrae of the spine don't completely grow over the cord and part of it is left exposed. Nothing below the defect works properly.'

'Bloody terrible.' The boy, who had stopped to talk to somebody, was laughing. I felt John's eyes on me.

'What?'

'I've been asked to set up a flying doctor service in Central Africa.'

'Will you do it?'

'Yes . . . Will you come with me?'

'No.'

'What if I offer you substantially less money?'

'Ah! Now you're talking.'

'I knew that would get you.'

'Well, yes. And of course Francesca will be delighted.'

John laughed. 'She's a tough cookie.'

'Nah, not really. She's a neglected cookie.'

'Yes, I know that. I don't know why I said tough. Silly. Sorry.'

'When are you going to Central Africa?'

'Not for a year or two. The other news is that I'm going to London soon, to St Peter's, to brush up my abdominal surgery.'

He smiled. 'And, as Sister McTeague said, I'm a little deficient in the obstetrics department.'

My mind filled with the extraordinary events of that day at Kamanga. The ether, the saw, the Giant afterwards, sleeping, patched and peaceful. John continued. 'Can I ask you something really personal?'

I was instantly curious. 'Of course. What?'

'Were you ever a medical student?'

'Christ, no. Why?'

'You seem so interested. I just wondered if you'd started, then chucked it. Maybe had a bit of bad luck and thought you'd killed some bugger or something.'

If only he knew. Killed some bugger? Killed lots. Bad luck? I did it on purpose. That's what I was best at. But I laughed and said, 'No. But you're right, I am interested. Too late now, I suppose. I should have thought about it twenty years ago. How long does it take to get to where you are?'

'About seven years after qualifying.'

'Yes, that's a bit long. Anyway I couldn't give up flying.'

'So will you come to Central Africa?'

'Yes, fuck it. *You* tell Francesca.'

John shook his head, 'Why don't you resolve this with Francesca? Marry her or let her go.'

'I could ask the same question of you and Joan. She adores you and you love her, don't you?'

'Yes, but this job's too demanding. I worry about Joan being neglected, it wouldn't be fair to her.'

'Rubbish. You worry about Joan anyway, so why not wrap up warm together while you do it?'

'There's something wrong with us, you know that.'

'I know, but what is it?'

'We're men.'

'That's bad?'

'It's not bad, but somewhere we got hold of the wrong end of the stick. Or maybe that we got hold of a stick at all was the problem.'

'But we had to have a stick otherwise how could we have brought the elk home for the cooking pot.'

'Yes, but after we brought the elk home, we didn't put the stick down. We became accustomed to holding it – and using it.'

'We don't beat women.'

'Maybe we do. Not with a stick but in some way maybe we want to exercise control. Is that what we're doing now?'

'On the pretext of protecting them?'

'Yes.'

'You're right, there's something wrong with us.'

One of my greatest concerns, as time passed, was that, although I was still truly in love with Francesca and couldn't imagine life without her, there were occasions when I didn't like her very much. This endorsed my conviction that the age gap was too great. In her raw, youthful perception, there remained large areas of black and white, whereas my skill to distinguish multiple shades of grey became ever sharper.

We looked at the Mercedes that John wanted to buy but there was an expensive whine from the gearbox so I warned him off and drove him back to the hospital. I called Francesca in the hope that she would have found something else to do in the afternoon.

'Hello?'

'Hello, it's me.'

Silence from Francesca.

'What are you doing?'

'Waiting for you. Are you calling to cancel?'

'I told you, I'm on standby. I didn't say I would come over.'

'What's the difference if you standby there or here?'

It was a fair question. There really wasn't much difference and anyway John had to get from the hospital to the airport.

'I'm not paid to standby in your house, I'm paid to standby at the airfield.'

'You're being pedantic.'

I was.

Francesca opened the door wearing just a T-shirt and lacy knickers. As I came in she pulled the T-shirt off, dropped her knickers and sat down on a small sofa in the hallway. She had a deliciously dirty way of moving forward in the seat, legs open and thrusting her fanny at you. Sort of . . . 'Go on. Wouldn't you like to shove it up?' I always would.

'Where's Gertrude?'

'She's around somewhere. Do you care? I don't – and she doesn't.'

The idea of fucking Francesca, with the possibility of Gertrude watching, was an amazing turn on. I said, 'You want her to watch, don't you?'

'Yes. Don't you?'

'Yes.' So I got on my knees, Francesca did her fanny thrusting thing and pulled me into her. After a few moments, I saw Francesca smile over my shoulder and I knew that Gertrude was behind me. There was a complicity between them that hinted that this wasn't the first time. I caught another shared look. Francesca pulled off me and stood up.

'Swap.' she said. I turned to sit. There in the dining room opposite, on a carver turned to face us, sat Gertrude, clothed, her dress pulled up and her hand moving between her legs. I smiled, she smiled. Francesca got on, straddling me, her tits in my face. She was giving Gertrude a good view. I could feel Francesca's body begin to tremble, which was her overture to orgasm – then the front door was open and Angela was in the hallway, yelling, 'Oh for Christ's sake!'

Gertrude, unseen by Angela, was up like a flash and through the door to the kitchen. My instinct was to rise, but Francesca's was not and she, being on top, was somewhat in command of the situation. My second thought was that I was more protected where I was than scrambling to my feet and going through the comic ritual of pulling up my trousers.

We were spared the move by Angela sweeping by and contriving to wallop my knee with a bag containing cans of something. As she passed, she couldn't discipline her eyes against flicking down to the pillar of fire firmly embedded within the golden palace of the Himalayas. Score one for the human reflex. We were laughing like schoolkids, pulling on trousers and knickers when she came battering back out into the hallway.

'Please do that in the bedroom if you must,' she snapped, eyes down, fiddling for something in her handbag, 'that sofa's just been re-covered.' And she was gone. The car started and we heard shale being flung by spinning tyres. When we had recovered from our mirth over the re-upholstered sofa, Francesca said, 'She needs to be fucked by about five Masai at once. I just feel it would be a bit boring for the Masai. Let's see if Gertrude's okay.'

'You go. I'll wait in the bedroom.'

'No you've got to come. We were all in it together. Otherwise she'll feel used by you.'

Francesca was right. 'Okay. I just have to call in and tell them where I am.'

I called Joan at Wilson Airport to tell her where I was. Joan, although ever perfectly polite and pleasant to Francesca, gave me the impression that she didn't greatly like or approve of her.

We found Gertrude with a broom, on the veranda, brushing nothing. Francesca was laughing as she ran to put her arms around her.

'Gosh, that was close. You okay?'

'You get me in trouble, Francesca,' she said quietly.

'You don't need me to get you in trouble, Gertrude, you're perfectly able to do it on your own. Hal, give Gertrude a hug and tell her everything's okay.'

Gertrude turned to me to accept the hug, which she returned warmly, her breasts pressed against me. She obviously loved sex – like us.

'Sorry Gertrude. Everything is okay. And that was very sexy.'

'Francesca is a sexy girl,' Gertrude said seriously, then smiled. 'Now I go home.'

'We're going into the bedroom. You can come if you like,' said Francesca.

'No, I better go home now.' She looked at Francesca and put her hand on my arm. 'I think this is a good man for you.'

'No, I'm not very good, Gertrude, but thank you,' I said. And she was gone, running. I was intrigued.

'So what's the story here? How did this all start?'

'I told you. When I caught her at it in the kitchen.'

'No, it didn't go from the kitchen to this afternoon in one jump.'

She smiled her wide smile. 'Oh, look at you. You're all excited. Did you like it?'

112

'Of course I liked it. That's why I want to know more about it.'

'I'll tell you if you put your cock back up me,' she said over her shoulder as she headed for the bedroom.

I fulfilled my part of the deal. 'Right. So?'

'Well, after it happened, she was in a state. She thought I'd blab and she'd lose her job, so I chatted to her for a bit, to put her at ease and stop her worrying.'

'What did you chat about?'

'I told her I'd been caught at school.'

'My God! You were caught with the French master?' I imagined Francesca, in her school hat, tearful in the courtroom as some poor bastard was put away for life.

'God no! He'd have gone to jail.'

'My thoughts exactly. So who?'

'Another girl.'

'At school! You did it with a girl at school?'

'Are you shocked?'

'No. Can we get her to come over now?'

'You'd love it, wouldn't you, you beast. All men love girls together.' It's true.

'What were you doing?'

'We were sitting on the bed, one at each end, showing each other how we rubbed off, and Mrs Sprunt walked in.'

'Mrs Sprunt? That was her name? Sprunt?'

'Yes, poor thing, because of course we called her Mrs Cunt, or Cunty Sprunty.'

'Well, she should have thought of that and changed it, the silly sprunt. So what did she say?'

'That Maggie and I should report to Thackeray at 7 and 7.05 respectively.'

'Who was Thackeray?'

'Head of House's room. Their rooms were named after writers.'

'And what on earth did she say when you got there?'

'That was Miss Carruth. She was a good egg. She brought us both in at the same time and said that as far as she could see, the only thing that we did wrong was get caught, but we weren't to say she said, and that she'd reminded Mrs Cunt that it was school policy to knock on dorm doors before entering. Then she said could we please leave because she wanted to have a wank before supper.'

Francesca delivered this line in such a straight fashion, that for a second I believed her. I said, 'How did Gertrude take this?'

'She said she had a friend she did it with, too.'

'So have you done it with her?'

'We've had a feel.'

'Of each other?'

'Yes.' This conversation, as we were gently fucking, was getting us both very hot, so the talking gave way to serious sexual pursuit. For over an hour, we thrashed around the bed, until Francesca got up to get us some water. I said, 'For God's sake put a dressing gown on or something.'

Instead, she put on my shirt and walked bare-arsed out of the bedroom. I heard her call, 'Hal?'

'What?'

'Joan just drove up.'

'Joan?' Odd that she should come here. I put on my trousers and went into the hall, Francesca behind me. I opened the door to a startling image. Joan's face was white and tear-stained – her eyes were wide and she was shaking. She saw Francesca, naked but for my open shirt. An unreadable expression crossed her

114

face an instant before she flew at Francesca, slapping and punching her.

'You bitch!' Joan screamed, 'you selfish, awful bloody bitch!'

I pulled Joan off, pinning her arms and holding her tightly, yelling, 'Joan, for Christ's sake, stop. What is it? What's wrong?'

There was a moment of silence then she made the most awful sound. A shout, a scream and a cry all at once. A phrase from my childhood came to me, 'the howl of a soul in hell'. Then, 'John's dead. John's dead.'

I didn't understand what she was saying. 'Wha—'

'And Alec. They crashed.'

Time stopped. A buzzing in my head. A gear change, a time-shift in the universe. Everything had moved and nothing would be the same again.

'They crashed? How? Silly words but I had no others. Joan shouted, 'Alec took John up in the big Piper.'

'Alec? Why didn't you call me?'

'I tried. I tried. I thought . . .' She couldn't breathe. 'I thought you'd put the phone off the hook.'

I ran to the bedroom, followed by Francesca. There, on the bedside table was the phone, but the handset was dislodged from the cradle. I turned to Francesca. Panic blazed from her face. 'I didn't! Hal, I didn't.'

Joan was now in the room, her eyes on the useless telephone. I said, 'Couldn't someone have come for me?'

Joan, spent, her arms limp by her sides, spoke so quietly that we could hardly hear her.

'John said to leave you because you were with her, that Alec would be fine, but he lost an engine on take-off and couldn't hold it.'

We had no words, we had nowhere to go, so we stood, and stood. I became aware of the bed linen. Unnoticed, Francesca's period had started. The sheets were streaked with blood.

Two days later the red, stony earth slid from my spade and clattered on to the lid of John's coffin. I had brought Death to John, my friend, whose entire nature was dedicated to the preservation of life. Who would I damn next? Francesca?

For the wake, the hospital had taken a function room at the New Stanley Hotel. Francesca went home after the burial. Convinced that the telephone story would have been spread by Joan, she said that she couldn't face the looks of accusation and loathing. No amount of protestation from me would persuade her otherwise. Perhaps she was right, I don't know. I didn't want to go either, but I did. Perhaps, in my own festering guilt, I wanted them to stone me to death.

The room was depressing. A table at one end was set with sandwiches and stuff. There were upright chairs placed side by side around the walls. People stood in small groups or sat uncomfortably, balancing plates on their knees. Knees have to be kept together to hold plates. Some held their heels off the ground. Everyone looked slightly silly. I hadn't eaten and was slightly woozy from two whiskys. It seemed that the entire hospital staff was there. An exclusive club, the medical profession. I felt alone – and envious.

A man in his sixties, an English 'gent' approached me, hand outstretched. 'How do you do? Brian Whittaker.'

'Hal Sinclair. How do you do?'

'You the pilot who cleaned up the amputation?'

I wondered if this was going to be a reprimand. 'Yes, I am.'

He sat. 'John said you did an amazing job.' I was spared having to respond by the noisy arrival of a large, red-faced, bull-necked Scotsman, spitting vitriol.

'Christ! There are times, boy, there are bloody times.'

Whittaker, ignoring the choler, said, 'Hello Reg. Do you know Hal Sinclair?'

'Hal Sinclair? Oh aye. Pleased to meet you.' He pulled a chair away from the wall, turned it to face us and sat, heavily. 'So you're the latest in a long line of untrained surgeons eh?'

I tried to smile. Reg continued. 'Naw, it's all right. At least you tried to treat the poor bugger.' Then to Whittaker, 'You know what that bastard Mbutu's just done? He's written a paper on spinal tumours and wants my name on it. *Bastard!*'

Then he addressed us both. 'Know what he did? A bloke comes in eight months ago, says he's got a tingling in his toes and a bit of a headache. They give him some aspirin. Fair enough.'

Whittaker nodded, Reg ploughed on. 'A month later, he's back, can't feel his feet. "Right" says Mbutu, "it must be hysterical." Out with the old valium. Next time, he's *carried* in. Canny bloody *walk!* "Ah," says the bold quack, "it must be sciatica! Up the aspirin dose." But – a glimmer of medical genius here – "Due to the severity of the symptoms, send to X-ray." No elementary neurological examination anywhere along the line, not even a kick on the fuckin' knee. A couple of weeks later, he gets an X-ray. Guess what, pals.'

He looked at me 'C'mon doc. Have a go. What do you suppose they found? C'mon now, what?'

'A tumour?' I said softly.

Reg, his thumb cocked at me, turned to Whittaker, 'An' this bloke's a pilot. Give the boy a consultancy immediately!' He turned to me. 'Right! A tumour. A *gianormous* fucking tumour. That bastard's got a stack of cases like this. Star-class ineptitude all down the line, an' he has the gall – the te-fuckin'-merity to write a paper – with my name on the foreword? Cunt!'

I asked if the patient was dead.

'Dead? Oh Christ aye. He is *totally* fuckin' dead, no two ways about it. Sorry I missed the burial, by the way. How did it go? Okay?'

'Terrific,' I said. 'I think he'll stay down all right.' It was an unnecessary barb at a man who meant no harm. To his credit Reg didn't rise to it.

'Aye, well . . . His face dropped. 'It's a terrible thing. He was an awful good bloke, John.'

That unadorned little phrase 'awful good bloke' spoken with such simple heart by this big, gruff man, almost finished me, but his returning anger diverted.

'He gets killed and bastards like Mbutu go on fuckin' people up – and even if the arsehole had written a definitive paper instead of a pile of shite, it still doesn't justify his malpractice.'

'That's always a difficult one, Reg,' Whittaker said, on the hunt for a philosophy.

Reg's eyebrows scrunched down. 'Not for the bloke with the tumour. Of course you could always ask him.' His voice assumed the tone of an imbecile, '"Excuse me, do you mind if I don't treat you so that I can observe you on your way to death? Your name will go down in history, my son." You know, I'd have no quarrel with him if he told you to go an' get fucked in the arse by a gnu.' He shook his head, sadly, 'No, no. If you're in agony, you want someone to take the pain away an' be nice to you. Pain is sore – an' death is utterly fuckin' depressing.'

*

Sweet Sunbeam took me to John's house. I don't know why I was drawn there. Maybe I just wanted to hold on to him a little longer. It's an odd thing, a house adrift; all the signs of a life, a personality, but frozen, dehydrated.

On a table by the door was a teacup, stuck to its saucer. Beside the sink in the kitchen was a glass, still with a whiff of alcohol. Whisky. I washed them then spent a few moments thinking whether to dry them or leave them on the drainer. I couldn't decide. I put a packet of salt and the tea caddy back in the cupboard then sat at the kitchen table and cried.

I cried for many things. John, my own and the world's loss of him, Francesca, in my heart of hearts, for whose happiness I feared; all those and the families of those I had destroyed, and my parents, who died before I could show them that I loved them and was grateful.

Curiously, I also wept for a girl I didn't know, and had not thought about for years, a plump little squatter child of about ten, whose family had been bombed out of its Liverpool flat and was then, with others, existing in a disused slate factory near our house in the Lakes. I was running home from cricket practice and she was ahead of me. Hearing my footsteps she had turned. I saw fear in her face as she mistakenly saw me as a threat. A tragedy of the class system. She was 'common', I was 'posh' and therefore dangerous – and she began to run. I slowed to a walk but she continued to run – and fell heavily. As she hit the ground her dress flew forward exposing her bottom. She had no knickers. She scrambled up as I got to her. Her knees were bleeding, as were the heels of her hands. She didn't know what to hold to make it better and she knew I'd seen her bum.

'Are you all right?' I asked.

She was crying and couldn't or wouldn't answer, so ran off. Now, a quarter of a century later, the images of those ripped knees, frightened eyes and poor, white bottom made my heart break for her.

I sat for a while at John's desk, thinking of the terror of his last moments and wondering if he'd said anything. We knew what Alec's last words were because he had the transmit channel open. 'I'm sorry Mum. I love you.' Pilots in most cases, when they know they're going down, talk not to their lovers, wives or children, but to their mothers. The spiritual umbilical, it seems, reaches across the cosmos.

On John's desk was an open file, marked World Health Organisation Documents spilled out of it. Looking at the top one, my eyes fell on the words:

. . . delighted that you have agreed to head the project in Central Africa.

As to your concern, we are pleased to grant your request for a two-year study period and have arranged a position for you at St Peter's Hospital in London so that you may revise your knowledge and practice of abdominal surgery.

The most terrifying idea wrenched at my stomach and somewhere a goose walked over my grave. Was this destiny – or insanity?

The following weeks fed my new obsession and much time was spent in planning and research. Francesca knew there was something in my head and asked constantly what it was. I couldn't tell her. Never had I been so frightened, or determined – and so afraid of the loss of Francesca, which had to come.

The doctor with whom I now most frequently flew was Reg Fraser, the rough Scottish diamond. It was John's quiet confidence and gentleness that reassured his patients but Reg's open assault on them and their condition, whatever it was, seemed to have exactly the same effect. Healing, it appeared, could take many forms.

I passed this thought to Reg, who said, 'Oh aye, I think that if you were sufferin' from a real nasty but ye had time and money, eventually you could find some bastard that'd cure you. Could be anybody, could be Harley Street, could be a fuckin' witch doctor but it would be the cunt that somehow communicated to you that you were now in safe hands and that it was gonnae be all right.'

We had dinner with Reg a few times. He couldn't take his eyes off Francesca, for which I couldn't blame him. Afterwards, Francesca always asked about him. She was attracted to his fusion of extreme coarseness and gentle understanding.

All was now prepared. It was the moment to tell my love that our lives would be shattered.

'Oh God, don't. Oh please don't, Hal.'

'I'm not going from simple choice. I can't stay here.'

For the hundredth time, she asked, 'But where are you going?' and for the hundredth time, I replied, 'I can't tell you.'

'But why won't you say that you'll come back?'

'Because you mustn't think of me coming back. You have to learn to stand on your own feet, darling. I'm not good for you – and I'm too old for you.'

'But I'll never find anyone like you.'

She was so earnest and sad, it was unbearable.

'Now you know that's not true. That's what everybody thinks at these moments, and they always find someone else.'

'No. No one does things like you do. I love you, Hal. I just love you so much.'

'But you go to bed with other men,' I said, gently, 'if you love me so much, why do you do that?'

'For protection.'

I understood and told her so.

'See? You always understand. You always know why people are unhappy and in pain.'

I took both of her hands. 'And now I'm asking you to understand that I'm in pain. I'm devastated by this, Francesca. I'll go to my grave believing that I killed my friend. I feel worthless. And I'm terrified that I'll bring harm to you. I've brought harm to people all my life.'

'What harm? How?'

'I was a soldier. I harmed people.'

'But how?'

'I can't talk about it. I can't. But I might have found something that'll help – and you must let me try.'

She could see it was hopeless but couldn't let go. 'But why can't I come with you? No, I know. Don't say it.'

'Darling, darling. I *know* you didn't put the phone off. You were involved but you're not to blame. I'm to blame. You did what your emotions compelled you to do. Now I'm doing what I'm compelled to do.'

We sat in silence for perhaps five minutes, then, 'Try and say you might come back' – her voice broke – 'so I have something to hope for.'

I couldn't continue the utter brutality. 'I can't say that I'll come back . . . but I can't say that I won't.'

She threw her arms around me.

I said, 'There now, you see? You're left in uncertainty. What you always say you hate most.'

'But I must have something to hope for.'

'So must I.'

Our loving that night was desperate and angry – and tender. There were no orgasms, just tears.

The following morning at 8 a.m., I went to the airfield. As I passed the office window I saw Joan inside, at her desk, her head in her hands. So much pain everywhere. As I approached the door, I coughed to give warning of my arrival. I opened the door and walked in. Joan looked up, smiling, no sign of distress.

'Hello Joan, how are you?'

'Well, you know . . .'

'Yes, I know. The new pilots will be here tomorrow. They're good lads. A bit wild but they'll never let you down.'

'From where do you know them?'

'We flew military missions together.'

'Military missions! Where?'

'Where we had no bloody business to be.'

She looked at me and smiled a sad smile, 'What a life you've led.'

'I suppose.'

'We'll miss you.'

'Thanks, Joan. I'll miss you.'

She smiled brightly as she said, 'It's not fair, losing John and you at the same time.'

'I'm deeply sorry, Joan.'

'I know, Hal.' She rose and hugged me.

I said, 'I want you to know that I really believe that Francesca had nothing to do with the phone being off.'

'That's good, Hal. I'm glad.'

'I'll be around for a few days yet,' I lied.

At five o'clock the following morning, I took off from Wilson Airport having left a note for Joan saying that I was going to take the Cessna up just to make sure that the new boys had nothing to complain about. Two hours later I was over one of the most remote parts of the country, 500 feet above a lake, flying level with the cliff edge surrounding it. The ground beyond the edge was flat for miles. I climbed a further 1,000 feet, tuned to the emergency frequency, pressed the transmit button and said, 'Mayday Mayday. This is Five Yankee Alpha Foxtrot Delta. I have a serious fire on board.'

Immediately, back came, 'Mayday acknowledged. What is your position, Five Yankee?'

I gave my height and a position, which was over dense jungle and four hours' flying time from where I actually was, then shouted 'Tell Francesca I love her'. I blew hard into the mic and switched off. I turned and landed 500 yards back from the cliff edge.

In my canvas bag were a money belt, a safari hat, a water bottle, salt tablets, two cans of tuna fish, a loaf of bread, four bananas, a map of the area, a compass, a large hunting knife which I would have in my hand at all times, two shirts, one pair of trousers, two pairs of underpants and socks, a woolly jumper and two tomes, *Bailey and Love* and *Bell, Davidson and Scarborough*, both essential textbooks, copies of Francesca's poems and John Koston's birth certificate.

I threw the bag out, turned the aircraft to face the lake, set the flaps to a quarter and climbed half-out. I reached back in, opened the throttle halfway then jumped to the ground. The aircraft sped away from me towards the edge. A wheel hit something and it slewed off course. If it got to the cliff edge too far below flying speed it would simply fall off and drop 500 feet into the shore of the lake, remaining visible. It slowly turned though, and was again accelerating towards the edge. It shot off and disappeared from my view. A few seconds later, it reappeared, climbing. Its speed had increased in a dive so it had gained altitude. It was doing what all good aircraft are supposed to do – fly. The nose was coming too far up though, for its speed. It lost its grip on the sky and stalled. It slid back, tail first, turned into a leaf spin and fell into the lake. It was gone in seconds. Sad.

I was in shock at the enormity of what I had done. I had stolen and destroyed an aircraft. Even more horrifying, I had released Francesca from me in the most brutal way. There was no going back.

The heat was almost solid to the touch as I set off on my 20-mile hike. I imagined an aerial shot of myself; an ant in the vastness of Africa.

I had experienced many dangers, indeed life-threatening situations, but this one was different in that there was nobody in the world on whom I could call for help – even if I had a radio. Hal no longer existed. My fear now was not of bullets, nor terrorists with diabolical methods of torture and killing, but of providing lunch to one of the many surrounding but unseen and always hungry predators. Lions hunt during the cooler parts of the day and in a group, therefore they're easier to spot. That's the girls, of course. The boys lie around in the leonine equivalent of smoking and stinking of drink.

The leopard is more dangerous. It hunts alone both day and night and could silently get to within ten feet, so that the first thing you'd notice would be that you were lying on your back with its teeth in your neck. There are also cheetahs, hyenas and wild dogs, any of which might happily attack and munch. I could be unlucky and surprise a resting rhino which would run at me at 20 miles an hour and buffet me into oblivion. There are many ways to die out here.

There was no possibility that I could go unnoticed, my footfall and smell being detectable from a long way off, so I reasoned that if I couldn't be invisible, at least I could be peculiar. Animals tend to be cautious of what they don't know, so I sang a lot. Hits of the sixties, the Stones, the Beatles, best-loved operatic arias without the words. I tried singing the first movement of Beethoven's Fifth but, inexplicably, failed.

Only one extraordinary thing happened on the journey. I crested a hill and there on the other side was a herd of elephants. They were all turned in my direction as if they had been waiting for me to appear. I suppose they *had* been waiting, they would have known for some time that something was coming, they just didn't know it was me. I altered my course to pass fifty yards from them. As I passed, they turned to keep me in vision, then, at a respectable distance, they followed me. Elephants are huge creatures and a herd of them is a pretty awesome sight – and when they're walking behind you, it's a pretty awesome experience. I had no idea whether or not it was in their minds to charge, but I thought not. They were neither snapping their ears nor shaking their heads, two signals of impending doom. I tried 'M'appari tutt' amor' from *Marta* on them but they didn't join in. Probably didn't know it. They didn't know 'La donna e *mobile'* either, so I gave up. I knew that they wouldn't yet know any of the Beatles stuff so didn't try.

Suddenly, it got scary. They came closer. Closer and closer until they were all around me. There was no point in my running, they could easily out-run me. It was one family. I think I counted twelve. They didn't crowd me, but left an area around me as we continued to walk. We walked like this for perhaps an hour. About four miles. As my fear subsided, I chatted to them, told them all that had happened; about Francesca and me. They nodded sagely as they walked. Abruptly, it was all over. They broke ranks and stopped. I stopped. I don't know what had changed, why they had stopped – why they had started in the first place. A curious idea presented itself; they had been protecting me. Perhaps one of the big cats had come nosing around me. I'd heard of dolphins protecting people in the water, indeed of taking the drowning to the surface. The elephants perhaps provided the same service. I thanked them and we went our separate ways.

A further two hours took me to the road which was my first waypoint. The most difficult thing, as I waited, was staying awake. I was now exhausted, having walked for over eight hours, but to sleep unprotected was to be totally vulnerable, not just to big cats, which would be awake and hungry by now, but also to reptiles. A rock python could wrap its sixteen-foot length around me in a trice and I'd be devoured alive.

An hour later, I heard the whine of an old, stressed gearbox, and a bus appeared, bouncing along, smothered in people. It hit a particularly large rut and some men fell off. They chased it, yelling. Some, on the bus, shouted encouragement but the bus showed no sign of slowing. I stood in the centre of the road but as it approached, it still showed no sign of slowing. Closer and closer it came, until I could see the driver's face, which showed no signs of life. Just as I was about to jump clear, I saw a hand grab at his shoulder and he jerked, saw me and hit the brakes. He'd been in a deep reverie and was lucky still to be on the road. Despite the fact that road traffic is extremely light, there are a huge number of accidents and, because buses are so over-crowded, the carnage can be considerable.

I climbed in. It might have been less unpleasant to travel on the roof but I was too tired to be able to hang on for every second of the two-hour journey which would take me to the train bound for the port of Mombasa. This entailed a further journey of about sixteen hours because the train could not travel safely at over 35 miles an hour. At Mombasa docks I looked for the *San Vittore del' Lazio* but no such luck. I found a freighter, the *Marie Jeanne* bound for London, bribed a crewman to take me as a stowaway and spent the following four weeks imprisoned with my textbooks. The most intensive study period of my life.

Normally, I would have enjoyed such a journey, rich with event and every kind of hazard but my heart was for ever broken and all of my will now intent on learning – and holding together the tatters of my mind.

Francesca

'Francesca, Hal's missing.' With that small collection of sounds I was consigned to an alien and desolate world.

Ten minutes after Joan's call, I was in the office at Wilson Airport with Joan, Daniel the mechanic and, from the Wilson control tower, Colin, who had taken Hal's Mayday call. He said, 'The army will help with the search.'

I seemed to be having difficulty understanding language. I had to run each word through my brain a couple of times to make sense of it.

The door opened and a smiling young man came in. 'Hi, Bob Bishop reporting for duty.'

Joan turned to him, 'Oh. Mr Bishop.' Then to us, 'Mr Bishop is one of the new pilots.'

We looked at him. He sensed the atmosphere and said, 'Is something wrong?'

'I'm Joan Ashplant-Beer. I'm sorry, this is no way to greet you, but there's bad news. Hal may have gone down.'

There was a moment as he took it in. Hal? Hal? Gone down! 'My God, that doesn't sound like him. What happened?'

Colin said, 'He put out a Mayday, reported a fire and gave his position. There was a noise, then transmission ended.'

'Did he give his height?'

'Two thousand AGL.'

I ran the young man's previous speech again in my head. 'That doesn't sound like him.' I was abruptly alert. I said, 'He's right'.

'What, Francesca?' said Colin.

'He's right. Hal wouldn't die in an aeroplane. He's too quick, too resourceful, he'd do something. He's spent his life surviving bad situations.'

Bob looked at me. It was the kind, sympathetic but patronising look of the sort that only officers of the British military can impart. He said, 'Yes, but sometimes. you know . . . it . . . '

I saw him think better of concluding the sentence.

He continued, 'At least we have his position. Is there a search up?'

'They're just sorting it out,' Joan said.

'Can I join it?'

'Of course. They're over in Hangar Four.'

'Can I come, please?' I pleaded.

'Of course.' He knew it was unreasonable to refuse me.

As I moved to the door, Joan said, 'Francesca?'

'Yes?'

'I'm so, so sorry.'

I knew it was heartfelt. 'Thank you, Joan.'

The search area was divided into equal squares, the search patterns being designed to minimise risk of collision. We were at five hundred feet above dense jungle. I expected at any moment to see Hal on top of a tree, waving. After about 45 minutes, Bob said, 'The difficulty is that any falling debris would just penetrate the trees and vanish.'

'Then we'll have to have a ground search.' I knew from his silence that he had little hope. I wanted to leap from the aircraft. I imagined that the Fates would be kind and I would crash through the trees and land in Hal's arms.

Back in the office the following day, I sat with Joan and Bob, in despair, going through the 'what ifs'.

Finally, Bob said, quietly, 'I've as much faith in Hal's ability to survive as you, Francesca, but there's just no sign, which probably means that the aircraft disintegrated in the air.' He paused. 'No one could survive that.'

Later, Angela pretended sisterly sympathy but I knew she was secretly pleased. Everyone tried to persuade me to return to England but there would be no sense of Hal there, apart from in Cambridge, which now seemed in another era. All memories were here and even though they all hurt, I could no more have left them than I could have left Hal. The only person to understand that was Reg. Reg, the most opinionated man I'd ever met, had withheld all opinion on what I should do. He simply listened and was kind about Hal.

But Hal had left me. Before the accident he had left me. He had done this. He had denied our love, our future and now our lives. I tried to summon the guts to end my life but failed. I asked Reg why I lacked the courage.

'It's nuthin' to do wi' courage, Francesca. People kill themselves when they're less afraid of oblivion than they are of waking up – and when they've lost hope of that situation ever changin'. You're a survivor, Francesca.'

'What makes you think that?'

'Your anger.'

He was right. I was angry. I was enraged at Hal for dying and enraged at everyone else for living. I was angry at Reg for being so big and so kind and so intelligent. It was out of anger, that I let him fuck me. Afterwards he apologised, as if it had been something to do with him.

'I'm sorry Francesca, I shouldn't have done that.'

'Didn't you want to.'

'Yes.'

'So why are you sorry?'

'Because you're in mourning. You're vulnerable.'

'Did you think, she's vulnerable just now. If I play my cards right, I might get my leg over?'

'Of course not.'

'Then don't be sorry.'

Before he could stop himself, out came the words,

'I love you, Francesca. Oh fuck, I didnae mean tae say that. I'm sorry, I'm sorry.'

'For God's sake, stop being sorry. It's not the worst thing in the world to say to a girl.'

We saw each other more and more. The tittle-tattle was terrible. Angela was disapproving. 'Isn't this behaviour a bit hasty, Francesca?' She didn't like Reg for lots of reasons, not least of which were that he was from Glasgow and coarse and because he referred to the Embassy as 'the fuckin' shambassy'.

She was afire with rage when I told her I was pregnant.

Hal

Getting back into the UK was easier than leaving it. Crew members on merchant ships were rarely troubled for passports. It was understood that they would go into town, drink, find women, then return to their vessels. Customs had more important things on their minds. I thanked Maurice, who had stowed and fed me through the voyage, and walked down the wooden plank which served as a gangway, on to British soil, well, British concrete. Some seamen got out of a taxi, I climbed in.

'*Centre ville, s'il vous plaît.* Er . . . Soho.'

The cabbie said nothing, just re-flagged and moved off with the traditional jerk so that I was thrown back into the seat. At the dock gates, a policeman stopped us and asked the driver, 'Who've you got?'

' Frog. He's goin' up west . . .'

The copper opened my door. 'You crew, sir?'

'Crew? *Ah, oui*, crew, *oui*.'

'What vessel, sir?'

'*Comment, monsieur?*'

The cabby shouted as if to one deaf, 'What *bato* you off, mate? *Kwel bato?*'

'Ah! *Marie Jeanne.*'

'All right, sir. Thank you.'

And out into London we drove. Apparently I was being followed but I wouldn't know that for some time. I was unaware that Cadell had known of my being in Kenya and of my 'death'. I had been spotted at Mombasa docks by watchers on the lookout for a Soviet mole who had fled London and was seeking concealment in an African country which enjoyed good relations with the USSR.

St Peter's Hospital was situated in the Bloomsbury area of London so I rented a tiny, one bedroom, unfurnished apartment in Harrison Street, within easy walking distance. Despite paying for 'furnishings and fittings', there were none. This was euphemism for key money, which was now unlawful. Anyway, what it meant was that my first few days were spent in visiting second-hand furniture shops. I had also bought a large, leatherbound notebook. In it, on my first evening, I wrote:

'My darling Francesca,

It seems as though I've entered some strange land, where reality and fantasy battle for superiority. Strangest of all is knowing that you will never receive this or any subsequent letter.

I must talk to someone, but there is no one on whom I can place the burden of knowledge. The news of my death will of course have reached you, and your anguish will be immense – or is that vanity on my part? What a hideous irony that to embark on a course to alleviate pain, I should first have to inflict it.

I have decided to become a doctor, so that I can return to

Africa and continue John's work, but, I'm afraid, distant from all of you. Unhappily, time is not on my side, so I am forced to take a short-cut. Should I lose my way in this, then the best that can happen is that I proceed directly to jail without my £200. The worst – is indescribable.

You are there when I wake and with me till I sleep.

I love you so.

Hal

For the following eight weeks, I studied as a man demented. The most difficult subject was chemistry. What reacts with what to do what. How blood is made, the complexity of the fabulous 'endocrine orchestra', the system which is responsible for growth and maintenance, which analyses all stimuli, physical and emotional, and responds accordingly. It is *stunning*.

Finally, on a cold, wet, English morning, I walked toward St Peter's Hospital, the dominant principle of medicine in the forefront of my mind: 'First, do no harm.' I asked for Andrew Parker, Head of Surgery. A porter took me to his office where I met Parker's secretary. A Miss Moneypenny, she knew everything but dispensed information only when required so to do.

'Good morning, I'm John Koston.'

'Dr Koston, how do you do?

Dr Koston. The title came as a shock. I wanted to give something back that I'd destroyed but now I felt like a monstrous interloper.

She continued. 'I'm Alison Richards. Mr Parker's in theatre but he shouldn't be much longer.'

With that, from the next room, which I took to be Parker's, I heard a door opening, slamming shut, then a raised voice, old school, cultured. It reminded me of Cadell.

'Well, that was a waste of bloody time. Stupid woman, I told her to lose weight. Not an ounce . . .'

Alison smiled, 'Excuse me.' She said, picked up a file and headed through the door. The voice resumed. 'It'll take them half an hour to get theatre ready again. We'll never get through. What's next?'

Alison's voice, muted, 'Dr Koston's here.'

'Who's he?'

'The chap from Africa.'

Parker, irritated, 'What chap from Africa?'

The door was tactfully eased shut. A few moments later, it re-opened, but a fraction too soon.

'Why is he coming here?'

'Because that's the way the world is.'

As Alison came back in, he mumbled, 'Oh . . . I hope he bloody speaks English.'

She shook her head and smiled, whispering, 'Sorry about that.' She indicated that I should go in. 'Dr John Koston,' she announced.

Parker stood and smiled. He was fifty-ish and, the first word that came to my mind, was 'noble'.

'Koston, good to meet you. Sit down, sit down.' He pulled a small electric fire towards himself. 'As a matter of fact, you've arrived at an opportune moment. On of our chaps, young Lamont, has just piled his motor bike into a wall so we won't see him for a few months. Bloody things, motor bikes. Ought to be banned, don't you think?'

I elected to be politic. 'Yes.'

'You obviously mean no.'

'Obviously, obviously.'

Parker smiled and removed some papers from a file. 'Right. Where are we?' He read aloud: 'John Koston, educated New

Zealand, MB Auckland, since then, working in East Africa.' He looked up. 'What, you a religious type, are you?'

'Not at all, I . . .'

'Good, good. You don't sound like a kiwi.'

'My parents were from here.'

He was back in the file, muttering, 'Intention to get fellowship and return to Africa. Ah! So you want to refresh your abdominal surgery. What have you been doing?'

'I did flying doctor work, so a lot of general practice, as it were. The surgery was mostly orthopaedic.'

'Well, look, all of this seems fine. Just make yourself at home. Attend the clinics, assist in theatre, come and go as you like. Once you're settled in, they'll soon work you into the receiving rota. That okay?'

'Fine, thanks.' I couldn't resist it, 'How's my English?'

He considered the question a moment, 'Not a patch on your hearing.' I knew we'd be friends.

He rose and headed for Alison's office.

'I've got to get back to theatre. What's next, Alison?'

'Mr Griffiths's bronchial fistula.'

'I hope he's got more stamina than that stupid Martin woman.' He nodded in my direction. 'Sandra'll show him around, yes? Don't worry, anyone could do Lamont's job. Bright but slow. *Very* slow.'

'Except on motor bikes.'

Parker smiled, said, 'Well, see you everywhere,' and was gone.

'Breathtaking, isn't it? You'll get used to it,' said Alison.

'At least it saves you having to speak. Do you mind if I look at your system?'

'You'd better.' She indicated a pile of files on a side table. 'Tim Lamont's case sheets. You'll be doing the discharge summaries. Tim *was* a bit behind.'

I was about to pick up the files when a young woman came in. 'Sorry, am I late?' Alison introduced her as Sandra Mason.'

'Did you hear about Mrs Martin?'

'Yes,' said Alison. Sandra looked as though she expected Alison to say more, but nothing came.

Sandra continued, 'It's so awful. A woman died in theatre this morning. Mr Parker was really angry.'

'I'll see you later, Dr Koston,' said Alison, pleasantly indicating that we should get the hell from under her feet. As we walked, I asked Sandra,

'What was it about the death that made Mr Parker angry?'

'He'd been explaining to her for months that before surgery, she had to get her weight down and stop smoking. He really pleaded with her, but she did neither. What made him angry is that she's got two teenage daughters and now there's no one to look after them.'

'No father?'

'Not in evidence.'

We arrived at Casualty where I was introduced to Parker's senior registrar, Jack Paton, and Sister Meg Williamson, 'who helps him to remember the difference between a tibia and a fibula'.

'How long will you be with us?' from Jack.

'Quite a while, I think.'

'Good. Coming to the rave-up tonight?'

'Thanks. If I can stay awake.'

Introductions were made to the relevant people. The whole thing was so *Doctor in the House* I couldn't get over it. Same cast, same attitudes, same jokes. We arrived in the children's ward. A boy of about eleven had made a paper aeroplane and was throwing it about, trying to make it fly. I asked, 'Having trouble?'

The boy grabbed the paper plane. He had the look of one who is frequently reprimanded. 'I just . . .'

'You were just trying to kill the pilot.'

'What?'

'Can I look at your plane?'

He reluctantly handed it over. 'I won't do it again.'

As I refolded the toy, I said, 'If I make it airworthy will you do it again please?'

'What?' He was suspicious and bewildered. Perhaps because he didn't understand the word 'airworthy'.

'Do people often scold you?'

He looked at me warily. 'Sometimes.' He meant 'often'.

'I'm sorry to hear that. When you grow up, you can be a pilot and fly away from them all.'

He permitted himself a small smile. I went on, 'Look, an aeroplane needs a proper tail to keep it balanced when it flies.' I launched the new model which flew almost the length of the ward. He looked at me. I said, 'Now look at how it's folded then make another one.'

'Okay.' He ran to retrieve it.

'Bye,' I called. He didn't answer.

As we left the ward, Sandra asked, 'Do you have a child?'

'No, I am one.'

As we walked the corridor away from the ward, 'That's pretty well it,' she said, 'but you'll probably keep getting lost for a bit.'

'If I do, I'll just stand crying till I'm found.' It took her a second to get the joke. Francesca would have got it in a flash.

139

'Do you think you'll make the party?' she asked.

'I still have some unpacking to do, but I'll try.'

'It would be really nice if you came.' In other words, 'My fanny's yours for the asking.' I wouldn't be asking. Not that she wasn't attractive, not that I wasn't flattered. After the first time that Francesca and I had split up, I had gone to bed with Lorna and others but the trauma of this experience had laid waste my libido. I was also permanently tired.

Sleep was an unaffordable luxury. As long as I could stay awake, I studied. That night, it was the appendix. 'If you can't find the appendix, trace one of the taeniae coli of the caecum, leading to its base. The appendix is then freed by a finger passing along it towards its tip, any filmy adhesions being gently disrupted . . .' On and on. I did anatomical drawings to familiarise myself with the structures – and fell asleep over them.

The days and weeks went by with my time spent mostly in theatre, observing and occasionally assisting. Nothing spectacular. Using retractors, holding this, applying pressure to that, stitching. I learned a huge amount in addition to the considerable knowledge I had gleaned listening to and watching John. The actual business of surgery, although requiring skill, is not all that complicated. A lot of it is common-sense plumbing. It's knowing where everything is, what it does and its order of precedence that is vital. And knowing what to expect post-operative, such as the reduction in kidney function after major abdominal surgery.

I had established a reputation as a loner. Inventing a past was more than I could cope with. One afternoon, I met Parker in a corridor. He hailed me.

'Koston, how are you getting along?'

'Fine so far, sir, thanks. Do you have a clinic this afternoon?'

'Yes.'

'Mind if I sit in?'

'See you there in ten minutes.'

In the consulting room, I was going to sit well away from him but he pulled a chair to beside his at the desk. 'Always present a united front.'

The nurse brought in a black lady and her child. 'Mr Parker, this patient has been sent over from Casualty, could you have a look please?'

Parker stood, giving them a huge reassuring smile. 'Good afternoon. Sit down, sit down.' He addressed the child. 'Hello, what's your name?'

Nothing from the child.

'Got something the matter? A sore bit?'

'No, sir, it's Mrs Nkoyo,' said the nurse.

Parker laughed. 'That's a good start. First identify the patient. 'Sorry, Mrs Nkoyo, what's the problem?'

'Thank you,' said Mrs Nkoyo.

'That's all right. I haven't done anything yet.'

'It's her hands, sir,' the nurse informed again.

'Ah!' As he looked towards her hands, she raised them for inspection. They were covered in reddish purple lumps.

'Ah, yes. Do you speak English, Mrs . . . er Ko . . . er?' He moved round to her side of the desk and took one of her hands.

'I don't think she does, sir,' the nurse again.

He raised his voice a little, 'Do you understand what I'm saying?'

Clearly, she didn't. 'Uhuh,' he grunted, and turned to me and giving nothing away by his tone, said, 'Well, I don't much like the look of this. Very nasty macules. Haven't a bloody clue what that is. Never seen it before, have you?'

I was taken aback at being asked for an opinion but on this occasion, I was lucky.

'It looks like something we were coming across now and again in Africa. Kaposi's sarcoma.'

'Well, I'm damned. We live and learn. So tell me.'

'It's a bit strange, it may be the precursor of further serious conditions. It's got people a little baffled.'

'How do you treat it?'

'I don't know that you can. We sent them to the dermatologist.'

'That's good news.' He turned to the nurse. 'Take her over to Eastwood's clinic. Slip her in Kaposi's sarcoma, eh? That'll straighten his face for him.' He courteously showed them out.

The next five were routine question and answer sessions with the patients, so no alarms. Then there arrived a man in his fifties who had been referred because of leg pain. Parker put him on the examination table. People look so vulnerable like that, in their undies, their flesh white and lumpy.

'Any pain or discomfort apart from the legs?'

'I seem to get indigestion a lot, Doctor.'

'Right, let's have a look.' He palpated the man's abdomen then turned to me. 'Have a prod. Right there.' He went back to the desk, I laid hands on the patient and did as Parker had done. The man gave me a half smile, which seemed to say 'I'm sorry if I'm putting you to any trouble.' I smiled back as I tried to feel what Parker had felt.

The man said, 'Is there something wrong, Doctor?'

Parker came back. 'Feel it?'

'No.'

He pushed deep into the abdomen. 'Just there. Feel it?'

I did the same. I could feel what I knew to be his liver. If anything, it might have felt larger than it ought. 'Ah, yes,' I said.

'Are you a drinking man?'

For a shocked second I thought Parker was addressing me, thinking I'd have to be drunk not to feel whatever it was, but –

'Now and again, Doctor,' said the patient.

'Well, cut down on the "nows" and lose the "agains" completely. Your liver's tired.'

I made a mental note to examine my own liver as soon as possible and compare.

At the end of the clinic, Parker said, 'Thanks for your help. Thank God you seem to know something.' He was being kind and encouraging of course but it astonished me how easy it was to get away with this – so far.

I said, 'I was afraid I'd forgotten my way around the abdomen a bit.'

'Thrust a hand or foot under my nose and I experience a mild sense of panic. Did I see your furrowed brow looking over Jack Paton's shoulder in theatre this morning?'

'Yes, you did.'

'Done anything yourself, yet?'

'Not yet, no.'

'I'm on my way to theatre now. Last of the day, hopefully. The GP diagnosed haemorrhoids, turned out to be a tumour. It might be quite interesting. Got the energy to come along?'

'If you've got the energy to do it, I've got the energy to watch.'

As we were being gowned and gloved, we discussed problems of the colon. I knew, from John, that the Africans rarely suffered from bowel disease, so passed this information to Parker.

'It's the diet. I'm always telling the nurses. No smoking, no booze. Eat nothing but maize. Which reminds me. Lotte, that's my wife, said would you come to dinner sometime?'

I had dreaded something like this. Parker and I liked one another so I knew that this invitation might come and that there would be no ducking it.

'Thank you. I'd be delighted.'

'Good. We'll fix a date and make a night of it. Nice bowl of oats and a couple of glasses of liquid paraffin.'

We went into the operating theatre. I was now feeling the same thrill that I felt going on to an air base. The team was ready and waiting for the big chief. Anderson, an anaesthetist, Vivien Hesketh, the theatre sister, and two nurses.

'Good afternoon, sir,' they chorused.

''Afternoon, angels. Even *you* look angelic this afternoon, Mr Anderson.

'Thank you, sir,' laughed Anderson.'

'Must be all that gas you sniff. John, would you like to open?'

'No, I'd like to see how *you* do it.'

'Fine. Just say though. I'm inclined to do it all myself, you know. Get finished and off to the golf. Tell you what you can do for me, though.'

'Yes?'

'Take some of my clinic in the morning. I won't give you anything hairy, unless of course it's a fanny.'

A single chirrup of laughter from the younger nurse. Sister Hesketh said, 'Ah, yes, the old ones are the best ones.'

'Yes, sir, of course I will,' I said, noticing the instant chemical change in my system. What I once thought of as my stomach turning over, I now knew to be the release of adrenalin which inhibits the production of insulin. Insulin enables absorption of glucose from the bloodstream into fat cells, liver and muscle, so, being inhibited from doing that, more glucose is instantly supplied to the brain. That's just part of the phenomenal chain of events, precipitated by the release of adrenalin that will enable you to run like buggery if you find a panther in your bed. Clever, no?

Anderson spoke. 'Would you like to start, sir?'

'Ah! The gas man flareth,' said Parker. 'Right, Dickie. Have you got a nice, sharp knife there, Sister?'

I'll spare you the details of section for the removal of carcinoma of the arse.

Following a couple of hours in the hospital library, hoping to be forearmed for anything Parker might be throwing at me in the morning, I got back to the flat about nine o'clock with some shopping and a new toy. Fatigue drove me on to the sofa – three hours later I woke up, grabbed a banana and some bread and opened my toy. This was a slide projector to use with a new American study aid: a series of slides to accompany lectures on tape. The more common surgical procedures, appendicectomies, hernia repairs and so on, gone through, step by step, including the hazards occasionally encountered. The last thing I remember, was something about 'superficial epigastric and pudendal vessels' before the clinking of milk bottles brought me back to consciousness.

On my way to the hospital, I had two fried eggs, bacon and sausage, toast and marmalade and a large mug of navvies' tea at a local greasy spoon. You want it now, don't you? Your salivary glands are in action. Your imagination can't get over the bacon, can it? If you're reading this in bed, you're even considering getting up and making it, aren't you? The bacon, that is, not the bed.

With a heart rate of about a 110, I called in the first patient, a man in his fifties, in a sports jacket, cavalry twill trousers, yellow waistcoat, white shirt and regimental tie.

I had learned from Parker's idiosyncracy of, rather than reading the GP's referral letter beforehand, to have the patient tell him what's wrong. That way, the possibility of acquiring information missed by an overworked GP – or indeed, not passed to the poor bugger by the patient was far greater. Then you also read the letters, of course. Diagnosis is the following of paths. Ask X. If the response is A, ask X+1. If the response is B, ask Y, and so on; acquirement and elimination.

'Sit down Mr Whiting. What's troubling you?'

'Well, it's not bad really, Doctor. I don't know why I'm bothering you with it.'

I smiled. 'Well, since we've both struggled in here this morning, we might as well deal with it.'

'Yes, well, thank you.'

'Is it a pain somewhere?'

'Well, yes. It's been getting worse I suppose.'

'Uhuh. Where is the pain?'

In the effort to get over his embarrassment but at the same time show he didn't care, he shouted, 'The anus.' It must have been heard three rooms away.

'Okay. Haemorrhoids?'

'Mmm.'

This was the moment to read the GP's notes. Nothing untoward. I examined him and gave him the bad news that surgery was the only option.

Next was a very pretty twenty-five-year-old. What we would come to know as a 'Sloane Ranger', one of the brigade of county girls hunting in Chelsea, not for fur and fox but fun and fux. She was in a mini skirt, fitted shirt and the year's latest fashion items, thigh-length boots.

'Hello Miss Ruskin. Please sit down.'

'Yes, hello.'

'What's troubling you?'

'I've got piles! HaHaHa! Terribly silly really.'

'More sore than silly I'd have thought. Good that you can laugh, though. Most people crawl here in tears.'

'Oh dear, do they really?'

'How long have you felt discomfort?' I asked.

'Oh, I don't know. A month or two.'

'You've waited a long time.'

'Ha Ha Ha. Oh well, you know.'

'Yes, I know. If you'd like to pop behind the screen and slip off your bottom half.'

'Oh. Yes, absolutely.'

I handed her a gown. I looked at the notes. Nothing unusual. She emerged, wearing the gown and boots. She could have been on the cover of a glossy mag.

'All gone. Ha ha!'

'Fine. Just lie on the table. On your side, please.'

She lay on the table – facing me. 'Yes, but round the other way,' I said.

'Ha Ha! Sorry. Yes, of course 'cause you have to ... er ... Yes. Sorry.' She turned over.

'That's it. Good. Now just bring your knees up as far as you can.' She brought them up a quarter of the way. 'Right up, please.'

'I can't bend them any more than that.'

'Really? What's wrong with your knees?'

'Nothing. My boots are too long.'

Next was a huge man in his sixties with the face of an ex-boxer. He hobbled in.

'It's no use Doc, I'll 'ave to 'ave 'em done.'

'What?'

'These fuckin' piles.

Before the next patient was brought in, I said, 'Hold it a second, Jenny.' I leafed through the referral letters. As she saw me smile – 'All of them?'

'Every one.'

'I love Mr Parker,' she said. 'He's the only one who makes us laugh.'

At the end of the morning, Parker's head came round the door.

'Get to the end of them all right?'

I said, 'If they ever tire of the fingerprint system, they could try arseholes. No two are ever alike. Thank you for the opportunity to study them.'

He beamed. 'Pleasure, pleasure. Now, *you* can do something for *me*.' I raised my eyebrows. He went on, 'I've double booked myself this afternoon. Could you take the intensive students for me?'

More insulin inhibitors rushed through me. Teaching!

'I was going to do a ward round.'

'No, don't worry. Nothing but convalescents. Get cracked into the learners.'

'Well, I . . .'

'That's the ticket. I was going to talk to them about immunity, tissue rejection and so on, but do whatever you like. Bye.'

When I'd finished writing up the case notes, I sat quietly and considered what lay before me. Teaching. Me, teaching mature students, whose tuition was paid for by the state? (Those were the days.) I couldn't do this. I had to find someone to pass it to. Their knowledge far exceeded mine. Except, maybe . . . I grabbed an apple and a textbook and headed for a nearby town garden where I could read undisturbed. The thrill of fear brightened my mind. Glucagon again, great stuff.

There were five students, two female, three male. I recognised all of them but had spoken only to one, a girl.

'Good afternoon. I'm John Koston. I bring apologies from Mr Parker and some information on the procedure of amputation, with particular reference to the upper arm.'

The girl I knew, raised her hand. 'Excuse me, sir, Mr Parker said he was going to talk about immunity, so we all read it up.'

'Then you'll have read enough to know that there's no cure for it.' They laughed, thank God. 'You will also have read enough to know more about it than I do, and I am reluctant to spend the next hour looking like a pillock.'

Up spake one of the boys. 'Do you think there's much point in learning how to amputate limbs if you're going to be a family doctor?'

No form of address, no 'Sir', no 'Doctor' preceded the question. This was a well-spoken lad with a lock of dark hair over one eye.

I replied, 'Why teach all pilots to land on one engine when so few will ever have to do it? But emergencies can happen. One happened to me. Why shouldn't it happen to you?' I could see him dismiss the idea.

'Maybe,' he shrugged. I was irritated but remained pleasant. 'Why do you want to be a doctor?'

'My father's a doctor and he's done all right.'

'You mean financially, socially and so on?'

'I don't see what this has to do with amputation.'

I kept it light hearted. Was this the real boy talking, or the troubled one who had to impress with his apparent challenging of authority?

'If I was having a limb removed, I might be mildly interested.'

'If you were in the kind of condition where you needed emergency amputation, I don't think you'd be asking that question.'

'You're right. You're absolutely right. I would readily imagine that the doctor would be unstinting in his effort to save me; that his diligence and his motives would be above reproach. He would simply have my trust. How sad that it might be misplaced.'

There was a savoury moment of anticipation when no one could divine what would be said next. I said, 'All right, off you go.'

He looked at me.

'You want to go? It's all right, you can go.'

He gathered his stuff and headed for the door, driven more by his ego than any good sense. I said, 'Hey, why don't you just stay?'

'Why?'

'You'll only go and waste your money on that lousy coffee. Listen, what would be better is if you wasted even more of your money and brought us all a cup of that lousy coffee.'

He looked bewildered, and left. I turned to the others. 'That was a great start. Sorry.'

'No, we're sorry, sir,' said one of the other boys. We introduced ourselves.

'What was the emergency, sir?' from a girl, Carole.

'Oh, yes, the emergency. This was in Africa. A man had been mauled by a lion and lost an arm, so it was more of a tidying-up job really. My problem was that I wasn't too practised.'

'How did it go?'

'He wasn't exsanguinating the last time I saw him. It's bizarre in Africa. Often the patient just buggers off back into the bush. You presume that if he doesn't come back, then he's okay. I suggested that we adopt that practice here, but I found patients to be unenthusiastic.'

Polite laughter was interrupted by a tapping noise on the door. I opened it and there was the boy I now knew to be Roland, bearing a tray of cups. Remembering Captain Arcangeli, I started a round of applause. Roland took a bow and the clouds cleared.

'Now,' I said, picking up a piece of chalk, 'let's examine the anatomical structures you would encounter during amputation through the upper arm. Anyone know the route and destination of the ulnar nerve?'

A silence while they look at each other for inspiration, then from Carole, 'It ends up beside the brachialis.'

'No, that's the radial.'

I knew more than they did. And I now knew how exciting teaching was, and why John had never tired of answering my questions. That night:

My darling Francesca,

My life is lived in a state of permanent but controlled terror.

I've so far avoided any major procedures but have

discovered that much of surgery is like motor engineering but on a machine which, although much more sophisticated, is considerably more forgiving. An engine needs all of its components to keep running. The human will tick over quite happily for decades with whole bits missing. The trick is to remember which bits.

I am taken absolutely for granted. It simply doesn't occur to anyone that I'm not exactly what I say I am. Fortunately, I learn quickly and have already overtaken students who have been at it far longer than I.

My diagnostic powers are better because I suppose that age has taught me how to listen – not just to the words but how they're spoken. I like people much more than I realised and enjoy helping to make them well.

Colleagues are curious that I've formed no relationship, nor even taken Nurse Bloggs into the sluice room for a quickie. Liaisons are dangerous because I have no real past. I also fear talking in my sleep.

I wish I knew how you were.

14

Francesca

'Do you, Francesca, take Reg to be your lawful wedded husband, to have and to hold, to love and to cherish, from this day forward, for richer, for poorer, in sickness and in health until death you do part?'

'I do.' Did I? I hadn't a clue. Nor, I'm sure, had anyone else in the building. When intent to marry is declared, the world smiles and congratulates, says how lovely it is. No one ever says, which in many cases would be more helpful, 'What? Are you out of your fucking mind?'

That's not wholly true, Angela said it, well, she didn't say those words, she said 'You're completely stupid, Francesca.' This opinion came not from a historical examination of wedlock but simply because, as I've said, she considered Reg to be a savage. No matter that he was a highly qualified professional and a wonderfully decent man, he said 'cunt' a lot. I felt sure that Angela didn't have one, and so felt excluded.

I had so many times, in my imaginings, sworn the marriage vow to Hal, until Death us did so untimely part. Why now did I marry Reg? Many reasons. He loved me unconditionally. I loved him in my way, because, like Hal, he had honour and was kind and, of course, I was pregnant; at that time, for a girl out of wedlock, still a terrifying condition. I couldn't imagine my father reassuring me, telling me not to worry, that we'd be looked after. But Reg did. Immediately upon telling him that I was 'up the duff', he asked me to marry him. He said he'd wanted to ask me anyway but had considered it to be indecently hasty. I smiled and said, 'You didn't consider it indecently hasty to fuck me.' It was the only time I remember seeing him lost for words.

The baby growing inside me saved my sanity. She was my new friend – I always knew it was a girl – who was with me everywhere, awake and asleep. I played Mozart and Bach to her. I spoke to her constantly and asked for her guidance, imagining that since she was unborn she might yet bestride two worlds and have access still to the wisdom of the other. New and frightening words entered my vocabulary: 'glomerulone-phritis', a kidney disease; 'pre-eclampsia' detected by protein in the urine, and God forbid, 'eclampsia'. Don't even think about it. Thankfully, none of these I suffered, and Reg resolutely stayed away from medical terms, giving me only such information that was helpful and reassuring.

In the early months, the pregnancy was more of a fantasy, for it was really difficult to grasp the reality of what was to come, despite the obvious changes that occurred. My libido, which I normally bore on outstretched arms for all to witness, became, for the first few months a total recluse, somewhat to Reg's annoyance. It was something of an irony then, that later, when I was overwhelmed with randiness, Reg discovered that he couldn't face sex with me being so heavily pregnant; an atheist with Calvinist tendencies.

Gertrude was not so inflicted and helped out with pleasure. During this time, the intensity of sexual sensation was, well, sensational. Greater even than with Hal. I wanted to ask Reg if there was a physical reason for this, but my relationship with him was not conducive to the revelation of my dalliance with Gertrude. In desperation one day, when Gertrude was not available, I bought a cucumber.

Alongside my randiness, I was driven to engage in pursuits which hitherto had held no interest for me, such as baking, cleaning out cupboards and rearranging furniture. When confronted with Reg's question, 'What the fuck are you doin' darlin'?' I realised that I was building a nest. Weird bird.

I was also eating for England. This may have been as a result of depression. When I was not raging at Hal for having died – and it was a towering rage – I was aching for him. I worried that any depression might travel through my placenta to my baby, whose name, I had determined, would be Claire. I tried to avoid all unhappy thoughts, which meant strict censorship of most literature. I therefore rediscovered Jeeves and Wooster and listened only to concerts and nice plays on the BBC World Service. My pregnancy was proceeding nicely. I thought.

The baby came prematurely – and horribly deformed. It seemed to be made partially of what looked like Lego. There were lumps of hair and bits of skin from which bare bone protruded. My sister, who was present, turned it to reveal that the other side of its body was one huge mouth. My screams could have been heard in Uganda. Poor Reg almost had a heart attack before he woke me. This was the first of a number of such dreams. Consciously, I suffered no more than the normal apprehensions, but subconsciously, terror. It was obvious that I had a fear of my tits being damaged, because all the creatures to which I gave birth had huge mouths which clamped themselves over them and pulled. But then of course, they weren't 'tits' any more. It all became clear one day, looking at them, observing how they were growing. No longer were they assets to display and with which to entice, a source of pleasure for me and whoever happened to be fondling them, they were now mammary glands, changing shape and content for one purpose only, to be plant and machinery in a new baby factory. I was in production. Perhaps I should apply for a royal appointment. Francesca's Fallopians by appointment to Her Majesty the Queen.

One afternoon, while shopping, I ran into Jeremy, Angela's husband. He bundled me into his Land Rover and insisted on taking me to tea at the embassy.

'We never see you, Francesca.'

'I know, Jeremy, I'm sorry. I like to see *you*, but Angela's acid is bad for my baby.'

Inside the embassy, we were hailed by the ambassador, Sir Ralph Haggard.

'Hello Ralphie,' I greeted him with a best smile. Ralphie had always fancied me but his terror of being stripped to the ranks far overwhelmed his lust so he restrained himself to amiable flirtation. Most of those who achieve rank in the Diplomatic Service have great charm. It's what they do. In fact it's pretty well all they do, but so armed, they can accomplish a great deal. My father, I could see, had great charm, he just rationed its use with me. I expect Ralphie's family suffered similar privations.

'Francesca, I do believe you're now fatter than I.' I told you he had charm. 'Have you had tea, you two?' continued Ralphie.

'Just heading towards it sir.' said Jeremy.

'Perfect timing. You'll have it with me.'

And we did. And while munching a piece of Madeira cake, some went down the wrong way and I choked. With each violent cough, I involuntarily gushed a quantity of pee into my knickers. No matter how hard I squeezed it made no difference and I couldn't stop coughing. Observing the fall of liquid on to the ambassadorial Aubusson, Ralphie calmly reached for an ornamental copper coal scuttle and placed it beneath the drip.

He smiled and said, 'We'll withdraw Francesca and allow you to come to yourself. Please avail yourself of my loo. It's that door there.'

As he and Jeremy cleared the room, he said, 'Please don't be embarrassed. When my wife Rose was carrying David, she peed on Mrs Khrushchev.'

Hal

The evening that I approached with curiosity, pleasant anticipation and dread, was upon me; supper with the Parkers. I hadn't told anyone at the hospital, partly because in discussions about Parker, no one had mentioned ever being there, thus leading me to suppose that, perhaps, no one had.

He lived in a pleasant, Edwardian house set in a large garden in a wealthy area of London called St John's Wood. I expected the door to be opened by a butler or maid, but no, it was Parker, still in his dark grey chalk stripe.

'Koston, dear boy! Good, good, come in.' He closed the door behind me. 'I'll lead the way, shall I?' And he did, down a hallway with a black and white marble floor, to a delightful large drawing room with comfortable sofas and armchairs, beautiful lamps, and the walls covered in paintings. Exactly the kind of room that I imagined that Francesca would have made for us. I was spared from dwelling on the thought by the arrival of two beautiful women – identical twins in, I suppose, their late forties. Parker who, like Cadell, knew the rules, presented me to them.

'This is John Koston. My wife, Lotte and her sister Milla.'

'Hello. Which is which?'

'I'm Lotte, this is Milla – but sometimes we change if we're feeling to be mischievous.' But she spoke in a most delicious accent – 'I'm Lotte, zis is Milla – but sometimes ve change if ve're feelink to be mischievous.'

This was totally unexpected. I had imagined Parker to be married to either a grand, elegant English rose or something stocky in tweeds which regularly beat the hell out of him.

'How do I know that you haven't already switched?' They looked at me.

'Milla,' said Lotte, indicating me, 'this one, we'll have to watch!'

I asked them where they were from.

'You haven't time to listen to the answer,' said Milla, 'Anyway, Andrew thinks we're from outer space.'

'You see what I'm up against here,' said Parker. 'What can I get you to drink? Whisky?'

'Thank you.' I prayed that the women weren't doctors. Should the conversation unavoidably turn to medicine, it would be hard enough to hold my own with one expert, but three? Actually, medical chat was less of a fear than the lack of an authentic past.

The next surprise of the evening came when we moved into the dining room. They pulled back their chairs but didn't sit, so nor did I. At Lotte's place lay a pleated bread loaf, covered by a small white cloth.

Milla spoke. 'Tonight is Friday, so we have a special dinner. You see, Lotte and I are Jews. Andrew, not. We don't really believe, but it's a very ancient culture and we don't like it to die, so we continue with the customs.'

'Yes, absolutely. I understand,' I said.

Lotte struck a match and lit the candle before her. She then shaded her eyes with her hand and spoke some words, which I took to be a grace in Hebrew. She laid her hand on the bread and spoke a little more, ending with 'Omen'. Milla and Parker repeated it. I took it to mean 'amen' so I said it too. The women looked at me.

'You learn quick!' said Lotte. The bread was broken and some little pieces cut. A little wine was poured into a silver goblet and this was passed round with the bread. I had thought that sharing bread and wine was a Christian communion but it had evidently been going on for thousands of years before Jesus gave up carpentry and got himself in trouble. At school, we'd been told that communion originated at 'the last supper'. More tosh.

I was slightly apprehensive that the food might be strange and part of a ritual, but no. There followed the best smoked salmon I'd ever tasted – from a local shop with, I thought, the rather unfortunate name of Panzer – then a magnificent Chateaubriand. All washed down with first, a Pouilly Fumé then a grand cru from Paulliac. These people knew how to party.

Mercifully, Lotte and Milla were not medics, but string players, both in the London Philharmonic Orchestra. Lotte, a fiddle player and Milla, a cellist, were both on the first desk of their sections, so these women were considerable musicians.

All went well, the ladies being great story tellers. They entertained me with tales from behind the scenes and about the great figures in music. One I particularly liked was a letter to someone from Tchaikovsky, in which he wrote: 'I have just read through the music of that scoundrel Brahms. God, what a giftless bastard.' Parker had, of course, heard them all before, but sat smiling, evidently taking great pleasure from Lotte and Milla.

When I was least expecting it, 'Milla, we're talking too much about music. Enough. John? Where are you from?'

'No, please, I love hearing about music.'

'So maybe later. You're from where?'

'New Zealand.'

'It's very beautiful. We were on tour there with the orchestra. You remember, Milla?'

'Of course I remember. I'm stupid all of a sudden?'

'Not all of a sudden.'

I loved them. They were so beautiful and intelligent and funny. Francesca would have loved them too. The age difference between Lotte and Parker wasn't much less than between Francesca and me. How was it that he could do it and I couldn't? I was about to ask how they met, when, from Milla, 'Where in New Zealand?'

'Auckland.'

'I can never remember, is that on the north island or the south?'

The north island or the south? Jesus! I hadn't a clue. *Panther in the bed!* Glucose inundated my brain.

'It's on the . . .' My eyes flicked to the window. 'What was that?'

'What?' they chorused.

'I thought I saw something pass the window.'

Parker rose. 'What sort of something?'

'I don't know. Just a shape. I take it that there shouldn't be anyone in the garden at night?'

'Damned right,' said Parker, heading for the door.'

Lotte and Milla were on their feet in a flash. 'Andrew! Stop! Don't go out.'

'I'll get the shotgun. I'll shoot the bugger up the arse.'

'Aha! No!' yelled Milla. 'Then you'll go to jail, and really you will learn something about buggers and arses.'

Milla's sodomite warning made me weep from laughter. It was spoken thus – 'Zen you vill go to jail unt really you vill learn somesink about buggers unt arzes.'

Anyway, since I knew that there was no one out there, I could afford to be brave, so said, 'Sir, I'll have a look around. It may just have been a shadow or a reflection or something.'

'Take this,' said Lotte, handing me a poker from the fireplace. Clearly she was less concerned about *my* incarceration, and its concomitant perils to my arse. I took the poker and was shown to the back door.

'I'll come with you,' said Parker, 'always present a united front, remember?'

We circumnavigated the building, the concerned faces of Lotte and Milla appearing at every window as we did so.

'Such brave boys!' said Milla as we re-entered.

'That's us, Koston,' said Parker, 'hearts of lions.'

'So now you must have coffee and cake.'

I felt such a heel, alarming them so, and all because I didn't know at which end of New Zealand sat Auckland.

As we tucked into coffee and a cake straight from the god of chocolate, I asked, 'How did you all meet?' I addressed the question to the women, who looked to Parker, then looked down.

I looked to Parker, who said, 'At the end of the war, in Germany. I was an MO in the army. I met Lotte and we took a bit of a fancy to each other, so when it was all mopped up, I went back to find her. Then Milla came over.'

Looking at the women, I said, 'That's very romantic.'

'Oh yes,' said Lotte, quietly.

'Yes,' said Milla, also quietly.

They looked at Parker and smiled, then dropped their eyes. Then I realised. Jews? Germany at the end of the war? Something big had happened here. There was more to be told, but it was unlikely to be tonight. Was Milla spoken for, I wondered? Highly inappropriate to ask. The evening ended with Lotte playing a Mozart Violin Sonata, with Milla at the piano. (E Minor K304. Have a listen if you don't know it.) I was pleased for Parker that his life seemed so splendid. At the hospital, he was like a god, driving everything with an intense energy. At home, he seemed truly tranquil.

In his office the following morning, he asked, 'Have you met Dougall McKay yet?'

'No. I know who he is, but we've never met.'

'I think it would be valuable, don't you Alison?'

Alison gave a bright smile. 'Yes, very helpful, I'm sure.'

Parker continued, 'He's a man who enjoys an extraordinary rapport with his patients. Find out where he is, Alison. Join his ward round this morning.'

'Fine,' I said.

Half an hour later, at a ward doorway, I stood with a group of junior registrars, Jack Paton, two nurses and Penny Gregson, the ward sister, awaiting the arrival of McKay. He appeared from a doorway midway along the corridor, stood a moment, looking about him as if completely lost, then set off in the wrong direction. Sister Gregson indicated that we should move. We caught up, and she said, 'Good morning, sir.'

McKay, probably approaching retirement from state medicine, had thin hair, carefully parted and an extremely Presbyterian expression. The latter, not surprising since he was from the highlands of Scotland.

'Good morning,' he said He looked at her but neither spoke further, nor moved.

'Would you like to do the ward round, sir?'

'Why else would I be standing here?'

Jack Paton, for reasons known only to himself, said, indicating me, 'Mr McKay, this is John Koston, on secondment from Africa.'

McKay turned his sin-searching gaze on Jack and said, as though he'd never heard of the place, 'Africa?' He blinked with one eye only, and headed for the ward.

Sister Gregson turned her eyes to us to pre-empt any smart-arsed looks or remarks. In those days there was a tremendous discipline to hospital life. Occasionally tiresome, but on the whole, I think, of great benefit.

McKay walked past the first bed, on which lay a middle aged lady. Sister Gregson spoke.

'Sir, this is Mrs Rogers.'

McKay stopped, looked at the sister then the chart. 'Well, I don't remember her.'

Jack Paton bravely spoke up. 'You did a hemicolectomy on her, sir.'

'Mhm? And how did that turn out?'

'Very well, sir.' He attempted a reassuring smile at Mrs Rogers which, from her expression, I deemed unsuccessful. A vague wave of McKay's hand indicated that the wound on her abdomen should be exposed. It duly was. He looked and fingered gently around it. 'You'd better tell her to go home.'

And he turned away, never once having looked his patient in the eye.

He moved to the next bed, occupied by Lucy, ten years old. This time he looked – and looked. Then, 'Yes, this was Crohn's disease.'

There was an uneasy silence. Lucy's eyes furrowed and she looked at Sister Gregson, who said,

'Sir, this is Lucy. She had an appendicectomy following peritonitis.'

'Not at all, Sister. I remember this procedure particularly well.'

Lucy spoke. 'Will I be able to go home?'

McKay's head jerked like that of a startled bird. 'Who said that?'

'Lucy, sir,' said Sister. 'She'd like to know if she can go home.'

'Not at all. There's no question of going home.' He turned to Jack Paton. 'You keep a careful eye on this.' He moved on and they all followed. I looked at Lucy who was now in tears. I sat on the bed and took her hand.

'Lucy?'

She was enduring what we all remember from childhood, those involuntary spasms, a combination of sobs and hiccoughs.

'S . . . ss . . . s sister s . . . s said I'd be going home t . . . t . . . tttoday.'

'Did she?'

'My d . . . ddaddy was coming back *specially* from France, 'c . . . c . . . cause he doesn't live with us any more and he was cc . . . coming back *specially*.'

'I understand. I don't know your case, Lucy. Do you know what you had?'

'Yes, it was appendicitis, like Sister said.'

'I see. Then don't worry. As soon as we finish the ward round, I'll talk to Sister and we'll straighten it all out.'

I looked up, to see that the ward round had stopped and that all eyes, except McKay's, which were fixed on the ceiling, were upon me.

I said, 'See you in a little while, Lucy.' And rejoined the group. McKay altered his gaze to his feet and asked, 'What are you doing?'

'I was talking to Lucy.'

'While we are waiting?'

'While she was crying.'

'Perhaps she has reason to cry.'

I gave him my 'are you really sure you want to take me on?' look which I'd learned from Cadell, and said pleasantly, 'Yes, I think she has.'

I could feel the excitement rise in our little group. The story would be round the entire hospital in ten minutes. All my care to remain grey had gone for nothing. I was now ablaze. Though, if they had expected fireworks from McKay, they were disappointed. Predictably, he said nothing but moved to the next bed and stood silent, waiting.

'I'm waiting, Sister,' he said.

We were at a loss. We looked at our feet, at each other, at him. He was waiting by an empty bed.

The rest of the round was uneventful. McKay's parting shot to me was – 'A pity they don't teach you manners in India.'

'China,' I replied, to the great amusement of Jack Paton.

'What's your name?' he asked, looking at a point some-where to starboard of his right shoe.

'Wong, sir. Helmut Wong.'

'Right, Wong, I'll remember that.' And he strode off, probably in the wong direction.

'Chancing your arm a bit there, old son,' said Jack, grinning.

'Oh well,' I said. 'Sister, can we sort this problem with Lucy?'

'Yes, of course. I'll get his secretary to slip him a discharge sheet to sign. He won't read it.'

Fifteen minutes later, my beeper sounded and I headed for a phone. It was Alison, Parker's secretary. 'He wants to see you.'

'I'm on my way.'

Parker was lying on the treatment table in his room. For a moment I thought he was ill.

'Are you all right, sir?'

'Ah, Dr Wong. Yes, just straightening the back.' He remained recumbent. 'So you took on the Tartan Terror.'

'God! That was fast. How did you hear?'

'I was operating. The news came in alongside a bottle of blood. Cheered everybody up.'

'I didn't mean to take anyone on. I'm sorry, sir. Is it likely to go further?'

'He's not a good man to cross. He'll always remember that something happened but he won't remember it accurately.'

'Well, he doesn't even remember his patients – or his way around the hospital. Why is he still operating?'

'We need the hands. There aren't enough to go round.'

'But doesn't he kill more than he cures?'

'That's the extraordinary thing. When he's inside the abdomen, he's absolutely unerring.'

'He never makes mistakes?'

Parker looked at me. 'I believe that's what unerring means, yes. He has no compassion, he's a pure mechanic. I'd rather not ask him to my party, but if I had something wrong with my gut, he's the man I'd call. It takes all sorts.'

'Hmm,' I grunted.

He pulled himself off the treatment table. 'Anyway, how are you getting on? All right?'

'Fine, sir, thanks.'

'Right then. I'm perfectly confident that you're able to start operating.'

So there it was, sudden and simple, the last chance to back out. Start operating. What an enormous little phrase. Could I do it? Simple procedures, yes. Did I have the guts? 'Hearts of lions, that's us,' so Parker had said on the night of the hunt for the non-existent prowler. He meant surgeons of course. *Doctor in the House* again. 'To be a surgeon, you need the heart of a lion – and the hands of a lady,' said Sir Lancelot Spratt. Sounds neat but the hands of a lady aren't going to be of great use in, for example, trying to pull against the natural tension of a powerful muscle; then you need the heart of a lion and the brawn of a weight-lifter.

I wouldn't be left unattended of course. Jack Paton or one of the other senior registrars – and indeed Parker – would always be on hand if I felt insecure during a procedure. Also I knew that I wouldn't be thrown anything massive. The introduction to surgery was, at that time, a much more hands-on affair than now. Youngsters would watch a couple of simple herniotomies, for example, then have a supervised go. 'Get in and learn' was the attitude. Now there seems to be a great reluctance to let a student touch a patient.

That evening at six o'clock, we assembled in Parker's office to look at the theatre list for the following day. There was everything from partial gastrectomy, through gall bladder removal, to haemorrhoid repair. I was handed two biopsies, one to take a tissue specimen from the bottom of the oesophagus and another from the breast, and a hernia repair.

Sorry to disappoint you if you were expecting a drama but there wasn't one.

There was nothing complicated about any of the procedures. I was slower than the other team members but that was anticipated. And so the months passed, in the accumulation of knowledge and skill.

Dearest Francesca,

I am now operating. No transplants yet, just herniotomies, appendecectomies, removal of varicose veins and such. I didn't expect to get to this point so quickly, but they were clearly thinking that I should take my share of the workload. I am, after all, supposed to be fully qualified, just a bit rusty in the abdominal area.

I am certainly very rusty in the lower abdominal area. I wonder if you are.

Selfishly, I want to know how you're coping. It's something of a luxury to be allowed the possibility of knowing the reaction of one's friends to one's death. I feel guilty about being flippant like this about your pain. I miss you more than you could believe. And I want you to share in my achievement. Every time I drop an inflamed appendix into the bucket, I imagine you smiling fondly from the observer's gallery, before vomiting over the students.

I'm much less tired than I was.

Always, my love.

16

Francesca

I so wanted Hal to see what I'd done, how clever I'd been. Claire was born on a Saturday morning during week thirty-nine. On the previous evening, my presence had been demanded by Angela at a drinks thing she was giving at home for a visiting American diplomat and his elegant, delightful wife, Diana. The sofa on which Hal and I had been caught doing it had been moved on to the veranda. There I sat, with Diana, chatting about child rearing – what else? – when a warm feeling enveloped my bum. I thought I'd peed myself again, but when the gush continued in some abundance, I realised what had happened. 'Oh! I think my waters have broken.'

'Nothing to worry about, Francesca,' smiled Diana, 'your baby's on the way. We should get you to hospital though.'

'Yes, absolutely,' I said, standing up. As I did, the water, which hadn't yet soaked into the sofa but was still trapped in my dress and knickers, hit the floor with a wonderful splat just as Angela approached. What would have been a shrieked, 'Francesca, for God's sake what *are* you bloody doing?' was, on seeing Diana beside me, diminished to, 'Francesca, are you all right?' delivered through a smile of bared fangs. It was delivered loudly enough though, to make everyone turn. Their eyes dropped as one, to the puddle at my feet. Of course the eyes that I did meet were those of Ralphie, the ambassador whose Aubusson I had recently watered. He smiled affectionately. A shared secret.

'Oh, Angela,' I said, looking at the large dark patch on the sofa, 'isn't that the one that was re-upholstered?'

I had determined to have Claire naturally, without the support of painkillers – until the pain started. The contractions are completely manageable at first but when the actual birth begins? Jesus fucking Christ! 'Give me drugs!' I gasped, hardly able to spare the air to form the words. It is appalling, even with pethidine. But you know, the strange thing is, I can remember the pain only intellectually. I know that it was immense but I can't *actually* remember it. I can bring other pains to mind more readily, like going over on my ankle, or having my arm broken at lacrosse, but that's because those pains were relatively minor. We seem to have a safety cut-off in the memory of childbirth, probably because otherwise, we'd never, ever, do it twice.

The moment I saw Claire as she was handed to me, stained and squashed from her traumatic passage from under water to dry land, my world changed. She was now the centre of the universe. Everything would be for her. She would be first, always. Reg was magnificent. At all times supportive, unselfish and adoring of Claire. How would my Hal have been? The same, I'm sure. I held my baby to the wound of my lost love and dreamed of restoration.

17

Hal

One of the frustrations of the hospital system is that a patient may attend your clinic, be referred for surgery which someone else does, and is never seen by you again. Likewise you might never meet a patient on your operating list until just before knife to skin. You meet them after surgery, of course, when they're still groggy.

'Hello Mrs Smith, I'm Dr Koston, I sliced open your abdomen this afternoon.'

Oh, thank you, Doctor. Am I going to be all right?'

'Yes, it went very well. You'll be walking slowly for a week or so, but you're going to be absolutely fine.' And she smiles, and loves you.

Hospitals are wonderful places. People are often heard to say 'I hate hospitals, they're so depressing.' Indeed, I said it myself. It's a shame, really, because they're far from depressing. They're places that, for the most part, make sick people well. How can that be depressing?

It was now almost two years since I had presented myself at Parker's office as John Koston. No one in that time had for a second questioned that I was anything other than fully qualified. Every day was as exciting as, and more fascinating than, the one before. I had bought myself a Mini, what Francesca would have called, 'A completely delicious little car but slightly tight to fuck in.'

One afternoon, as I sat having tea in the doctors' mess, the phone rang. 'John, for you,' said one of the residents. I took the receiver and said, 'Hello, Dr Koston.'

The voice said, 'Hello Hal. Uncle Humphrey.' My heart muscles engaged low gear and shot to 190 beats a minute. It was Humphries, Cadell's subordinate sidekick.

'Oh, hello,' I said, with great outward calm. 'How are you?'

'Fine, thank you. We were just wondering if we might have a moment.'

The answer 'no' was not, of course, an option. I kept smiling for the benefit of those around me, whose ears would be quivering for a snippet, having been starved of all information about me.

'Yes, absolutely. When would be convenient?'

'When do you get off today?'

'I don't know but I can probably take a break from six till seven.'

'Fine. Shall we say your place about 6.15?'

'Yes, fine. See you then. Bye.'

Jelly-legged, I headed for my afternoon ward round. Would this be my last day as a doctor? Was I to be flung in jail – or blackmailed into returning to the skies of blood? The answer would be neither. I had long ago decided what I'd do if it came to this. At the door to the ward, Jack Paton caught up with me.

'John, I've got a problem. Can you cover for me tonight?'

I smiled. 'Yes, sure. What did we do?'

'What?' He looked puzzled.

'We'd better have the same story.'

'Oh!' He laughed. 'Christ, is my reputation that bad.'

'Pretty bad, yes.'

'No, it's not that. I'm on tonight but I've got a bit of a family problem. Any chance you could take my stint?'

This was awkward. Cadell wouldn't take kindly to being stood up.

'Do you trust me? I haven't done anything spectacular yet.'

'No, I've checked the wards. No one's likely to blow up tonight.'

'I've got to be away myself until about half past seven. How is that for you?'

'That's great, John, thanks. See you then,' and he was off.

As I approached my flat, Humphries walked towards me.

'How are you?' he said, offering his hand.

'Less well than I was a few hours ago.'

'Nothing to worry about, I'm sure. We just wanted to say hello.'

'Jolly decent of you.' I looked around, checking for what we called 'thump wallahs'. If this looked like turning nasty I would make a run for it. Humphries poured balm.

'It's unofficial Hal, he only wants a word,' he said this as he opened the passenger door of his half-timbered Morris Minor. I got in. We drove around the corner and stopped.

'He's in the green Rover.' Poor Humphries spent much of his life doing silly stuff like this.

'How are you anyway, Uncle Humphrey?'

'Thank you Hal, reasonably well. Quite busy at the moment, with this Cambodian stuff boiling up. Could have done with you a couple of weeks ago, I can tell you.'

A stomach heave as my most dreaded memory crashed into my head. I was saved by Humphries saying, 'Anyway you'd best get over there. Nice to see you Hal.'

'You too, Ronald.' That was his name, Ronald, but I'd never before used it. I crossed the road and got into the 3-litre Rover. Cadell hadn't changed a bit.

'Hello, Hal.'

I laughed. 'That business of driving me round the corner was one of the most suspicious manoeuvres I've ever seen.'

'Well, we've never been caught yet.'

'Who the hell do you think would be trying to catch you?'

He ignored it and said, 'It all seems to be going pretty well for you.'

'Until now.'

'No, no. That's nothing to do with us. That's the arthritic arm of the civil law and it'll never feel a touch from my people. I like to see my boys doing well.'

'My membership has lapsed.'

'Don't worry, it's for life.'

God, what hell was he going to try to place me in?

'Please come to the point. I've lost my appetite for suspense.'

He reached into the glove compartment. 'Want a Malteser?'

'Thanks.' I took one. It helped my desert-dry mouth considerably. He continued while munching . . .

'If someone disappears from the service because he's dead, then that's perfectly acceptable and jolly good luck to him. But if he buggers off without telling me, then turns up in Africa doing good works, I'm suspicious, that's all. The trouble with these things is that you can't stop eating them. Want another?' I took another Malteser, he took two and continued, 'Then when he appears in a London hospital professing to be a doctor, I'm bloody fascinated, so, I confess to being a little curious as to why you're doing this.'

'Because I want to.'

Cadell looked at me and mused. 'Because you want to . . . Hmmm. Do you do abortions?'

'Ah, that's why you want to see me. You're pregnant.' He smiled his charming, English smile, but said nothing.

'It's what I *should* have been,' I said, 'a doctor that is, not an abortionist.'

'Is it really? Well, well.'

'So what now?'

'Nothing. Nothing at all. Don't give it a second thought. Merely a social call.'

'Are you serious? You want nothing and you'll say nothing?'

'At first, I thought you were up to something, which, I may say, knowing you, would have surprised me, but you seem to be doing exactly what you seem to be doing, so I'm calling off the hounds. Scout's honour.'

'Really?'

'Mmm.' He nodded slowly, then, 'Why did you just walk away?'

I didn't answer.

'Something bad happen?'

'Yes.'

He looked at me for quite a long time, then said, 'Okay.'

'That's really it?'

'I suppose it is, yes. But membership *is* for life. Yours, not ours.'

And there it was. 'Always leave a door open.' You might want out – or back in.

A cloud had enveloped me. I liked Cadell but dreaded him, well, not him but what he represented, and I knew that the one thing he did want, was to let me know that he knew. I felt a bit adrift suddenly, a bit bloody alone, actually.

I had intended to have something to eat but Cadell and his sodding Maltesers had undone my appetite, so I walked back to the hospital to relieve Jack. He headed off and I grabbed the moment of calm to catch up on some paperwork. Ten minutes later I was summoned to Casualty by Jane, a junior resident. A creature of great earnestness, she was standing beside her patient, peering at an X-ray. Her head was tilted back, her nose crinkled upwards, exposing her upper teeth to the gum. Not a hugely attractive expression and one almost certainly employed throughout her life to aid concentration. She would always be unaware of it, despite her mother's no doubt constant nag, 'Don't do that thing with your face, dear.'

The patient was a man in his sixties, who really didn't look well; pale and obviously in pain. Beside him, fretful, stood a woman in too many clothes for the warm room. I said 'hello'.

'Oh, Dr Koston, this is Mr and Mrs Blackburn.'

'How do you do? What's the problem?'

'He's got a terrible pain. Terrible,' said Mrs Blackburn.

'Oh, terrible pain, Doc, terrible, in me stomach.' echoed the patient.

'What's on the X-ray?' I asked, taking it from Jane.

'I think there's a lot of air under the diaphragm,' she said. I looked at the plate.

'Absolutely right, Jane.'

'He's got an ulcer and they won't do anything,' Mrs Blackburn again.

'My doctor said I might have an ulcer,' offered Mr Blackburn. I touched his stomach and he jumped in pain.'

'Oh, sorry, Doctor.'

'That's all right, you're entitled to jump. That's pretty tender. Did your doctor have you X-rayed?'

'No, just gave me some medicine.'

'Just gives 'im medicine an' 'e needs an operation,' spoke the fretful spouse.

'Uhuh. Well, your wife's right, Mr Blackburn. You do have an ulcer. And it's made a small hole in your stomach and allowed air to escape into the peritoneal cavity. That's what's so painful.

'Can you make it better, Doctor?'

'Oh yes. You'll be fine,' and to Jane, 'Fix up theatre and call me, okay?'

'I already have, they'll be ready in a quarter of an hour.'

'When did you last eat, Mr Blackburn?' I asked.

'Just a cup of tea this morning. I'm sorry I don't really want anything.'

I smiled. 'No I wasn't offering you dinner, we just don't like to give anaesthetic on a full stomach.'

I explained the procedure in what detail I thought they could handle, then I was off – to bury my nose in a tome on the subject of repair of the stomach. I had assisted Parker three times in similar procedures. It's not just a repair, but in this case one which also involved division of the vagus nerves to reduce the acid secretion, and a drain put in place. I wanted back-up, so lifted the phone.

'Hello, it's Dr Koston can you get Mr Parker please? Tell him I need him in theatre.' I returned to the book. The phone rang.

'Dr Koston, can you get to theatre as quickly as possible please.'

'Yes. What's the problem?'

'The patient's losing blood.'

As I made for the door, the phone rang again. They thought that Parker might be in the hospital but they couldn't find him. Jesus!

I was scrubbed and gowned in minutes. As I walked into the anaesthetic room the first thing I saw was the red bottle. A tube had been passed through the patient's nose into the stomach to suck out gastric fluid, but what was coming out, was blood. Bad. Anderson, the anaesthetist spoke.

'We've got a bit of a problem here.'

'How much blood have you laid in?'

'Two pints, but there's more coming. I'm sorry, I shouldn't really have put him to sleep yet but I've got a case in the eye theatre at nine.'

'Maybe a good thing that you did. Let's get him in.'

We opened him. I was being cautious. The first thing was to find the bleeding vessel and tie it off. Nothing looked right. The moment I touched it, catastrophe. Blood everywhere.

'Suction please. Clamp.' The suction tube was introduced as I applied the clamp to a ruptured vessel. Another rush of blood. More clamps. More blood. We were awash. I'd never seen anything like it.

'My God, he's bleeding. Suck, suck.'

From Anderson, 'His BP is dropping. I can't keep it up.'

Sister Williamson said, 'Would you not be better to pack it?'

Anderson again, 'He's going to arrest. Get the crash team.'

The 'crash team' is a dedicated unit called to action in the event of cardiac arrest.

I was filling the wound with packs of wadding in an attempt to stem the massive haemorrhage.

'He's arrested!' from Anderson.

I immediately began thumping the patient's chest in an attempt to start the heart again. Nothing.

'I'm going in,' I said, meaning that I was going to open the chest and massage the heart.'

'I don't think it'll help. I can't get blood in fast enough.'

I heard a familiar voice. 'What's going on?' It was Parker.

Then from Anderson, the chilling words. 'He's gone.' I stood back. The enormity of the death had placed me in a different universe from everyone else. I had to stay apart. In the distance I saw Parker's hand in the wound, probing. He indicated for Sister Williamson to look. She did, then they looked at each other.

It was over. All of it. The dream, the hope of redemption. I left the theatre, changed quickly and was out of the hospital in minutes. It was Cadell. He'd brought death again. Maybe he was Death. I remembered a movie about a medieval knight to whom Death came, incarnate. The knight, for his life, played chess with Death. I was offered no such contest, for my life or anyone else's. Or perhaps *I* was Death. Yes. I must be Death. Or perhaps there are lots of Deaths, who move casually about, laying their cold fingers on the unsuspecting. I'd laid them on so many, and finally, by my monstrous conceit, on poor Mr Blackburn. He would be the last – well, second last. That was the only way to break the curse. I was in the car on my way to a high headland on the south coast.

The sun would soon set. How symbolic. I had ahead of me a couple of hours' driving, so I reviewed it all and summed up:

'Considering a promising start and the many opportunities afforded him, this boy has been not only a sad disappointment, but a disgrace.'

I was approaching the most glamorous gate to the UK, the White Cliffs of Dover. To a wartime pilot, there cannot have been a more welcome vista. They are high, they are mighty, they are home and they are hope. But today I was leaving. I was interested only in their height. I turned off the road on to a tractor track and headed for the edge.

Will I be conscious after the impact, will my brain still function for a few moments even though I'm in bits? Don't think. Drive. It'll soon be over. I imagine what I'll look like. Bone splintered into the frontal lobes, cerebral tissue oozing through the skull, thoracic cavity agape, revealing the heart, convulsing like the wounded animal it is. Fibulas and femurs stabbed through the flesh. I deserve it.

Nearer it came, my release. I remembered Lorna in the aircraft and what she'd said: 'And when the moment came it had no drama. I just thought, this is what I do now.' The edge was maybe 200 yards away. The highest speed I could achieve over the grass was 58 miles an hour. That should be enough to take me over the water. Then a thought crackled, *Suppose good old God decides to have a last laugh, and thinks, Wouldn't it be hysterically funny if on the way down, he saw a boat with a couple of kids in it and knew he was going to hit them. What a hoot!*

I braked and bumped to a stop. Was it actually cowardice? I don't know. I had no sense of relief but I knew I couldn't take the chance of killing again. I didn't want it to be cowardice so I resolved to return and take my punishment. If it was prison, fine. It might make me feel better. But then why should I be entitled to feel better? Oh, what a fucking mess. I drove home.

'Good morning,' said Alison, smiling. 'Go straight in, he's waiting for you.'

Now she would know. Now they would all know that I was a fake, an intruder. I was so sad to disappoint Parker – and Lotte and Milla, whom I would never see again.

'Good morning, John.'

'Sir. I don't know where to begin.'

'The place to begin, in this case, is the end.'

I felt sick.

He went on. 'I see by your expression that you take full responsibility for this man's death.'

'Yes, sir.'

'Yes.' He opened a large envelope and spilled photographs on to the desk. There it was, in glorious colour, evidence of my crime.

'It's part of my job to try to prevent situations like this.'

'I know there isn't an excuse. I'll tell you exactly what happened?'

'I know what happened. And I know that it'll happen again. Did you know a retractor tore the spleen?'

Worse and worse. 'No, I didn't even know that. There was so much blood . . .'

He drove on. 'When I was a serving registrar, I had a consultant whose favourite occupation appeared to be buggering up spleens. 'Oh bum!' he'd say, "that's another one fucked." A minute later, he'd whipped the whole thing out and it was in the bucket. By the way, have you taken a spleen out?'

'No, but . . .

'All right. We'll cover that.'

'No, you don't un—'

'Now I'm going to tell you what killed him.'

'I killed him.'

'Oh, shut up! A tumour killed him.'

'A tumour?'

'If you'd been able to get any further with the procedure – and if you hadn't buggered off like a guilty Girl Guide, you'd have seen a bloody healthy cancer which had eaten the splenic and all the other arteries down the greater curvature. Poor chap was dead long before he came through the door. No surgeon on earth could have prolonged his life by five minutes.'

Confusion! What had just happened? I'd come here in the tumbrel, I'd placed my head on the block, I'd heard the swish of the blade – and it had stopped halfway down.

Parker's voice again. 'Has this actually never happened to you before?'

'Not an anaesthetic death, no. People have died, but . . .'

'Well, you'd better get used to it.'

I didn't ever get used to it.

18

Francesca

The first years of marriage passed in child rearing. As with childbirth, no one can possibly communicate how relentless and overwhelming it is. I enjoyed every minute – except those when I was convinced that Claire had diphtheria or peritonitis or dengue fever or some such nonsense.

Reg would finally explode. 'But I *know* she hasn't got dengue, yellow, or any other kind of fuckin' fever, 'cause I'm a fuckin' doctor.'

'No, you're not,' I'd yell, 'you're a fucking surgeon.' Actually there is a difference. Things like sore throats and fevers under 102 degrees simply don't impinge on a surgeon's consciousness. 'Give her an aspirin, she'll be fine.' Of course, I did, and she was.

I wasn't fine, though. Now that Claire was spending time with other children, I was given to reflecting on what my life meant. It was Claire, yes, first and for ever, but shouldn't there be a bit for me as well? Reg was a good man, and fun, and I loved him. But I'd never been in love with him. It's a distinction we all understand, isn't it? I had to admit to myself that I no longer wanted him sexually. In fact I never had. So why did I do it? Anger, as I've said and also, in a perverse way, I was punishing myself for Hal's death – and John's. I wasn't proud of any of it, so I soldiered on, but I worried that it was affecting me physically. I was experiencing stomach pains and every couple of weeks would have a severe attack of the trots. The weight of guilt was about to increase.

In 1972, Jeremy had been sent, as part of his training, to the embassy in Nicaragua. The Foreign Office mandarins considered that the political climate generated by rising support for the Sandinista movement against the corruption of the Somoza family, which had ruled for almost 40 years, would give Jeremy invaluable experience in the art of the diplomat. Angela, of course, accompanied him. A massive earthquake struck the capital, Managua, killing them both. Every barb thrown, every mean-spirited thought generated against Angela, grew into a mountainous pile in my head – and made me angry with her for dying. I even entertained the thought that she was waspish because, subconsciously or spiritually, she divined that she would not live. It had never, ever occurred to me that Angela might die. It simply was not one of the possibilities. Kill someone? Maybe. But die? Never.

Their bodies were taken to England. We were advised not to look because there was not a lot left to recognise. My parents were stunned, but their public school Brit grit saw them through the horrifying business of interment. For the entire period of our visit, I noticed that Daddy was particularly sweet and attentive to Claire. Perhaps a memory of little Angela was rekindled. He even spoke a little to me.

Back in Nairobi, as time wore on, proximity and grief had brought Joan and me together and we became good friends. At tea in the Norfolk one day, we discussed, yet again, my increasing difficulty cohabiting with Reg.

'But you get on well, don't you?' Joan asked.

'Oh, yes. He's a good man. He's kind and scrupulously fair – which makes it harder. What would you do?'

'I don't know. When you started with Reg, I thought that probably you were right to. I was trying to cope with John's death and I think I envied your courage in being able to make the decision. Of course I also thought that you were a total tart,' she added, laughing.

'I've always been a total tart. No, I don't think it was courage.'

'We were all surprised.'

'I was running for cover and he was the biggest rock to hide under. It's just turned out to be a bit crushing – in the gentlest possible way.' Joan looked at me and nodded slowly, in understanding. I continued, 'Why do we look for a man to offer salvation?'

'That's what nice girls are told to do.'

'Oh God, Joan. Is that what I'm turning into – a nice girl?'

'Well, Reg certainly wasn't your usual type.'

'Shit and derision! How do you know what was my usual type?'

She smiled a smug smile. 'We know everything that goes on here. It's a tiny community.'

'What do you know?' Ignoring it pointedly, she took a piece of cake. 'Come on, you complete cow. What?'

'No, nothing.'

'*What?*'

'Everything.'

'All right. Tell me one thing you know. C'mon. One thing.'

'No.'

'See? You can't.'

She licked a crumb of cake from her finger and said, 'The boy at the embassy.'

'What boy at the embassy?'

'What was his name? He fancied himself rather. Sandy!'

I was astonished.

'Joan, you complete cunt. How did you know about that?'

I'm not a complete cunt. I've tried all my life not to be any kind of a cunt.'

I loved it when Joan cursed. It always made me laugh. Her English was so pure, slightly old fashioned now, and beautiful to listen to. She said 'cunt' in exactly the same way as she'd say 'primrose'.

I said, 'Well, you've slipped up, for once. How did you know that?'

'Because he told everyone, silly. You were a great conquest.'

'Conquest! The complete little shit. I led him like a lamb to the slaughter.' I told her about the book falling on his head. She was pleased.

'Mummy!' Claire was running towards me, followed by Reg, who was not.

'Mummy, Mummy, look. Daddy bought me a car and all the doors open and you can see the engine.'

Reg sat down heavily. 'I'm telling you, toyshops are all for bloody boys. Hello Joan.' And to me, 'Hello darlin'. How's your stomach?'

'It's all right, thanks. Just the same really.'

Joan gave me a questioning look but said nothing.

Reg went on. 'Brian said he could see you at the hospital about five o'clock. That all right?'

'It's fine, Reg. Thanks.

Claire was 'fixing' her new car with a spoon. Reg said, 'What are ye doin' darlin'?'

'The bloody door's stuck, Daddy.'

Reg looked at us and shook his head. 'Christ! he said. And Claire muttered, 'Christ'.

Reg suffered my physical rejection of him in silence. I asked him if he would rather I left, and he said, 'No darlin'. I love you. I'd rather have some of you than none of you.'

And anyway, there was Claire, who loved her daddy.

Hal

Parker's retirement from state medicine coincided with my fiftieth birthday, though I didn't mention that to anyone. We still met socially of course and in the private consulting rooms we now shared in Devonshire Street, but it took a lot of getting used to the hospital without him. The ten years that I'd been in medicine had seen enormous changes. Organ transplants were becoming more frequent and more successful, the heart could be stopped and operated upon, its function being taken over by a heart-lung machine. All sorts of tremendous advances – and probably most astonishing of all, I was now a 'consultant', what the public calls 'a specialist'.

And where was Hal? To the world, long gone, buried under piles of case sheets, X-rays, and the rubble of hundreds of clinics; washed by gallons of blood – none of it wastefully spilled. He was still there though, suspended, sustained by memory of his Francesca, a small warmth in his chill vault.

It had taken quite a long time to respond instantly to being called 'John' but it was now a natural reflex. Of course, I was no longer Dr Koston but 'Mr Koston', a title peculiar to British surgery. My consultancy – or specialty – was in vascular surgery. That is, the blood system, but in practice I did a great deal of general abdominal surgery. And I was no longer an impostor. I was a doctor. I knew as much as anyone. I'd sat and passed my 'fellowship'. I was now John Koston FRCS. Fellow of the Royal College of Surgeons. And the consultancy which had passed to me? Andrew Parker's.

We celebrated with dinner at his house. I had been there countless times over the years and we had all become great friends. Sometimes there was both Lotte and Milla, sometimes just Lotte, sometimes Milla. I still had not heard the story of their meeting, despite our closeness. An appropriate moment to ask had never presented itself. This would be the evening and it happened thus:

Milla was wearing a cream silk shirt with blouson sleeves. As she passed a silver jug of cream to me, the button of her cuff popped off. The sleeve dropped away and there it was – a number on her arm. Her reflex was to hide and, since she was holding the jug, she slopped the cream. Parker and Lotte looked up and saw. We looked at each other. I said, 'God, Milla. I'm so sorry.'

She smiled and said, 'Oh well.' Then laughed and said, 'Anyway, God is the one who should be sorry.'

I looked at Lotte. 'You too Lotte?'

'Oh, yes.' She smiled. 'We do everything together. We should tell him, Andrew. Tell him the whole story. Yes, Milla?'

'Why not?' said Milla, smiling. She looked at me and raised her arm to me in a gesture of acclamation. 'He's a consultant now! Here, have the the cream. Where did the button go?'

I retrieved it for her in wonder at the capacity of certain human beings to order their lives and make jokes despite having experienced circumstances of a horror that cannot, by the most sensitive, inventive mind, be imagined.

Having survived until late 1943, hidden in the wine cellar of an Austrian country house belonging to their friends the Schragers, the Suschny family, father, mother, their nine-year-old son Stefan, and a pair of twin girls of sixteen, finally fell victim to a foul farmer loyal to the Reich. His suspicions alerted by the slight increase in produce bought from him by the Schragers, he had toadied to the local Nazi Party official. The Schragers were arrested and shot. The Suschnys, at least some of them, were less fortunate. They were transported first to the concentration camp at Dachau, thence to Auschwitz.

As they were herded from the train at Auschwitz, a guard shouted '*Zwillinge!*' (twins) SS men moved in and separated the girls from the family. Mrs Suschny attempted to pull them back but a soldier stepped forward and smashed his rifle into her face. As Mr Suschny bent to help her, the soldier's boot cracked into his head. The twins, stiff with terror, were taken before a handsome, immaculately uniformed officer in a peaked cap, which he wore at the tilt. He smiled at them and asked their names, which they gave. Reassured by his gentle demeanour, they told him what had happened to their mother. 'Don't worry,' he said 'she'll be looked after.' A flick of his cane indicated that they should be put into a nearby truck. Inside, were another two sets of twins. The officer with the cap at a jaunty angle was, of course, Dr Josef Mengele, the Angel of Death, himself recently arrived as senior 'physician' at Auschwitz.

The last vision which Lotte and Milla had of their parents was them lying bleeding in the mud. Stefan and his mother were immediately dispatched to nearby Birkenau and gassed within hours of their arrival. Herr Suschny was detailed for slave labour at the Krupp factory. There he survived for about seven months until his broken heart faltered and failed.

Dr Josef Mengele. A grand irony that the monstrosity of Mengele is what would save their lives. Mengele's twins were given special protection. Their heads were not shaved and they were permitted to wear their own clothes. They had separate barracks and were, if not properly, at least better fed than the other prisoners. No one was permitted to abuse, or indeed kill them. Those privileges were reserved for Mengele himself. In the warped sensibilities of the environment, Mengele could be an avuncular figure to the children; some even called him Uncle Mengele. He could seem affectionate and often brought chocolate for them. But every day, the trucks came and the selected twins, known never by name but by the number that had been tattooed on their arms, would be transported to the laboratories. There was revealed the true Mengele. His seeming kindness was rather like bringing a lettuce leaf to a rabbit in a research lab. The rabbit would be gently held and softly spoken to before being laid on the table.

It is hard to imagine though, any researcher treating a rabbit with the degree of barbarity shown by Mengele to the children. Twins were laid side by side. Every part of them that could be reached was measured and compared. If a part to be measured was in a limb, then the limb would be cut off. If the part was in the abdomen, then the abdomen would be sliced open and the part measured in situ or removed. No, anaesthetic was not used. There was chloroform but it was administered only after the butchery. When the child was of no further use, the drug was injected directly into the heart; death was mercifully quick. There were experiments which the children might survive, such as injecting dye into the eyes to determine if they could be turned Aryan blue, but the result could be blindness, septicaemia and even death. Twins would be infected with dreadful diseases then carefully observed. If they recovered at different rates, then Mengele would try to find out why. Blood and spinal fluid would be drawn and sometimes exchanged. Again, in the interests of genetic discovery, sisters would be impregnated by brothers. Sex-change procedures would be attempted resulting in ghastly mutilation. Such horrors were visited not only on twins but on any person who was genetically damaged, dwarfs, hunchbacks, the deranged; anyone with an obvious deformity would be supplied for the delectation of the doctor. When all parts of them that could be used had been used, they would be thrown, like potato peelings, on to the fire.

Lotte and Milla were given tuberculosis. There was a beneficial side effect in that tuberculosis suppresses the appetite. The disease did not fully develop however, and they recovered. After the war, proper medical examination revealed old, hardened scars on their lungs. They had, without knowing, contracted it as children and had overcome it. Consequently, they had developed antibodies.

Mengele then turned to his interest in procreation. They were impregnated by another set of twins. Fourteen weeks into the pregnancy, Mengele attempted to swap the uterus of each to the other. Hysterectomy, even sub-total, is deeply invasive surgery. It is performed usually because of the presence of carcinoma or if the uterus impedes access to the operative field in, for example, excision of the rectum. The surgeon must concern himself with the protection of adjacent vital structures, the bladder etc. To remove a uterus takes the greatest care, but the arterial and venous connections which would have to be remade in an attempt to attach one would take the surgeon further into the territory of nightmare. Transplant surgery was a long way off, and not as far as I know has anyone, to this day, ever tried to transplant a uterus.

Transplantation was first attempted with the kidney, because of the simplicity of there being only one artery. It doesn't take a genius to imagine what happened to the twins. They suffered massive haemorrhage. Mengele immediately abandoned the procedure, leaving the girls to die, but his assistants, Jewish doctors who had been ordered into his service under threat of death, whisked the screaming girls out of the 'theatre' and packed them with wadding in an attempt to stem the bleeding.

Against all odds, they survived; survived not only the haemorrhage but the sepsis that followed the botched procedure. The twins therefore became medical curiosities to Mengele and so were not immediately murdered. They did remain certain though, that they would be subjected to further experiments. What they could not know was that the war was in its final months. The Soviet Army was approaching. Mengele fled Auschwitz and began planning his escape. The twins no longer had any protection. As the Russians closed in, the Germans moved thousands of women from camps in the east to those inside Germany. Lotte and Milla were transferred in November 1944 to Bergen-Belsen. If life had been harsh in Auschwitz, it was nothing compared to Belsen. Belsen had not been designed as an extermination camp with purpose-built gas chambers and furnaces. In this camp, death was by neglect; starvation, disease, and in the winter, exposure.

Incredibly, a spirit of civilisation remained within the prisoners. Orphaned children were looked after with great devotion and a school was established. Even in this extremity, children were excited about learning. Then in December, there arrived Josef Kramer, ex camp commandant at Auschwitz-Birkinau. It was his intention, in accord of course with the German government, that all prisoners should die. He stopped feeding them and denied them water. Sanitation was neglected. Inevitably, infestation by lice followed, and with lice, comes typhus. Typhus presents with rapid high fever, headache, nausea and prostration. A rash appears after about five days. If unchecked, delirium and coma will follow, usually ending in cardiac failure. In no time the disease was rife and unstoppable. People lay where they fell, so piles of bodies, some still with a glimmer of life, littered the entire camp. Huts which, at a squeeze might have held 80 people, held hundreds. The living lay with the dead and didn't seem to notice. In an absence of cleanliness, intestinal problems rage, so those on upper bunks who were unable to move, fouled those below them. The camp was one vast latrine. In addition to the everyday misery, Kramer and his thugs beat people. According to those who witnessed it and survived, the beatings were done not with any sense of detachment or indifference, but with amusement. They smiled and took pleasure. March 1945, the month before liberation, saw 18,000 people die.

In this savage world, Lotte and Milla lost hope. When, towards the end, the Germans in panic tried to kill as many prisoners as possible, the twins determined that they would allow themselves to die, rather than be murdered. Under one of the huts, the ground had subsided just enough to admit their bodies of skin and bone. In they crawled, and with two spoons and bare hands, they slowly hollowed their own shallow grave and waited for Death, the merciful friend, to gather them into his arms. As they had formed in their mother, so would they decay in the earth. Enfolded.

A few days later, on 15 April, 1945, British soldiers walked into the camp in disbelief at what assaulted their gaze. The twins were now alerted by new sounds. A loudspeaker announced that they were free. The gate from hell had opened but they were too weak to crawl through it or make themselves heard and, since their existence and position were unknown to anyone, they lay forgotten. Night fell, and with it, the small hope they had recovered.

At dawn, an exhausted young doctor, as he walked through the camp, paused, thinking that finally he was going to throw up. He didn't but he sat down against a hut for a few moments and out of the silence came tiny voices. He looked under the hut and said 'Hello?' and back came a barely audible 'Hello' – twice. Being too large to slide into the space which had admitted the skeletal bodies of the girls, he sought assistance. Soldiers entered the hut, tore up the floorboards, and Dr Andrew Parker met Lotte and Milla Suschny. 'Two pairs of huge eyes, attached to strange-looking featherless birds,' he said.

Many came through the gates of Auschwitz with severe malformations, many were disfigured by barbarous surgery but it is surely unlikely that ever there could have walked upon this earth a more grotesque mutant than Josef Mengele.

Parker, because he had hauled the girls from Death's maw, saw it as his personal duty to order their survival. Investigation revealed that the British government was unenthusiastic about welcoming Jewish refugees, so Parker devised a bold plan. He took advantage of the prevailing chaos as the people of Europe, scattered to the winds, struggled to re-assemble their lives. When he considered the twins strong enough to travel, he enlisted the help of Jamie, a pilot chum, to smuggle Lotte and Milla back to England. Jamie was flying military personnel back and forth in a Lysander, an aircraft designed to take off and land in short distances. On his way back to base, he would land in a field in Kent and drop the twins. It went without a hitch. In those days, it being impossible to track them, aircraft could come and go with no one the wiser.

Waiting in the field was Parker's father, Mortimer – 'Morty' also a doctor – who drove them to the family home in Cornwall. There, they were introduced simply as friends of the family who had been rescued from the Nazis. Morty had a word with the village copper who had himself miraculously survived the trenches of the First World War. Having no desire to see anyone suffer ever again, he turned a blind eye to the fact that the twins had no papers. Those were times when everyone was required to carry an identity card. They were also times when people were grown up enough to make their own decisions.

At last, the skies fell silent, the flames were extinguished, and the ground shook no more. Andrew Parker, who went to war an *ingénu*, came home bearing a burden of wisdom. Lotte and Milla, under the gentle care of Morty and his wife Hetty, were nursed back to health. They were transformed – on the outside. They had regained their strength and were the loveliest girls Parker had ever seen.

'They still scream at night, sometimes,' Morty had said as he and Parker sat over a late whisky. 'I offered them separate rooms but they want to be together. I suspect it's more "have to" than "want to". Another thing happened. In her solicitous way, your mum put sanitary towels on their dresser. Some weeks later they said that the tap was dripping in the washbasin in their room, so we called old Tommy Clapp. You mum went into the corner cupboard by the basin to turn off the stopcock and there at the back were the towels, unused. She was a bit worried, so she had a word with them. Do you know about this?'

'No, what?'

'They were butchered by some mad bastard in the camps. Rendered barren. God knows what kind of a shambles there is in there.'

'God almighty.'

'We could go in and have a look of course but my feeling would be to leave well alone. If anything presents later, deal with it then.'

Never in his life had Parker experienced such rage.

The old coach house was converted into living accommodation for the girls. It was basic, but they were very happy, feeling less of an intrusion on Hetty and Morty. Having no papers, proper work was out of the question, but they were skilled at dressmaking and soon had local clients. Then one day, the only piano teacher in the neighbourhood fell off her stool stone dead, and life changed. The twins had never mentioned that they were musicians but now they did. Contact was made with the dead teacher's sister, who immediately proposed that, if the parents were willing to have the twins as teachers, they could gladly use the studio, because, 'I will miss the children coming around.'

One of the parents heard Lotte playing to the children and recognised the sound of a real musician. In the ensuing conversation Lotte revealed that she was really a fiddle player and Milla a cellist, but that they no longer had instruments. 'But I work for Beare's,' he said.

'Beare's the fiddle people?' asked Lotte.

'Yes. I'm sure we can lend you a couple of instruments. They won't be from Cremona, but they'll be decent.'

All this while, Parker was still in the army but when possible he rushed back to Cornwall to be with the girls, whose high-school English had, through textbook diligence and keen ears, developed into considerable fluency – though with the thick accents that remained to this day. Whenever told that Andrew was expected home, they bloomed like cherry blossom and from the moment he arrived, the three were inseparable.

Alone with his mother cutting rhubarb one day, she had said, 'You're showing signs of being in love, Andrew. Are you?'

'I believe I am.'

'Which one?'

'That's the trouble. I don't know. I think they are one.'

She had straightened and looked at him squarely as she said, 'Then you'd better take them both, dear. Because you're right. You'll never separate them.'

'What are you talking about?' he said. 'Are you telling me to give them both up?'

'Darling, have you lost your command of the English language? I'm saying, take them both.'

'I couldn't do that. How could I possibly do that?'

She had sat down on the little stone wall which bordered the vegetable garden, the trug of rhubarb on her lap. 'We've just been through the second of two ghastly wars. Millions are dead, some of them our friends, some our family. When I was a girl, boys from around here were going off to fight in France. Those who came home on leave had to go back knowing that their chances of returning were very small. They were virgins, and desperate for girls. But we girls were all virgins too – and very proper, so we wouldn't do it. Well, a couple did. Most of the boys died. Now, I doubt any one of them died thinking, I wish Hetty had slept with me, but I can tell you that even now there are nights when Hetty lies awake crying, wishing that she had, wishing that she had given any small comfort to those lost and frightened boys.' Her eyes filled.

Parker, touched and stilled by this revelation of his mother as a woman, had laid his hand on hers and left it there.

'This is not quite the same situation though, is it?' he said.

'Only in that it would be a decision made through fear. I made the decision that I did because I was frightened. Frightened of discovery, frightened of the neighbours, frightened of my mother, frightened of the bloody vicar. Sod the lot of them, Andrew, sod them all. I sense something extraordinary between you and these girls. If it's what you all want, then find a way. Now I'll never mention it again.'

'You know there'll be no grandchildren.'

She had cupped his hand in hers. 'That makes me sad for you Andrew, and you must consider it carefully. We however, would benefit from having two lovely new daughters. Your father adores them. In fact, if you don't show some alacrity he might ditch the old bat here and run off with them himself.'

So, one sunny day on a cliff, caressed by a warm west wind, Lotte, Milla and Andrew declared all-out love. They discussed their future. He kissed them each in turn then lay with Lotte snuggled into his left side, Milla into his right, until the sun set; and none of them uttered a word.

They tossed a gold sovereign to determine for outward appearances, which twin he should marry. It fell to Lotte. The following year, they took their vows and in private, he and Milla swore them too. From that day to this, Parker spent night about with each girl.

There are nights still, when they scream.

Hetty and Morty are both gone, now. Morty was dispatched by two cerebral haemorrhages in fairly quick succession. Hetty was less fortunate and developed cancer of the lung. Milla and Lotte, her two loving and ever grateful daughters, moved back to Cornwall and nursed her till she died.

My decision to leave Francesca, my only love, and embark alone on this voyage, was, of course, made out of fear.

Francesca

I suppose that some things just aren't meant to be. 'Religious crap!' I can hear Hal say to that. 'Human relations are what they are. If you don't like them you can try to change them. You may succeed, you may not. If you can't, then it's not to do with fifth dimensional forces, but human taste and/or inflexibility.'

Here, it was both. My taste and my inflexibility as regards Reg – and Africa. You're either an Africa person or you're not. I'm not, Reg is. Irrespective of régime and circumstance, he loved Africa. There was much that I liked – and more that I didn't. It had changed considerably in atmosphere since I had arrived. Justifiably or not, I didn't feel as safe as before. Being grabbed to become a chunk of someone else's empire severely damages a country's natural development. Kenya finally became independent of Britain in 1963 but many structures survived, mainly through President Jomo Kenyatta's enlightened Forgive and Forget policy. Despite having been imprisoned by them for his leadership of the Mau Mau movement, which was instrumental in the gaining of independence, he remained pro-British. Indeed he called to them for help in subduing a military revolt.

Jomo died in 1978 and rule was handed to Daniel Arap Moi who continued many of Jomo's policies. As a nation slowly casts off the shackles of ownership however, it enters a period of great instability. Kenya, I felt, was headed exactly there and many at the embassy agreed with me. I feared for Claire. I considered that it would be difficult for her to make a life here as an adult, and therefore important that she spend the rest of her childhood becoming familiar with another culture. Reg disagreed. He thought that we should stay and help. I yelled, 'Oh yes. How the hell will Kenya manage without Reg and Francesca?'

We barely touched now. My fault. It was distressing for Reg – and distressing for me to see him distressed. I'm sure it was also distressing for Claire to sense our distress. That's a sodding lot of distress.

Reg, in his inimitable, wonderful way, gave me my freedom. Why couldn't I completely love this good man? Yet another grave flaw in the design of homo sapiens, but I didn't love him. Claire loved him. How could she not? And he loved her. How could he not? But Claire wasn't happy in Africa.

We'd been back to the UK at times, for the funeral, of course, to London, and once to Reg's family in Scotland. They lived in an area of Glasgow called Govan. Meeting them, it was immediately clear why Reg had fled. Despite his forewarning I was ill prepared. They were ghastly. His mother, Theresa, would you believe, was a splinter of a woman whose voice resembled the abrasive caw of the magpie and was rarely silent – with nothing to screech but complaint. His father, Billy, was mostly drunk and asked constantly 'So how are ye gettin' on wi the darkies?' and to Claire, who was terrified almost to the point of coma, 'Are ye no feert of the darkies, hen?' 'Hen', Reg informed us, was a term of endearment. Rather like 'bitch' I supposed. An hour in their company lasted a year. It was inconceivable that Reg, with his brains and his decency, could be the progeny of this awful coupling. What must have happened was that a delightful but inebriated medical student was granted a knee trembler by Theresa while she said her rosary.

'Naw,' said Reg, 'bright parents can produce some bloody thick kids. Why not the other way round?' I suppose. I couldn't really blame them for being the way they were. Where they lived was a Godforsaken place. Badly hit by the collapse of the shipyards, the men were on the scrapheap and Billy, a riveter, was one of them. There was nothing to look forward to but booze. As for Theresa, she was always running off to church to thank God for being so good to her. As Hal used to say, 'There are many ways that God may show his love – and none of them worth a damn.'

Claire loved London. She had read about it and had heard the ex-pats' incessant eulogising on the place. They didn't want to go back themselves of course. 'D'you know the cost of domestic staff there now?' To Claire, London was magic. The huge escalators at Piccadilly Circus, big red buses, cabbies with cockney accents who called her 'luv', Hamleys toyshop, theatres everywhere and people in them that she'd seen when we went to the pictures in Nairobi; everything invisible to Londoners. What delighted me greatly was our visit to the Festival Hall. Claire had never heard an orchestra live. The first item was Beethoven's overture, 'Consecration of the House', which opens with four huge orchestral chords. After the first two, she turned to me, smiling, her eyes wide with pleasure.

None of this made up for having to leave her daddy.

I became more and more fearful that if forced to remain in Africa I would become bitter and angry like Reg's mother. Reg resolutely refused to leave, so it was decided that Claire and I would go to London for a bit. 'Nothing definite, just a trial' but in our heart of hearts, Reg and I knew different.

On departure day, he brought the luggage down and we stood, looking at each other across the room.

'Oh Reg . . .'

'C'mon now. Your mind's made up an' your bags are packed. Let's not worry it to death any more.'

I ran and hugged him, 'Oh Reg. Oh, I'm sorry. I'm so sorry.'

He held me. 'Aye. I'm sorry too, darlin' but there we are. I should have been your daddy, really. Whatever happens, I can always see Claire when I need to, right?'

'Of course Reg. You know I'd never be an impediment to either of you.'

He gave me a squeeze. 'Right then, c'mon now, you'll miss that fuckin' plane.'

Claire came in from the garden on the verge of tears.

'What's up, darlin'?' asked Reg.

She just got 'Daddy' out before the sobs began. She ran to him and he swept her up in his arms. 'Oh Claire, ma wee girl. C'mon now.' He sat with her on his knee. 'Now listen. You and your mother are takin' this a bit too seriously. It's no' the end of the bloody world, you know. I'll be seeing you in a few weeks.'

Claire said, 'I'm not going.'

'Francesca, come here,' he said. I sat beside them on the sofa and Reg put arms round us both. 'Now listen, there's no need for this to be a whole big deal. You think that weeks is too long?'

Claire, through sobs, 'Yes'

'Okay, we'll take it a wee bit at a time. Now today is Sunday. Suppose we say that we'll speak on the phone two weeks tonight. If you say so, you can get on a plane and come back for a wee while. Just you. Your mummy'll stay in London.'

'Is that a good idea, Reg? She'll be starting school and everything.'

'If she's unhappy she'll get small bloody comfort from Pythagoras. This is more important.'

'Daddy's right. That's what we'll do.'

'P . . . p . . . promise?' she hiccuped.

We promised.

'Right. On your way. I've got to get to the hospital.'

We walked out to the taxi. Reg put his arms around me. 'Good luck, darlin'.'

'You too Reg. You're a wonderful man. You deserve the best.'

'Aye, right.' He lifted Claire who put her arms tight around his neck.

'Phone me as soon as you get to London.'

'Yes. Bye Daddy'

It was killing him. *I* was killing him, but Reg smiled on.

'Bye darlin'.'

Through the taxi's rear window we watched his huge form recede. Smiling and waving. Devastated, desolate.

Hal

'Beware the Hun in the sun' was an adage of the first dogfighters. The greatest threat is the one from which you have little time to defend yourself, as in, 'Is Auckland on the North or South Island?' from Milla.

It had taken some time to become accustomed to being the 'Parker', the one from whom a simple 'hello' could mean so much to a junior registrar. I was now accustomed to most other events of life, not that there were many. One of the pleasant ones was Harriet.

My libido was dormant only for a short while. 'Forget your dick until you find your feet' sort of thing. Relationships were impossible because the threat of exposure was ever present, and I didn't want to put anyone else through hell, but the monastic life was tolerable only for so long. Embarrassing too, that to the Parkers I was probably considered either neuter or a queen in a very deep closet. My only recourse was to the professional.

The doxy of the King's Cross streets wasn't the most seductive idea, nor did the headline, 'London consultant in tartoscopy scandal' have a particularly appealing peal to it, so, the Mayfair Ladies Escort Agency got my call. It served the purpose but was, as you might imagine, far from satisfactory. Sometimes we'd go to the pictures then a snack then a hotel room. The image which occasionally intruded during coitus was of a mother and child in my clinic discovering what I sometimes did in the evening. Decidedly detumescing. I indulged a few times over the years but with wilting enthusiasm.

Then Harriet appeared. Harriet was the real thing. A high-class tart. Twenty-seven, with a double first from Oxford, in Music and Medieval History but, as she soon discovered of the latter, who needs it? She couldn't get funding for research. It was a luxury subject for those with means, but Harriet was not so blessed, her high-bred family then suffering near beggary. As for music, she was an academic, not a performer, so one of her few options was to stay in Oxford as a tutor, an idea which palled. 'So,' she pronounced, 'the only other thing at which I'd excelled at Oxford was fucking, so I thought I'd give that a go for a bit.' She had found it scary at first – and who wouldn't – but had learned to be highly selective. Because she was so bright, she rapidly built a base of regular clients with whom she felt safe, and whose generosity allowed her a reasonable minimum of assignations. Three things particularly attracted me to her; her brain, her looks – she was the same 'type' as Francesca – and her love of music. Our evenings therefore were often spent at concerts. After one such, she said as we lay together, 'Can I ask you something?'

'Of course?'

'Are you married?'

'Yes – and I suppose I'd better go home.'

'Me too. Go home, I mean. I'm sorry, I shouldn't've asked. Are you angry?'

'Are you angry?' Immediately, there was the image of Francesca, on the night I met her, standing in the rain, calling me back as I rode away on Sweet Sunbeam. Such a long time ago. The ache was still fresh, though.

I smiled at Harriet, 'No, not at all.'

Saying that I was married was the first time I'd had to lie to Harriet and I hated it. I had become fond of her and I knew it was reciprocated. Danger. As we dressed, she said, 'I really enjoyed this evening. The music was good.'

'You didn't like the Beethoven.'

'Yes I did. It was just a bit slow. I'm a Toscanini fan. The food was good – and the bed was good.'

'It was. It always is.' I looked at her. 'You're a lovely girl.' She smiled and we continued to dress in silence. Then came the moment I found increasingly difficult. I passed to her an envelope containing £200. She said, rather sadly, '*Si possis, recte, si non, quocumque modo rem.*'

My brow furrowed. 'Oh dear . . . Ehm . . . 'If possible, rightly? Properly? . . . If not . . . however . . . What was it again?'

She laughed. 'It's Horace. "If possible, with honour, but in whatever way, make money." ' She kissed me on the cheek, 'See you in a month?'

'See you in a month. Thank you, Harriet.'

I felt wretched as I drove home. Ten years ago I could have saved Harriet but I was too old now. Always too old – or too late. Three women in my life had touched me. No, Francesca didn't touch me, she impaled me and I bled still. Lorna, who already had a family, remained in my heart since our night of extraordinary adventure. And now, Harriet, the whore, as she sometimes called herself. 'I'm Harriet the Whore, MA Oxon', she would declare in a grand manner. She wasn't a whore for much longer however, because around the globe there now thundered four horsemen, A, I, D and S, and she thought it prudent to be clear of their hooves. She became a music critic, and to the considerable amusement of us both, was on two occasions called upon to give an appraisal of the performances of previous clients. Pro that she was, she wouldn't tell me their names. Harriet and I remained good friends.

With the awareness of AIDS came the repeated mention of the condition Kaposi's sarcoma, words I hadn't heard since I spoke them myself to Parker on my first clinic with him at St Peters. There was the beast, living among us and none recognised it. That woman will be long dead by now, with millions of others. The conditions which take hold due to the breakdown of the immune system are ugly and unstoppable, but ironically, AIDS does have a saving grace, don't you think? It differs from every other terminal disease in one remarkable respect. Apart from the tragic infecting of haemophiliacs, we know exactly how to avoid contracting it. If only that were true for breast, bowel or any other cancer.

The armistice still being observed by Cadell had removed one huge threat to my security, and life as a surgeon was now so normal that it was hard to believe I'd ever been anything else – except when my patient was a child. That's when the struggle not to be overwhelmed by the horror in my mind was at its most extreme.

It was upon returning to my office after one such procedure that the Hun came out of the sun. I had inherited not only Parker's consultancy but also, just as valuable, his Alison. I was in my office four seconds before she came through the other door.

'Have you got a minute?'

'I don't know, you tell me. Why?'

'Yes, I think you've got about ten. There's a Dr Chigbo here from Africa would like to see you for a minute. He wants to thank you for helping him some years ago.'

I hadn't had such a glucose surge since the day I sliced through a major blood vessel in a place where humans don't normally have them. Alison would consider it uncharacteristic should I refuse to see him, and flight would be pointless. I needed a moment.

'Good heavens, really? All right, give me a few seconds then I'll buzz you. Give me four minutes with him then save me.' This had been one of Parker's recurrent instructions. She smiled and extended the evocation. 'Right, sir,' and was gone. It would be truly awkward if this chap had met John and me at the same time. There was nothing to do but play the cards I was dealt. I sat at my desk and buzzed Alison.

In came a giant in his thirties. He reminded me of the one-armed Masai. It couldn't be him though, unless he'd perfected brachial regeneration.

'Dr Chigbo,' said Alison as she closed the door on us.

'Dr Chigbo, how do you do. Come and sit down.'

'Thank you,' and he sat.

'Now, we met in Central Africa? Just refresh my memory, the years have tarnished us both a bit, I suppose.'

'Are you Dr Koston?'

'Yes, you were a student, were you?'

'Yes but not in Central Africa, in Nairobi.'

'Oh, Nairobi. Now I've never actually practised in East Africa but I spent a couple of holidays there. Was that it?'

He laughed and shook his head. 'No, it was at the Nairobi General.' He laughed again. 'I'm sorry, I feel a little foolish, but you look so different.'

I looked at him and held his eyes for a few moments, then asked, 'Was it the Dr Koston who was involved in the flying doctor service?'

'Yes, that's right. Yes, he was.'

'Oh dear. I'm afraid I have some bad news for you. There was a Dr Koston in Nairobi. I didn't know him. We weren't related, curiously enough, despite the unusual name. I'm sorry to tell you that he's dead.'

'Oh my God. From what?'

'He was killed in a plane crash. I don't know the detail, I'm afraid, but I remember news of it filtering through to us. I particularly noted it because of the name.'

'Did he have a family?'

'I don't know.'

'What a dreadful thing. He was a wonderful man, you know.'

I almost said 'yes he was'.

Chigbo continued, 'He was the best kind of doctor.'

I smiled at him. 'What kind's that?'

'I think, the kind who can imagine what it's like to be ill.'

'I can't argue with that.'

He rose. 'Well, thank you for seeing me. Sorry to have taken your time.'

'No, I'm sorry not to have been the right chap – for both your sakes. You can go out this way.'

I showed him through the door to the corridor, 'The stairs are down the end, there.'

'Thank you. Goodbye.

'Goodbye.'

I popped my head round Alison's door.

'Wrong bloke.'

'Oh, all right.' She handed me a cup of coffee. 'You've just got time for this.'

The training in Cadell's unit, as so often before, had saved me. 'Sometimes you have to take it on the chin, but at least try to convince them it's the wrong chin.' The shock of the morning, though, was well eclipsed by what happened later in the day.

I had been asked by a manufacturing company with whom I'd been retained as a consultant, to give a talk on 'Nuclear Magnetic Resonance', a new system which would enable us, without cutting or bombarding with X-rays, to examine internal tissue in great detail. It would later become known as an MRI scan. The do was held in a function suite at a London hotel. After the talk we were expected to trawl the many stalls which were set up to display the huge array of innovative surgical toys. I was chatting to a couple of sales reps when something made me look beyond them. Fifteen feet away, looking at me, was Francesca.

Francesca

I couldn't understand what I was looking at. I was unable to move or make a noise. I could reason only that I had died and we were together again. But Claire! What would become of Claire? He was coming closer. Maybe we could get Claire to come too. He was holding me. The smell of Hal. Hal . . . Hal . . . He was speaking . . .

'Please don't say anything. Call me John. John Koston. Please Francesca. Please.'

I couldn't say anything. It wasn't John. It looked like Hal. Death was so confusing. I was on the floor. People were looking down at me. John was holding me but he smelled of Hal, he looked like Hal. Maybe they were the same person. Perhaps that's why they were friends. It was important to understand this situation so I began to get up. Hal held me.

'Let's get you some air,' he said, and led me from the room. In an elevator I tried to ask, 'Did I do something wrong?' He looked at me and his eyes filled with tears. He put his arms around me and his face to mine. It was lovely but I knew that the bad thing would happen soon. I didn't know what it would be, though. He'd go away. I knew that. If I could only speak, then maybe I could find out. Maybe I could ask him not to go yet.

We were in a car with very soft seats. He held my hand – well, I held his really, in both of mine. I looked at him all the time but he was driving and could only glance at me now and again. He smiled, he was nice. I was trying to keep something away but wasn't sure what. I knew I mustn't do anything or say anything.

We went into a house. It was becoming too difficult to keep it away.

Hal

As I closed the door behind us, she moved away from me into the hallway – and cracked. She fell to the floor. I tried to put my arms around her but like a frightened, wounded animal, she was trying to roll herself into a ball. We remained there for perhaps ten minutes. She smelled the same. The olfactory memory is indeed the most powerful. Her sobbing ceased but for a time she lay, limp. Then I felt her body tighten. She sat up, pulled back from me –

'*What!*' she screamed, '*What!*' Then quieter, 'Is it you?'

'Yes.'

'You didn't die.'

'No.'

I felt as though I had known that this would happen. Perhaps even subconsciously, I had decided that one day I would try to find her and confess. She was shaking her head. 'Then wh . . . I ca . . .'

'Come and sit in here,' I said and led her to a sofa in the sitting room. I sat at one end, she at the other, her knees up, holding herself, and I told her the bones of the story. When I'd finished, she didn't say, 'That's amazing' or yell, 'You fucking bastard,' but said quietly, 'I knew you wouldn't die in an aeroplane.'

'Did you?'

'Yes, and you left a clue but everyone laughed at me.'

'What clue?'

'You told me that when pilots are going down they don't speak to their wives or children but to their mothers. Your last message was, "Tell Francesca I love her." I told them that, but they all smiled and said, "But that's a measure of how much he loved you." '

'I'm so sorry, Francesca.'

'Say it again.'

'I'm so sorry, I'm so sorry '

'No, my name. Say my name.'

'Francesca.'

It was the best word in my world so I couldn't but say it with love.

'Why didn't you trust me, Hal? I'd have done anything for you.'

'It was too risky. It was difficult enough for me do deal with my own fictitious past. People endlessly ask questions. We could have gone to jail for a hundred years. I still could.'

'You put me in jail for years . . . no, that's not true really. It's an open prison and the warder's very kind.'

My stomach flipped. 'You're married.'

'To Reg Fraser.'

'Ah. I liked him. Very straight.'

'Very.' A pause. 'We have a child.'

Why did I for a moment suppose that she'd still be waiting for me, like a nun for Jesus. Why was I always such a stupid oaf when it came to Francesca?

'Ah. Boy or girl?'

'A girl. Claire.'

'That's lovely. Which hospital is Reg working in?' I tried to make this sound casual even though the response might see me heading for the border.

'We haven't worked that out yet. He's still in Nairobi. He got me a job here with a surgical supply company, selling saws to cut the tops off people's heads. That's why I was there today. What about you? You married?'

'No.'

She smiled a dazzling, 'I know you though and I'm not going to be hurt by the answer' smile as she asked, 'With someone?'

'No.'

It hung for a moment. She continued, 'How long have you lived here?'

'Two years.'

'It's very nice. It's the way I'd have done it.'

'I know. Well, the poor man's version.'

The phone rang. I picked it up.

'Hello?'

Francesca

I was nonplussed. I've never been completely sure of what that means, but I think I was it. I was non-something. Non-everything, in fact. I looked at him as he spoke. He had quite a lot of grey in his hair and was more jowly and a little thicker round the middle. He was telling someone to 'get her down to theatre'. He asked the person 'Well, do *you* think you can do it?' Then he said. 'Good. Do you want me to come and look over your shoulder? All right. I'm on my way.' He put the phone down and said, 'I have to go to the hospital.'

I'd heard Reg have that same conversation over and over again. Hal was a surgeon – with authority – and he seemed – comfortable. I'd seen many sides of Hal but none of them would I say was 'comfortable'.

I said, 'This is bloody unbelievable.'

He gave a 'yes I know' shrug and said, 'Will you wait here for me?'

'No, I have to get back for Claire.'

'I'll call you a cab.'

'No, I'd rather walk for bit.'

'All right. Just pull the door behind you when you go. Will you leave your number?'

I looked at my knees and made him wait quite a long time. 'Yes.'

'Thank you. Bye.' He walked through the door, then came back and said, 'You won't say anything, will you?' I didn't know whether to laugh or cry at such brutal wounding. Didn't he know me at all, ever? In spite of my attempt to control them, my eyes filled. His expression told me he knew what he'd done. I said, 'What do you think?'

'I'm sorry,' he said, 'I'm always frightened.'

I looked at him. He left.

Hal was alive. My Hal. Hal my love. My treacherous love. This was too big. I couldn't get hold of it. I didn't know what to think. What did I think? No, what did I feel? That was it, it was about feeling, not thinking, so what did I feel? Shaken and angry. And wonderful. I felt wonderful. From the moment I saw him all those years ago in his Spitfire outfit, there was nothing for me to do with Hal ever, but love him beyond dreams.

I wandered round the book-lined sitting room. It had been two reasonably sized rooms but was now one huge one. I wondered why he wanted all this space. Hal had owned hardly anything. Now he had a house – filled with books. In the kitchen I drank some water. I opened the fridge. A bachelor fridge. The room, which was actually half kitchen, half conservatory, led into a small but well-stocked garden. Upstairs, overlooking the garden was a study; dark, polished wood against white walls, typewriter, filing cabinets and hi-fi – and books. A further, spare bedroom, unfurnished, and Hal's bedroom. On the bedside table, beside the phone, was a photograph of me – with my tits out. I fell on the bed and cried with relief.

Hal

Driving to the hospital through Regent's Park, I had to pull up in order to throw up; a curious reaction to being re-acquainted with the love of my life. I don't know what it was. Anxiety? Relief? Yes, relief that in at least one area of my life, the lie was over. Perhaps that vomit started the moment I 'died' in Africa. Anyway, better in the park than the operating theatre. What a day. First Dr Chigbo, then to see Francesca again. To hold her, even though she may not have noticed that she was being held, such was her emotional state. But married, and a mum. I hoped Claire didn't have Reg's looks.

Later, back in the house, I learned that Francesca had been in my bedroom and had lain on my bed. The door wasn't properly closed, which it had been because of the burglar alarm, and the bedcovers were neater than I'd left them. She'd be a hopeless spy – or perhaps she meant me to know. I buried my face in the bedclothes to catch the fragrance, which had not changed. Guerlain's Mitsouko and Francesca's sweat. Ohhhhh!

In Kensington, three nights later, I rang the bell to her flat on the top floor of a apartment block, the *pied à terre* of family friends who were presently living in the Bahamas. Diplomats are well connected. There was no reply. Ten minutes later she arrived in a fluster bearing shopping bags and said in one breath:

'Sorry, sorry. They said the car would be ready but it wasn't. Claire went to a friend's house after school so I have to collect her, but a man's coming about the heating, so . . .'

'Suicide's your only option.' I said, and she laughed and kissed my cheek.

'Hello Hal.'

'Hello Francesca.' I took some bags and we went in. A small but very pleasant flat. Old money.

I said, 'You could take my car, but it's a bit peculiar to drive.'

'Why, what is it?'

'It's a Citroën DS. You change gear without a clutch and instead of a brake pedal, it has a sort of rubber mushroom.'

'Fucking hell, Hal.' I can't tell you how good it was to hear 'Fucking hell, Hal.'

'I know. Phone the friend's mother and tell her I'm coming to get Claire, and you wait for the plumber.'

'It's an electrician.'

'Damn, but you know, I think the plan might still work.'

She laughed and said, 'By God, Curruthers, I believe you're right.'

'Will Claire be uneasy if I go?'

'Not if you make her laugh.'

My fears of Reg's cell structures were groundless. Claire was in Francesca's image. She was lovely. I put her in the back of the car and got in beside her.

'It's very comfy, isn't it?' she said.

'Yes. It's French.'

'Are you French?'

'No. Are you?'

She laughed. 'No.'

We sat for a few moments. I looked at her, smiled. She smiled back, then asked, 'Where's the driver?'

'I'm the driver. Oh! I'm in the wrong seat.' Her eyebrows shot up. I began a sequence of clowning. Banging my head getting out of the car, catching my fingers in the door, opening the other door on to my nose. I could see Claire giggling inside the car. Having got back in, I looked round at her, 'Shouldn't you be in the front?'

'Yes,' she said.

'Right. Climb over.' While she did, I employed a feature peculiar to this car. I released the suspension lever so that the car slowly sank to its lowest position. I started the engine and said, 'Would you like to ask the car to get up?'

'What?'

'Ask the car to get up. Her name is Milly Moonbeam. Just say, Milly, please get up now, we're going.' She looked blankly at me. 'Go on. Really.'

'That's the silliest thing I ever heard.'

'But it's not the silliest thing I've ever said. Go on, try it.'

Clearly indulging me, she said, 'Milly please get up, we're going.'

I pulled the lever up and the car rose about a foot.

'Ha Ha!' she said, delighted. 'How did it do that?'

'Hydraulics. The power of water, or any liquid, really.' We set off.

'How can water lift a car?'

'Simple things can be very powerful.'

'Like what?'

Levers, for example. Do you know about levers?'

'I know the word.'

'Right. Well, a lever can be a piece of wood, or steel, that'll help you to lift something very heavy. There was an ancient Greek called Archimedes who is supposed to have said, "Give me a lever, somewhere to stand, and I'll move the world."'

'How does it work?'

'I'll show you when we get home.'

'Was Archimedes the one who spilled the water out of his bath?'

'That's him! Now, in fact, you've hit on it, because without Archimedes starting to think about fluids, perhaps Pascal, who was the first one to really think about hydraulics, wouldn't have done so.'

'Did he make this car?'

'No. I'm afraid he's dead.'

'Oh, should we send a card or something?'

I had no beer to snort down my nose, so I almost crashed the car. She was Francesca all over again. The same face, the same dazzling smile, the same sense of humour. And to make the same joke as her mother had done, also within minutes of our fist meeting was – bloody spooky. I pulled my mind back to dynamics.

'Who told you about Archimedes?'

'My daddy. He knows lots of science things.'

'You must learn a lot from him.'

'Yes. Except that Mummy and I don't live with my daddy any more.'

When we were back in the flat, Claire fetched a broom, we made a fulcrum out of a few books and she effortlessly lifted the sofa.

After dinner, Claire tucked up in bed, Francesca and I sat on the sofa and talked of the intervening years. There were silences when there was just too much to tell and we couldn't recall any of it. Francesca got up to switch off Claire's light.

'Asleep?'

'Yes.'

I told her about the 'send a card' joke. Francesca was as astonished as I. Not that she'd made the joke, it had become a family witticism, but that she'd made it to me on our first meeting.

We were silent for a little, then she breathed heavily and said, 'I hope it was all worthwhile. You left an awful trail of carnage.'

'I was wrong to do it to you.'

'Did you get what you wanted?'

'Actually, it hasn't turned out the way I'd planned. The original intention was to go back to Africa but it would have needed all sorts of forged documents. It seemed too risky.'

She laughed. 'Why stop at forgery?'

'I've never thought of myself as a criminal. I had no thoughts of Harley-Street wealth – though it seems to have come to me in part – or kinky ideas of seeing women without their clothes.'

She smiled. 'I know the old adage, "It may be a mammary gland in the office, but it's still a tit in the moonlight."'

I laughed, and again there was silence. It's not difficult to guess what was in our minds, but I didn't let the thought linger, so continued.

'Anyway, I had to repay a debt. I robbed the world of a doctor, but I've put one back in his place.'

She gave me a look that I remembered, again from that first night in Cambridge when she ran after me in the rain and asked, 'Are you angry?' Her brow furrowed slightly, but this time she asked, 'Am I forgiven?'

'You were never blamed.'

'Really?'

'Really. I never blamed you, Francesca. I know you thought I did, but I didn't.'

She held my eyes and nodded, slowly. 'What a terrible day that was,' she said.

'Yes . . . yes.' Another moment of silence, then she said, 'Apart from forged documents and stuff, wouldn't it have been a risk, going to Central Africa?'

'I don't think so. Africa's so huge. If you dropped the British Isles on Africa, no one would turn to see what fell.'

'I suppose. Did you ever make mistakes? Diagnoses and so on.'

'Yes. A woman was brought in one day, screaming blue murder. Totally bonkers and completely incoherent from some speech defect. She was gesturing wildly, holding her head. There was nothing I could do, so I called Harry Solomon, the head of psychiatry. He looked at her, looked at me, took me out of the room and asked in a withering fashion, "You think this is a case for the nut house?" I said I thought she did seem rather disturbed. He said, "You'd be bloody disturbed if your jaw was dislocated and you couldn't make yourself understood." An orthopod was called and she left the building, hail and hearty, ten minutes later. She'd fallen in the street and bounced her chin off a litter bin on the way down.

Left to me the poor cow would have spent the rest of her life in the funny farm. Actually, she did see the funny side – and it'd be a good story for later.'

'Claire will love it.' She laughed. 'She loves medical drama.'

'Reg must miss her terribly.'

'Well, it's not for long.'

I don't know why she wanted to give the impression that all was well, but I saw little point in games now.

'I know you've split up.'

She was thrown. She scratched her knee, looked at me. 'How do you know that?'

'Claire told me.'

Her eyebrows lifted. 'The little cow. You asked her?'

'Of course not. She volunteered it.'

'Shit and derision. Bloody little cow.'

'Gets it from her mum.'

She gave me a long look, at once distant and familiar, and said, 'Did you think about me much?'

'I don't have to think about you. You live in my head.'

I felt as I did when we'd first met in Cambridge, that I mustn't touch. Having done what I did, I had no right. It was ten to midnight when I rose to take my leave.

'You going?'

'I hesitate to overstay my welcome.'

Exactly as she had done in Cambridge, she slid inside my arms and offered her mouth. We kissed. Soft and brief. She pulled back. 'Want to see something beautiful?'

'I do see something beautiful.'

'Smoothie. Come on. The roof.'

'We can't leave Claire.'

'This is the top floor. If I'm not here, she knows I'm on the roof and she calls me.'

The large, flat roof gave a breathtaking view over London. We stood for a moment, enjoying picking out landmarks, then from Francesca. 'Wanna fuck?'

'How much?'

'Two pounds.'

'Too much.'

'If you change your mind, I'll be over there.'

She walked to the opposite wall and leaned on it, looking at the view. Then, without looking round, she lifted the back of her dress and pulled her pants down to just below her bum. I slowly walked across to her and said, 'Okay, two pounds, if you throw in a cup of tea.'

'No. I don't do kinky stuff.'

I laughed, and said, 'I thought you'd want the first time to be an all night affair in a big, comfy bed.'

'No, it's as though I hadn't eaten all day. I can't face a big meal but I'd love a Mars bar.'

'In that case . . .' I turned her to me. In each other's arms, the carnal gave way to relief and joy; the end of the years of loss and longing.

She buried her face in my neck, as so often she had, and for the first time ever with Francesca, I felt no qualms. Watching her with Claire, I'd seen a stability, a maturity. I supposed that she might have observed something similar in me. Perhaps that was it. *I* had grown up and was, for the first time in my life, ready to be responsible for someone other than myself. Bloody slow development, no?

For ten minutes we hugged each other nearly to death then went back in for coffee. I asked, 'What do you want to do?'

'About us?'

'Yes.'

'What do you want to do?'

'I asked you first.'

'I know, but I'm not telling. What do you want to do?'

I gave in. 'When Claire approves, I'd like us to stay together. You?'

'It's all I ever wanted. What do you think, you stupid bugger?' She hugged me. 'You're very solicitous of Claire.'

'She's vulnerable just now.'

'Yes. We should take it slowly. Let her get to know you in her own time.'

'Absolutely.'

'We'll know when she's ready.'

'Or not. She might hate me.'

'She's more likely to fall in love with you.'

'Then we can sell the story to a French film-maker.'

'Would we move into your house?'

The manner in which she was plunging forward made me smile. 'When the time's right, I think we should choose a new place that would belong to all of us.'

'Thanks, Hal.'

'Francesca?'

'Yes?'

'I didn't think it was possible for any human being to love another as much as I love you. From the moment we met, it's never been any other way.'

'Nor for me.'

'I love you Francesca. I love you. I love you. I love you.'

What catharsis, finally to say it.

Francesca

At last, he said it. 'I love you Francesca.' I'd always known that, of course, and why he spent all these years playing silly buggers, I'm not sure I'll ever understand. I knew also that we'd never, from choice, be apart again despite what would be a hazardous existence. As Hal said, 'We'll be like agents dropped into occupied territory.' In all conversations it was vital to side-step chat about Hal's past. A careless response to an innocent question could deliver us into the hands of the enemy, which suddenly turned out to be almost everyone. In time, I was introduced to the Parkers as a new girlfriend. This was the easiest relationship of all because, in addition to being completely delightful and brilliant, they knew Hal well. Hal said that they were pleased that I'd come along because it demonstrated that he wasn't a screaming queen, but I knew that the real reason was that I could make up a four at bridge. Hal had tried to learn but it's a skill at which, like driving, if not schooled relatively young, one will rarely excel.

Claire knew Hal as John, of course. Just John, never Koston. Their relationship was good from the start but we waited some months before our meetings together became more regular. In that time she had been back to Nairobi to visit Reg. Whether she mentioned the existence of 'John' to him, we didn't know. Reg never mentioned it in letters or on the phone. Claire's letters would become a problem.

We had moved into Hal's house about five months after our 're-acquaintance'. Even then, Hal and I didn't sleep together. There's no book of instructions on how to bring a new man into your bed without driving your child completely potty. Their relationship was wonderful. All matters were discussed and decisions taken democratically, but . . . possession is seven parts of the law – or is it five – or maybe nine and a bit. Anyway, Claire very much had to feel that I was hers and no one else's, and that her father was not being carelessly betrayed. We avoided speeches which began, 'You see, darling, when people are very fond of each other, they like to . . .' Poor, gallant Hal had put a bed into his study leaving the master bedroom for me. Claire had her own room. When we all seemed familiar enough with each other, Hal instituted, at weekends, breakfast in mummy's bed, so that his presence there was, as it were, with Claire's dispensation. In time it moved smoothly to his sharing my bed. Christ! What a fucking palaver, but worth it.

We found a lovely Edwardian house not very far from the old one, quite close to the Abbey Road studios: 2 rec, study, 4 bd, 2 bth, clkrm, Grge. Lg Gdn. £60,000.

The single nasty part of all of this was having to censor Claire's letters to Reg. Obviously, he wouldn't know it was Hal, and I didn't want him to be further hurt by thinking that I'd found someone else so quickly. I therefore, forging Claire's handwriting, rewrote them, leaving out all references to Hal/John. One day I was going to have to make my confession to her.

27

Hal

Francesca's parents, Sir Guy and Lady Virginia Trestrail, were about the most charming people this side of the Milky Way. Charm was a profession with them, but they were excellent company. Whatever troubles they'd been having when I'd first met Francesca seemed to have been resolved. As far as they knew, of course, Francesca and I had met only recently. Virginia was beautiful and at 58 still extremely fanciable. Where Guy exuded reason and diplomacy to a fault, she diverted with a wicked tongue; for example, on receiving the news from her husband of the demise of his mother, her *bête noire*, she was heard by Francesca to say, 'Oh darling how absolutely perfect, the bin men come tomorrow.' As for Guy, the coldness and distance which Francesca had endured from him as a child became warmth and merriment in his relationship with Claire. He adored her and through her, came to see for the first time, what a lovely daughter he had in Francesca.

He and Virginia were, of course, deeply wounded by the death of Angela. One evening Guy and I, sitting in his garden after dinner, discussed the tragedy. He said, 'Angela was never a happy girl. I don't know why. Francesca was, or at least seemed – or was it pretended – to be. And she didn't receive the same amount of attention as Angela. Second children don't, you know. I sometimes think I wasn't very nice to her. Francesca, I mean. I'm sorry about that.'

I felt sad for him. 'Tell her.' I said.

'Really?'

'Why not?'

'Yes, why not? You're absolutely right. Thank you John. I will.'

And he did, and that night in bed, she cried for him.

A few days later, Parker and I sat in our respective consulting rooms, talking shop. It was an afternoon in late autumn and the sun still shone. I was dreading what was to come. Rona, the nurse in our practice, brought in some X-ray plates.

As I clipped them on to the light-box, Parker walked to the window and looked out. He asked, 'Did you say Claire was coming here today?'

'Yes, on a Thursday she comes here straight from school.'

'Good,' he said.

There was no putting it off. I said, 'I take it from your studied lack of interest, that you know exactly what I'm looking at.'

'I wondered how you'd get out of that one. You've a gift for the sideways approach.'

'I wonder who taught me that.'

The X-ray, which was of Parker's pancreas, showed a carcinoma. He was dying.

'Do you want me to do a short circuit?'

No, thanks. I believe in palliatives only for others. Switch it off, would you?'

'Of course. Sorry.'

He sat down. 'No, silly, really. I know what it is. Somehow, I just don't want to see it. Seen enough of them. Care to give me an estimate?'

'How often have you been able to answer that question?'

'I just want to try to prove you wrong. Just a bit of a game. What's life without a goal, eh?'

'All right. At the inside, two months. At the outside, nine.'

'Bloody hell, be fair, it's only a game.'

'All right, five.'

'Done. That'll see me through Chanukah and Christmas anyway. Bloody unreasonable to die then. Sours it for everybody for years. Pity it's winter, really. Could have sat in the garden.'

Rona knocked and came in. 'Claire's here, Mr Koston.'

'Thanks, Rona, I'll be a little while.'

'No.' said Parker, 'send her in. We've finished.'

Rona looked at me. I said, 'Good salesman, difficult customer.' I called, 'Claire, come in.'

In she bounced, pure St Trinian's. Hair awry, the hated school beret scrunched in her blazer pocket.

'Hello Claire,' said Parker, the gentleman, rising from his chair.

'Hello Andrew, how are you?'

He smiled. 'Better now that you're here. Are you coming to hear the orchestra on Friday?'

She turned to me, keen. 'Can we?'

'Absolutely.'

The pair of them were silhouetted against the window. Parker, who was saying something about Beethoven, seemed smaller. In fact he was. The disease was already taking its toll.

The whole thing was too damn sad. I was sorry for both that they didn't know each other for longer and sorry for me that I didn't know him for longer. And Lotte and Milla – how would they fare when their knight in shining armour was slain. Claire and Parker stood, smiling, chatting. For one, it was just beginning, for the other, it was over. What I couldn't know was that life was about to change, alarmingly, for all of us.

A couple of months later, from the bedroom window, I watched Claire, in the garden, with a skipping rope. It was a dull day, the trees almost bare. Francesca, by me on the window seat, was 'vetting' a letter from Claire to Reg. I could feel irritation radiate from her. I knew what was coming, I'd been expecting it.

'This one will have to be entirely rewritten.'

'What does she say?'

'There are so many references to you, and she uses the name "Koston" a couple of times.'

'God!' I said. 'Censoring a child's letters.'

Francesca boiled over. 'Care to suggest an alternative? And while you're at it, could you run up a few conversational lines about your past that I can trot out when cornered? God!'

She got up, walked across the room and back. One of these pointless moves we make when frustrated. She went on. 'You don't know the half of it.'

There was no point in telling her that I knew it one thousand per cent, so I kept my mouth shut.

She stormed on. 'Come on. You tell me what to do. Claire goes to Africa in a month. What do we tell her to say? And suppose Reg is noticing a subtle difference in her handwriting.'

'Perhaps we should tell her.'

'And make her an accessory? Fucking brilliant.'

In the garden, Claire, attempting a complicated skipping manoeuvre, fell heavily.

'She's fallen,' I said. 'She's cut her leg.'

'Well, you'd better run, doc.'

I did.

That evening, after supper, her wound bandaged, Claire and I sat before an open fire, playing Scrabble. Francesca had been thundering around the house looking for something. Now she appeared in the room.

'Where the hell is that bloody Italian cookbook? My mother wants a recipe.'

'There are still some unpacked crates in the garage, maybe it's there.'

'Shit and bloody derision!' She left. Claire gave me a 'she's on the warpath' look. I said, 'Look, you can do a marvellous one on a triple word.'

'What? But you're not supposed to tell me.'

'But I've an unfair advantage, because I'm a doctor, and it's a word you wouldn't know.'

'Wait and see if I can find it. What's the first letter?'

'Z.'

28

Francesca

I was actually angry with myself for not coping more ably. Poor Hal, being told he didn't know the half of it. I knew he'd been living it since the day he left Africa. Regretfully, I did on occasion have bouts of my old delinquency. I missed Gertrude too. Not only sexually but as a chum. We were very close by the end of my time in Nairobi. True soulmates, we unburdened our greatest concerns to each other. Our last time together was extremely emotional. We cried. She said, 'I love you Francesca.'

'I love you too, Trude.'

'No . . . I love you . . . I'm in love with you.'

I had sometimes wondered if it might be so, but I still didn't know what to say when she told me. It's so hard when someone declares love, not to declare it back. I hugged her and kissed her. 'I'm so sorry that I can't stay with you, Trude.'

'I know you can't. I just wanted you to know that I love you. I wish I could be Hal for you, but I know that no one ever will.'

'I hope you'll find your Hal, darling Trude.'

'I already have,' she whispered, sadly.

What a perverse bugger of an organ the heart is. All of this was whirling in my brain as I thumped around the garage, throwing things. There was a tea-chest marked 'Motor books/Aircraft/Maps/Manuals'. I thought the cookbook might have been put there in error so I delved in. There was an unfamiliar wooden box – locked. I didn't favour secrets at that moment, so I unscrewed the padlock eye. Inside was a large, leather bound notebook. I opened it. Inside:

'My darling Francesca,
It seems as though I've entered some strange land, where reality and fantasy battle for superiority. Strangest of all is knowing that you will never receive this or any subsequent letter.

There were hundreds of them. I read about ten then I could stay away from him no longer.

29

Hal

Claire puzzled over the 'z' word for about five minutes, then, 'All right. I give in, but I'll only take half the score.'

'You like to be fair, don't you?'

'Yes. It's best, don't you think?'

'Yes, I think it's best. The word is "zygoma".'

'What does it mean?'

'It's your cheekbone. Remember that one when you play with your daddy next month.'

'I don't want to go to Africa in the holidays.'

I didn't want this to be the thin end of a wedge, so said, 'Your daddy would be terribly disappointed. You're the most important thing in his life, you know.'

She was silent. Despite all efforts to bring Reg into conversations, to keep as much of the relationship as alive as possible, we knew she was suffering emotional lesions and the most dangerous thought of all. So I asked, 'Do you think it's your daddy's fault that you're not all together any more?'

'I don't know.'

'Do you think it's your fault? That it was something you did?'

She was silent. I was aware of the tragic fact that children can blame themselves for events over which they truly have no control; a parent's death even.

'It's absolutely not your fault, Claire. And it's not his. If he had his way, you'd all be together. There are all sorts of things that conspire to affect people's lives. Even things that happened before you were born.'

'What things?'

'Oh, I don't know. But what's happening to you now can have an effect on your children, when you have them.' She looked at me and gave a little laugh.

'You must miss your daddy.'

'Yes I do. Why doesn't he come here?'

'His Christmas holidays may not be long enough.'

'He's not my real daddy, you know.'

What did she say? I must have misheard. 'What do you mean? Sorry . . . what did you say?'

'My real daddy is dead. He was killed in an aeroplane.'

Firecrackers exploded in my head. 'I'm sorry Claire, I didn't know.'

Then, just on the offchance that there was something else I didn't know, I asked, 'Did you know him?'

'No, he died before I was born.'

I didn't know where to put myself. I wanted more than anything to gather Claire in my arms and cry. She was speaking again. 'My mummy told me about him, of course.'

I'm afraid it was irresistible.'

'What did she tell you?'

'That he was crazy – but lovely crazy.'

And Francesca's voice, quietly, behind me, 'But definitely crazy.'

I turned. She stood in the doorway. In her arms, a large leatherbound book.

If it was possible to die of pleasure, I'd have gone, right then.

Later, in bed, cuddled close, Francesca asked, 'Why didn't you tell me about the letters?'

'For the same reason that you didn't tell me about Claire.'

'Which was?'

'Apart from your innate cussedness, a need to keep something back. A secret room.'

'Really? Why?'

'I remember a line from a marvellous play on television some years ago. It struck me quite forcefully, which is why I remember it, I suppose. "As long as he could keep just one chamber in his castle locked and its contents safe from scrutiny, Bluebeard was model husband, reliable father and responsible citizen." '

'Very neat. I would have told you, you know.'

'I know. And I would have given you the letters.'

'I know. Are you pleased, really?'

'That's the dumbest question you've ever asked. I'm drowning in pleasure. Of course there's also the pain of not being able to tell her.'

'We can when she's grown up.'

'I don't know. She's lovely. She's really lovely. You made something wonderful, you and Reg.'

She kissed my arm. 'Thank you. So are the letters. Really lovely. Aren't we lucky?' She snuggled in to me.

'You *are* a funny girl. There is one thing we have to do, though. We have to tell Reg that I'm alive. He'll find out sooner or later.'

She sat up. 'I couldn't. I couldn't tell him. I've given him enough bad news in his life.'

'It's not necessarily bad news. It's preferable to you meeting someone new. Someone who might make difficulties over you – or indeed Claire – visiting him. I'll reassure him that I won't tell Claire that I'm her real father and that he'll always be welcome and . . . you'll all come and go as you please.'

'You make it sound easier than it's going to be.'

'It's *all* been easier than I thought it was going to be. Do you think Reg will keep quiet?'

'Yes. I do. You're a good doctor. That's all he'd care about. Do you think you're safe from the law?'

'I think I won't ever be safe.'

'Jail?'

'I don't know. It would depend, obviously, on whether or not the police were involved. The profession would try to keep it internal because they wouldn't look good. It'd be difficult to say I was guilty of malpractice because, apart from the fact that I haven't practised badly, they'd have to admit that for years their sacred body had failed to notice it. They even made me a chief consultant, for God's sake. The journals have printed my papers . . .'

Francesca pulled away and turned her body to face me. 'Let's ask Reg to come over,' she said.

I was to meet Reg on Hampstead Heath. On the previous day Claire and Francesca had picked him up at Heathrow, taken him to his hotel and dined with him. Today, Claire at school, Francesca took Reg walking on the Heath. It was bright and very cold. Using no names, she would tell him of the man she'd met, of his unorthodox entry to medicine and his reasons for such. She would make a plea that the concealment of his identity be respected. I waited on a bench under a tree between East Heath Road and White Stone Pond. Should Reg's reaction seem favourable, she would reveal me; otherwise, she would walk on by.

As they came into view a hundred yards away, my scarper reflex revved up. Flight, though, would defy reason. Our survival together would be determined now. Closer they came. More rapidly beat my heart. They were not speaking. A few feet away, Francesca stopped.

'Reg?' She indicated me. 'Hal.'

I rose. He looked at me. I could see his brain riffling through memory files, reading, discarding, then picking one out. His reaction was actually comic. He looked at me, at Francesca, at the trees, at me, at the trees, at the ground, at me . . .

'Hal,' he said. 'Jesus! Fucking Lazarus!'

'Hello Reg.'

'What the fuck? I need to sit down.' He lowered his hefty frame on to the bench and looked at me. 'You faked the whole fucking thing?'

'The whole fucking thing.'

'And you're a surgeon?'

'Yes I am.' He continued to look, his jaw loose.

'What's the function of aldosterone?'

I laughed. 'Is this going to be a lengthy examination?'

'Depends. So, aldosterone?'

'A hormone. Part of the reabsorption process of sodium ions in the distal tubules; has an effect on the metabolising of electrolytes.'

'Okay. What does ANP stand for?'

'Atrial natriuretic peptide.'

'What's a nylonephrotic enzoid?'

'What? That doesn't make any sense.'

'Naw. I just made it up.' He turned to Francesca. 'He seems like the real thing right enough. Chancers that pretend to be doctors never know any chemistry.' Then to me, 'An' ye did this 'cause somebody died?'

'Yes. There were other reasons, but . . .'

'Was it John?'

'Yes.'

'Aye,' looking at Francesca, 'well, I've heard that story a thousand times.' And to me, 'An' d'ye feel you've atoned?'

'No, atonement doesn't work.'

'Aye, yir fuckin' right there.'

'I took John's name because he was on the medical register.'

'I don't think he'd mind.'

'Do *you* mind?'

'Mind what?'

'Well, do you want to come for supper tonight or do you intend to head straight for Scotland Yard?'

There was an alarming silence as he looked at us both in turn, then, 'I don't think the food's any good at Scotland Yard, so I'll take my chances at your place.'

On the walk to the car, we reminded him to refer to me only as John and discussed the knotty moral question of what Claire, if ever, should be told. This was not a decision in which the feelings of Reg or myself could be of account. The dilemma was whether, in order to protect her from law or scrutiny by, God forbid, the press, she should be denied knowledge of me as her father. Finally, Francesca, tiring of our philosophical *mélange*, spoke. 'Boys,' and so I suppose, we seemed, 'give your brains a rest. This is not a decision that has to be made. If and when the time comes that it is necessary, then we'll make it.' There was no disagreeing with that.

The evening was splendid. Claire was high with the excitement of it. Francesca was inevitably tense at first but quickly relaxed when she saw that Reg and I showed no intention to compete. Reg is . . . well, something you don't see all that much. Reg is a grown-up.

Claire, never told to go to bed, usually went of her own accord. Tonight she valiantly fought the sandman. It was ten past midnight before he downed her. Reg carried her up.

We chatted for another hour. I liked to be in the hospital by 7 a.m., so was fighting the sandman myself. Inevitably we discussed my deception. Before leaving, Reg summed up thus:

'Qualifications are to make others feel comfortable. We all know blokes with a string of letters after their names who sit on every high-level committee, and some of them are bloody awful doctors. Bein' a doctor's an attitude of mind. If you have that attitude, you learn all you can learn because you're desperate to know all you can know.'

The remainder of his week-long visit passed pleasantly. He took Claire out a lot, to the pictures and the theatre. She cried sorely when he left, so she and I talked a lot about him and about children and how they feel when their parents split up. Sad.

Christmas came and went. The problem of whether or not Claire should go to Africa was solved by Reg coming to spend it with us. Excellent. Taking Reg into our confidence enabled us to relax. Life again settled into routine – but nearby, already glowing, was the ember that would become the firestorm.

*

My decision to tell Parker my story wasn't taken until a few moments before I did.

I've always disliked February, the unequal segment thrust in to complete the circle and which somehow gives no impression of a move away from January. Perfectly fine in Sydney of course, but in grey London . . .

I was with the Parkers. We sat in their conservatory, on a Saturday afternoon, lit by a bleary sun. Parker was now a thin man wasted by the disease and yellowed by the jaundice that accompanies it. His eyes, although having retreated into his skull, appeared larger, doubtless from staring Death in the face. Here there were no hushed and respectful tones in the presence of Charon. There was no pretence that this was other than it was. People faced with the death of a loved one, in understandable fear for themselves, use denial as a shield, thus condemning the dying to face the abyss alone. Lotte and Milla were not going to allow that to happen to their beloved Andrew.

During my visits, he always asked about the hospital. Who was doing what? Who was doing whom? This time, he didn't. Making tea in the kitchen with Milla, I mentioned it. As she placed little Vienna cakes on to a plate, she said, in a manner entirely matter-of-fact, 'When the business is going under, you start closing departments.'

Why did I feel the need to confess to the Parkers? It wouldn't make the slightest difference to them whether or not they knew. Perhaps it was a way of telling them that I loved them. Anyway, I told them. The reaction was not the one I expected. They all found it hysterically funny. Then Parker said, 'Well, whatever, you're a doctor now. I know that better than anyone.'

Milla said, 'Hal? That's good. Much better. I never saw you as a John. But as a Hal? Yes.'

Lotte said, 'So you and Francesca are just like we three. Meant to be together. What is it, Andrew, that they say in *Romeo and Juliet*?'

'Star-crossed.'

'That's it, "Star-crossed lovers" That's all of us. Isn't it, Andrew? We're star-crossed.'

'Yes, that's us, that's us.' he said softly, smiling.

The following morning brought a letter, hand delivered in the night, from Andrew, Milla and Lotte, saying goodbye. They were dead.

Our dear Hal,

Please forgive us for leaving so soon but you better than anyone will understand why. This is not a decision taken recently. We had many years ago determined that we would proscribe our own time of death. The moment has presented itself rather earlier than we had hoped, but that's all right.

Please be so good as to inform the police and give all of the emergency services our sincere apologies for any unpleasantness we may have caused them. We take comfort in knowing that there is nothing that they will have not have encountered before. The back door is unlocked.

Please explain to Claire that we died in neither sadness nor despair, but in love.

We are grateful that you revealed your real life to us. How fitting that we should all have lived with great secrets and how agreeable that we should end our day with a good story.

Miss us but don't mourn us.

With love to Claire and Francesca and especially to you, dear Hal,

Andrew and Lotte and Milla

It was signed by all three. I waited at their house for the police to arrive. I showed them the letter, explaining that 'Hal' was their nickname for me. It was accepted without question. We entered together but I asked to be allowed to find them myself.

Self-dispatch is never simple – if you're in your right mind. Those overwhelmed by despair don't entertain the thought that if, for example, they throw themselves out of a window there might be someone beneath. Calculated termination requires careful planning. If it's by chemical means, how much do you take? Too little and you might wake up hours later with your kidneys destroyed. Too much and you might vomit it back. It is impossible to know exactly when death will take place, so might a concerned neighbour have your stomach pumped in the nick of time? If the wish is to die outdoors, location must be chosen which will prevent intervention from a well-meaning dog walker. Parker knew all this and more.

They were in bed, partly covered by a duvet. Andrew in the middle, Lotte and Milla close against him in his arms. Their uppermost arms had been across his chest, I presume holding hands until all muscle tone was lost. Rigor was well established so muscle had contracted and the bodies, if unimpeded, would have assumed a more foetal position. Their top halves were naked, in devotion. Parker knew that the introduction of toxins would have an effect on the bowel; post-mortem would reveal that their rectums had been filled with wadding. Their dispatch vehicle had been pentobarbital. Commonly an anaesthetic, it will, if taken in high dosage, reduce the central nervous system to coma. Respiratory failure and death will follow. There are worse ways to go.

Back in my own driveway, as I climbed out of the car, a figure appeared.

'Hello Hal.'

'Hello?'

'It's Humphries.'

And so it was. He had not aged well.

I instinctively made a connection between Cadell and Parker's death. Nonsense, as it happened, but indicative of my cynicism.

'How are you?' he said but without waiting for an answer, 'Cadell would like a word, if you can spare the time. He's just around the corner.'

I had no choice. There was the same Rover, looking not a day older. As I was about to open the door, Humphries offered his hand.

'Goodbye Hal. It's always a pleasure to see you. Good luck.'

He walked away. How odd. I was rather touched by his demeanour, but alarmed by his good wishes. I climbed into the Rover.

Shock. Cadell was an old man. His hair was completely white and his face heavily lined. Frail? No. Still powerful.

'Hello Hal.'

'Hello Cadell. Uncle Humphrey isn't looking too well.'

'No he isn't. He's been looking after aged, demented parents for years. He's quite likely to pop off before them at this rate.'

'Does he have a family?'

'Humphries? Don't be daft. He's as queer as a bag of bishops.'

'Really? It never occurred to me.'

'Well, it wouldn't. The chap's not a pansy, he's just an homosexual. Anyway. How have you been getting on? No need to answer that, we know you're doing extremely well. Congratulations on your consultancy.'

'Thank you. Are you going to bugger it all up?'

'Certainly not. Indeed you may continue with renewed vigour.'

'Hmm?'

'We're in a little spot of bother and we'd like you to help us out, if you would.'

'I'm sorry, I can't. Not now. Apart from anything else, I don't believe in that stuff any more. Not that I ever did, particularly.'

He tapped the steering wheel. 'I doubt that anybody does much, bar those of us in the dungeon.'

'No, I . . . No. I'm sorry, I absolutely can't.'

'No, *I'm* sorry Hal. It's the old non-returnable offer, I'm afraid.'

'Oh God. I'm too old. And I'm certainly not the flyer I was.'

He laughed. 'Oh Lord, we don't want you to fly. We want you to operate.'

My look to him and my silence prompted him to continue.

'This is the situation. A member of an Arab royal family, Prince Khalid, despite the benefits of a fine English education, is trying, secretly he fondly imagines, to establish, with other Middle-Eastern nations, a power block with a bigger fist than OPEC in the oil market, and a combined armed force supported by the Soviet Union.'

'That may be bad for you, but good for them.'

'Not all of them, no. Our concern, shared by the spooks of many western nations, is not so much that we would be seriously threatened by war, but that the political foundation upon which the new alliance would be built is terminally unstable. Its collapse would render the entire region a battleground. That's good for no one. Anyway, as luck would have it, Khalid collapsed last night. A suspected aneurysm. He wants a British surgeon.'

'So wh—'

'In return, we'll authenticate you. Give you a past. Passport, birth certificate, any documents you'll ever need. You'll have to go now, of course. He's just down the road in The Princess Grace. You can take five minutes to tell Francesca that you'll be missing lunch. I'd be happy to join her and eat your share of the roast beef, only I've never really liked it.'

'Stop, stop! Cadell, this is silly. He's hardly likely to abandon his entire plan simply out of gratitude to a British surgeon.'

'Yes, that's why we need you. We'd like you to do your best to save him but, in fact, actually let him go.'

'Let him go? You mean kill him?'

'Well . . . sort of.'

So, what to do? I'd learned to heal but the ironic adjunct was that I knew also how to kill in the simplest, least detectable way. And who was this man Khalid? A visionary? A tyrant? Could I be protecting the world from a Stalin? If I do it, we're free. If not? Cadell is an impeccably bred, politely murderous bastard. A few minutes later, I headed for The Princess Grace.

Prince Khalid, somewhat short of effervescent, but none the less stoic, lay listening to my appraisal.

'Your aorta has become weakened and distended at one point, rather like a ballooned bicycle tyre.'

A stony look flicked in my direction. I added, 'I don't know why I should suppose that you ever mended a tyre on your bike.'

'Perhaps you might construct a metaphor upon the leg of a camel?'

I laughed. 'Sorry. I suppose it has all been explained.'

'Does your skill equal your reputation? Forgive me, I shouldn't place you modesty in danger. Please tell me how you'll proceed, sparing me, if you will, any vehicular analogies. Let's begin with the incision. Where?'

'From the sternum to the pubis.'

And so it was. It's a huge incision. The sternum is where the lower ribs meet, the pubis is . . . yes, that's right.

Apart from the theatre sister and the anaesthetist, my team was from the Middle East. It was headed by Farrah, the family's personal surgeon, whose expertise evidently did not inspire quite enough confidence, Khalid's physician, whose presence was a mystery, three nurses and, at Farrah's request, some students.

In we went. To the students I explained my task. To remove the damaged part of the aorta and reconnect the severed artery with a dacron graft. The transverse colon was tucked up out of the way and the small bowel lifted out of the abdomen. It was packed with warm saline towels to reduce loss of body heat, and held steady by the youngest nurse. I could now have a look around. Providing that there was nothing to worry about above the renal arteries and there was no obvious disease of kidneys or liver, I could determine the state and size of the aneurysm.

This would be the danger moment. There was no way of examining it but by touch, and a touch is enough to rupture a badly eroded artery; it'll crumble. The heart is a helluva pump. If you cut an aorta and hold it like a hose, the blood will shoot a distance of 25 feet. If it did rupture, we had little more than ten seconds to avert catastrophe. The other danger was that if aortic damage extended too far up, then it would be difficult to clamp without damage to the renals. We'd therefore have to use a balloon catheter to stem blood loss until we could get the graft in place.

As I was poking about, Farrah said, 'Wouldn't it be safer to introduce the balloon catheter before examining the aorta, then if it ruptures, you're safe?'

'It might seem that way, but it's not easy to find the neck of the artery so we'd risk further damage. Also, if we do it now, we stop renal blood supply for much longer and we don't want to lose his kidneys.'

Nothing from Farrah, I said, 'If you want me to proceed that way, then I will. It's your show. I'm the hired hand.'

'But the expert one.' Because he was masked, I couldn't tell whether he spoke in grace or bitterness. He went on. 'Prince Khalid trusts you. So must I.'

I withdrew my hand from the wound. 'Good, the iliacs are fine. There's no pulsation of the inferior mesenteric artery. Some calcification. Right. Let's see what we have.'

All movement stopped – except for the anaesthetist, an old hand who leaned slightly out of the way of what he knew might be the blood firing line. My hand went back into the wound. I gave them a running commentary.

'It feels very fragile. There's a reasonable neck below the renals, so we should be able t—'

In an instant, blood everywhere. It bubbled up my arm to the elbow. A large glob hit the young nurse in the face and she loosened her grip on the bowel she was supporting. It began to slop back into the abdomen. I said, 'Packs and catheter.'

Farrah yelled at the nurse, 'Hold the bowel!'

'Please don't shout.' I said

Sister was thrusting packs into the wound. They immediately saturated with blood. Another nurse was applying suction. I pulled the bowel out again and said to the nurse, 'It's all right. Just hold it there.'

I glanced at her and saw her pupils dilate. She was going to faint.

'She's going. Someone get this bowel. Give me the catheter.'

But 'someone' went to her aid.

'Leave her, get the bowel.'

And as 'someone' did, the nurse hit the deck.

The catheter was passed to me. I fed it into the artery, eyes closed, the better to concentrate on my fingers. As you can imagine, everything's very slippery and one is trying to introduce something into a very small tube when every beat of the heart sends a pressurised volume of blood to wash it out. I felt it go in.

'Inflate.'

The blood stopped gushing. I don't know exactly how long that took. A lot happened but it all happened at once. Probably not more than ten seconds. There was 'Ohh' of relief from the team, then the anaesthetist's voice, 'Can you stop, please.'

When the gas man says 'stop' you stop. It was quite possible that Khalid was going to arrest. I admit that I don't know what I felt. I hadn't tried to kill him. I couldn't. On the contrary, I had done my best to save him, but if he died? A huge problem solved at no cost to me. But . . .

'His BP is rising. Okay, carry on.'

We carried on. We put the graft in place and closed him up.

Now what? I tried to imagine Cadell's reaction when told that the executioner had fired wide. He might smile – and then again, he probably bloody wouldn't . . .

Khalid was conscious when I went in.

'Hello there.'

'Ah, the transport manager.'

'We've given you a new inner tube. It's looking good.'

'Thank you.'

I was now enraged by what Cadell had expected me to do, enraged at what his trade had done to Francesca and Claire and Reg and so many more – and especially one; that little one. This prompted me to tell Khalid of Cadell's murder plot.

'But, as you can see, I didn't go through with it.'

There was a worrying silence, then he smiled. 'So, you're a traitor.'

'Her Majesty's heating bill may rise a little, but I think the realm is still safe.'

'Your intelligence friends may be less philosophical. Don't worry, what you told me will be our secret.'

'Thank you. They're nightmare people. They make the world a bad place.'

'It's a game. I play it myself.'

'I wish you'd all stop.'

'We will, when someone from the stars comes to steal our ball.'

I was driven home in one of Khalid's limousines. It was an absurdity of comfort and gadgetry. The rear seat was a sofa with down-filled cushions. There was a drinks cabinet, ice machines and a video recorder, with a camera pointed at the back seat. What did he film himself doing, I wondered. What a contrast it was to the poverty and affliction of Africa. The car stopped. I was home. Home to my pretty Edwardian mansion. Not much poverty or affliction here, either. I'd gone off course somewhat. I climbed out of the limo, half expecting Cadell and a platoon of paras to drop from the skies, but there was only rain.

I told Francesca everything, and that there might be serious repercussions. She was in near panic.

'God! God! What are we going to do? Would they try to kill you?'

I laughed. 'I never thought of that. No, I don't think so. What would be the point? Anyway, it's too much trouble, all that stuff.'

'Have you ever done it?'

It was time to come clean, time that Francesca knew the whole story. She would have to wait a few hours more, though. Claire was home from the pictures with her best chum, Lizzie. The evening was passed in a pretence of normality, then it was bedtime.

We sat in the bedroom, on a little sofa in front of the fireplace. Francesca would scarcely move during my disclosure. She sat forward, her hands clasped between her knees.

So, *have* you ever done it? Killed anyone?

'Not at close range, no.'

'My God. How?'

'By setting explosives, or from an aircraft.'

'Were you a mercenary?'

'That's what it was supposed to look like.'

'What do you mean?'

'The intelligence services, on behalf of the government naturally, ha ha, might . . .'

'What do you mean, 'ha ha?''

'Governments come and go. They're composed of individuals chosen by the people then booted out by the people. They're far too transient and self interested to be trusted with the security of the state. The intelligence service – and I don't mean the one which has an address, but the real one which operates in vaults within vaults, far from the sight or knowledge of any Cabinet rooms – is the real Foreign Office, and indeed, one could say, the real Home Office. When people are recruited, they're there for life. The continuity of the like minded, that's what's considered vital.'

'And you were one of them?'

'No. I had nothing to do with policy. I was a foot soldier. An elite one, but just a squaddie none the less.'

'So what did you do?'

'All sorts. There might be a British interest in the outcome of a seemingly unimportant skirmish – or it may not even be a *direct* British interest. We might give the French a hand, or the Chinese. We'd put a couple of people in to make sure it went the way everyone wanted it to.'

'As easy as that?'

'No, it's not easy. I don't mean that this takes just five minutes. An operation might last for months. Years even.'

'Doing what?'

'Often simply creating confusion. If combatants don't understand why or how things are happening, it unsettles them. Chaos is very effective.'

'And killing?'

'Yes, killing.'

'It's all so unlike you.'

'The model you see before you was a long time in the making.'

'What changed you?'

'It was gradual. In the places where we'd been operating – huh – funny. "Operating". Now it means save, then it meant destroy. Anyway, in those places, nothing ever got better. It was becoming clear to me that only the people of whatever country could sort their own problems. Powerful nations brought in to "help" simply perpetuated them. Then the uncomfortable thought insinuated itself that it was sometimes in our interest that the problem remained. Then . . . a couple of things happened.'

I could feel the shakes begin and the awful sob being born deep inside me. Could I get the story out before it overwhelmed me? Francesca could see that something was amiss.

'Do you want to tell me?'

I nodded. 'There were two airborne missions, months apart.'

'Where?'

'I really can't tell you.'

'Don't be silly, Hal. After what you've already told me?'

'All of that was general. It's better that you don't know particulars.'

'But I want to know.'

'I know. Everyone wants to know secrets. But secrets are very heavy, and awkward to hold – and make targets of their bearers.'

She held out her hand to me. I took it and she saw that I trembled.

'What happened, Hal?'

'The ops were similar in that both were air-to-ground attacks on villages which, we were told, were terrorist camps. As I let my rockets go, I saw a man break cover and run to untie a goat. The rockets hit. Now where, I wondered, does it say in the terrorist handbook "At all costs, protect your goat"? The next—'

I paused, feeling the corners of my lips twitch downwards as the tears came to my eyes. Francesca came close and hugged me. 'Oh Hal, Hal.'

28

Francesca

Hal's second story was long in the telling. I'd never seen anyone in such distress. At times it seemed that he might die of crying. For minutes between words he was unable to speak or, it appeared, even breathe. This is why:

'In the next, I was the second man in. There were huge explosions from the rockets of the aircraft in front. As I released mine, something appeared in the air ahead of me. We were flying low so it rose above me then fell towards me. It was a child. There's an antenna on the nose of the aircraft, like a swordfish. There was an awful thud as the child, it was a little girl, was impaled on it. Her blood ran towards me, up the cockpit glass and over my canopy. There was so much of it. She must have been unconscious, but for some moments after the impact, still alive. Her body remained there all the way back to base, held by a 500-miles-an-hour wall of air. Her hair blew in the slipstream. When I landed, the ground crew, shocked, brought ladders and we took her off. I held her . . . she was so broken. And hopelessly tried to say I was sorry. I wish that there was a loving God. I would have flown her to the top of the sky and passed her to his care.'

After a time I rose, pulled back the covers and he fell into bed. I undressed us both and curled into his back. He reached behind and clasped my thigh.

'I understand now, Hal. Why you did everything that you did. I understand.'

He said nothing, but squeezed my leg. Eventually his diaphragm spasms ceased and his breath evened. About half an hour after that, I felt him fall asleep.

At six in the morning, the police came and took Hal away. Claire didn't wake to witness it, thank God.

To those of us who don't break the law, and I include Hal as one, since he gave to society rather than took from it – and anonymously, he had by now paid for the aircraft which he'd crashed into the lake – to be abruptly on the wrong side, is very, very frightening. Hal appeared before a magistrate at ten o'clock, charged with personation, that is, 'to impersonate with criminal intent', and obtaining money by deception. To the former, he pleaded guilty, to the latter, not guilty. What chilled us was that bail was denied, reporting restrictions were imposed and the trial would be held 'in camera'. This was to prevent Hal, now considered a loose cannon, from shelling his own side in full view – not his intention. In these circumstances one is rendered instantly a non-person. I tried to speak to Hal but he was immediately taken away. No amount of pleading or reasoning would slow the mechanism of The Law. He was gone. Asking where he was being taken brought the response 'You'll be informed in due course.' It makes one want to scratch eyes out – or buy a machine gun.

Daddy came up trumps and spoke to a chum, an eminent barrister, Robin Maxton-Greene, who took the brief. There were aspects to the case that puzzled him. He said that it looked like someone had it in for Hal and asked if I knew whether or not that was likely. I said that I didn't know, and asked why he thought so. He said:

'For a start, bail was refused. Absurd. As for the personation, he's proved himself in medicine so that would bring a nominal sentence. If it was custodial, which I doubt, it would be suspended. However, the charge of obtaining money by deception shows a determined effort on someone's part. Also, hearing the case is Lord Crantleigh. He has the reputation of favouring the establishment. At supper some evening, a fellow member of the Athenaeum will mutter, 'We're relying on you for this one, Crantleigh.' So, he'll do his best to steer the trial and, if it's a guilty verdict that's sought and won, hand down a hefty sentence.' Then he added, 'I didn't say any of that, you understand.' I understood.

I think he fancied me – but then again, I foolishly imagine that everyone fancies me.

The press, despite being gagged, beavered away collecting opinions, anecdotes, half truths and, no doubt, downright lies with which to entertain the public should restrictions be lifted. Claire said that she didn't believe that 'John' could do anything wrong. She wanted to visit him in prison. The whole prison thing fascinated her. She asked about bars and chains and 'will he be wearing a striped uniform'.

Hal was worried about his patients.

It wasn't possible. After everything, we'd be parted again. Hal in prison? Hal? For *not* killing someone.

Hal

I was remanded in a hellhole called Belmarsh and tried at the Old Bailey. Something of an honour, I believe – if you're nuts. Almost all of the prisoners I encountered were bewildered inadequates treated as sub-human. Although they may have been inadequate, some were obviously intelligent, much more so than those in charge of them which, without doubt, added to their frustration and rage. Mandatory before becoming a prison governor, should be a voyage on Captain Arcangeli's ship.

Journeys while in custody were horrible. I had imagined that prisoners sat on long benches on each side of the prison van. Not so. Inside are individual cells, so small that one can barely turn around. The holding cells, and there seemed to be a great many of them at the Bailey, able to hold upwards of a hundred, are also tiny, about ten feet by five with a concrete bench at the end opposite the door. I noted that there was nothing to which a ligature might be attached should one be inclined to self-destruction – and many were.

My trial was held in Court 3, one of the old ones. Carved oak and rather beautiful, if you were just visiting. I was surprised at how small it was. The dock was dead centre, facing the judge who sat, not in the centre seat but on one to the right. Above the centre 'throne' hangs the Sword of Justice. No one may sit under it except the Lord Mayor, and he didn't come once.

Slightly below and to my left sat the legal teams, and to my right, the jury. Behind me, the empty public benches.

'All rise,' called the clerk of the court. We all did, and I set eyes, for the first time on Lord Crantleigh. Actually, he had rather a nice face, for a man with 'sold' stamped upon his soul. He had an odd way of looking at people. Sideways. His eyes to them, his face turned away.

The trial was at once both terrifying and silly. The charge of obtaining money by deception was based on my time in private practice, the allegation being that because I wasn't qualified, I defrauded my patients.

The prosecution produced experts who stated that there were no substitutes for qualifications. They also produced one Dougall McKay, the nutty highlander with whom I'd had a clash in my first weeks at the hospital, the fruitcake who had made the little girl cry, and who had waited at the foot of an empty bed. He, now shrivelled and pasty white, testified that I had urged the discharge of a seriously ill child. Parker had been right about McKay: 'He'll always remember that something happened but he won't remember it accurately.' His moment in the witness box ended with 'No transgressor shall escape the reckoning of the Almighty.' Maxton-Greene was on his feet.

'M'lud, I request that the jury be instructed to disregard the witness's last remark.'

'I'm sure, Mr Maxton-Greene, that the members of the jury will themselves know how best to consider Mr McKay's remark.'

Most distressing was facing Mrs Blackburn, whose husband I actually thought I *had* killed. She was called by the prosecution to say that I had stated quite clearly before her husband went to theatre that 'he'd be fine' – in other words, that I was incompetent.

Unfortunately, Andrew Parker, who would have been my star witness, was unavailable, but we countered with Alison, my, and formerly Parker's secretary, who testified that Parker did not in any way hold me responsible for the death. Further, we produced witnesses who attested to my skills and dedication.

The only time that I felt human was when in the dock. Although I couldn't speak, I was at least physically in the company of those in the free world. No Francesca, of course. Not even she was permitted to attend. The return to the holding cell, there to wait, sometimes for hours before being led to the prison van, was a stern reminder that there was nothing you could do about any of it. Well, nothing that *I* could do . . .

Taking the stand was a miserable experience. Maxton Greene questioned me over the accounts of the prosecution witnesses in order that I might rebut. I dealt with them, I thought, favourably, but then, cross examined by the prosecution, it seemed that everything I'd said in my whole life was a lie. Sadly, there was no denying it – and the words ' but you see . . .' were given short shrift by Lord Crantleigh. The following day, prosecution and defence made their final appeals to the jury. Crantleigh adjourned the court stating that his summing up would be in two days' time.

Francesca

I had been prepared to swear anything to help Hal but he wouldn't hear of it. Maxton-Greene had warned that, because I wasn't married to Hal and therefore protected from testifying against him, I would be called as a witness for the prosecution. I wasn't. He himself didn't want to call me because if I took the stand for the defence then the prosecution could cross-examine and I might then be open to the danger of being charged as an accessory. Hal had explained that none of this would happen because Cadell's own curious sense of fair play would disfavour any prosecution of me, an innocent, and that it wasn't even about punishing *him*, but was a memo to everyone in the firm making it clear what would happen if they stray.

Maxton-Greene called to tell me that the judge was about to sum up and that the jury would be out by lunchtime the following day. I was to be permitted to attend for the verdict. Not Claire, just me. Halfway through the evening, the doorbell rang. There was no one there, but through the letterbox had come a sealed envelope addressed to 'Francesca'; in it, was a typed message.

'Pack three suitcases, one for each of us. A car will pick them up at six o'clock tomorrow morning. Come to the court in the afternoon. Bring Claire. You'll have to leave her outside while the verdict is read. If it's not guilty we'll go home. If guilty, then immediately upon the verdict being given, before sentencing, call out 'I love you Hal' then leave the court in tears. Walk straight across Ludgate, down to the top of Wardrobe Place. Someone will meet you there. Do as he says. The plan remains in place for however long the jury deliberates.

There are other choices. Either wait until I get out of prison in however many years, or rid yourself of me and make a new life. I'll know of your decision by whether or not you leave the courtroom. Obviously, you should tell Claire nothing of this beforehand. Whatever you decide, I will love you both always. Hal.

Terror. What the fuck was this? Another Hal madcap scheme? Escape? How could he possibly arrange anything from prison? And anyway what would we then be? Fugitives. How would we get out of the country? To where – and as whom? It was insanity. Out of the question. I did pack the bags though, on the chance of receiving further information.

The Judge's summing up was torture.

'The accused's skill as a surgeon is not what is to be considered here. It is not in question. The charge is 'Obtaining money by deception'. Did the accused, by posing as a bona-fide member of the fraternity of medicine, deceive people who, weakened by illness, gave him their trust. And, on the one hand, the accused did gain a fellowship of the Royal College of

Surgeons, but, you may ask yourselves, given his skills for deception and manipulation, skills which he does not deny, was this fellowship obtained purely on merit?

On and on. Crantleigh's accomplishment was giving the appearance of being fair while branding Hal a liar and a rogue.

The jury retired.

This was by far the worst bit. Stomach-churning misery because there was nothing more to be done. Yes, if guilty, we could appeal but that still meant months in prison – and perhaps to no avail.

Again, I wanted a machine gun.

One hour and twenty minutes later we were informed that a verdict had been reached. A nice policewoman chatted to Claire, while I went into the court.

The jury filed in, little folk with their own problems and fears, holding our future in their hands; for a few moments elevated to the status of gods.

I looked at Hal. He smiled but seemed weary. His shoulders sloped.

'All rise,' said the clerk and we all did, as Lord Crantleigh came in. He sat, we sat.

The clerk again. 'Will the foreman of the jury please rise?' She did. An average, middle-aged, middle-class woman with proud tits, no, in her case it would have to be a 'bust', in a navy-blue crew-neck pullover. Probably perfect jury material, over whom in a few moments, I might want to evacuate my churning bowels.

Casually, Crantleigh asked, 'Foreman of the jury, have you reached a verdict?'

'No my lord.'

What? A courtroomful of eyebrows shot up.

'Sorry, my lord, I mean yes. Yes.'

Crantleigh looked at her sideways for a moment, then again, 'Have you reached a verdict?'

'Yes, my lord. Sorry.' Human after all.

'Will the prisoner rise.'

Hal got to his feet but supported himself with his arms against the dock rail. I'd never seen him like this.

The judge, 'Foreman of the jury. Please compose yourself and consider carefully what you are going to say. This is not the right moment for the wrong word.'

During the following exchange, Hal loosened his tie and undid the top button of his shirt. He seemed to be slightly out of breath.

'Yes, my lord.'

'Very well. How do you find the prisoner? Guilty or not guilty?'

'Guilty.'

Once more, those small sounds which maul. Hal and I looked at each other. He mouthed 'Sorry'. I couldn't bear to be parted from him again. It wasn't within my power to manage the loss.

I shouted, 'I love you Hal,' burst into tears, and ran from the court. In the hallway I grabbed Claire's hand and we ran from the building – into a mob of reporters. They were all around us, lenses and microphones as weapons, aimed.

'Will you be leaving him?'

'Will you be waiting for him?'

'Did you know he wasn't a real doctor?'

'How does it feel to be the partner of a criminal?'

'Mummy!' said Claire holding me around the waist.

'Claire, did he ever treat you when you were sick?'

That did it. I yelled, 'He has never treated my daughter with anything other than love and respect. And you're frightening her. Now *please*, let me pass.'

I moved forward and they immediately made way. I realised then that they couldn't by law impede me. A cab appeared, then slowed, as the driver saw what was going on. I waved and he stopped. He reached around and opened the passenger door to admit us. He had the thickest specs I had ever seen.

'Where to, lass?'

'I'm so sorry, we're not going far, we just needed to be rescued.'

'Aye, I could see that.'

'If you wouldn't mind dropping us around the corner in Ludgate.'

'Right.'

We alighted a few seconds later. I took out my purse.

'How much?'

'No, yer all right.' I saw that he had no teeth.

'No, really, I . . .'

'It were just a few yards. I don't mind helpin' out.'

'That was kind. Thank you.'

We crossed the road and headed down to Wardrobe Place.

'Where are we going Mummy?' She was crying.

'We're going to meet someone.' I hugged her. 'I'm so sorry Clairey, we have to be strong and brave just now.'

'All right.' Watching her pull herself together I was so touched and so proud of her. There, in Claire, I saw Hal, her daddy, who so many times in his life had been required to marshal all the warriors of his intellect in the battle to stay alive – and on course – and sane.

'Who are we going to meet?'

'Someone your d— John. Something John arranged.'

And as we rounded the corner into Wardrobe Place, a man got out of a large black car and came towards us.

'Miss Trestrail?'

'Yes.'

'Please.' It was a foreign, perhaps Mediterranean, accent. He opened the rear door for us. It was a very large car. A Daimler, I think, with black windows.

He got into the driver's seat and lowered the glass division. 'We must change location now.'

'Where to?'

'Very near. Please, be comfortable. There is a bag. Please wear the clothing you find in it.' And he raised the division and moved off.

Clothing? Be comfortable? I was terrified. And that which I had been denied depositing on the forewoman of the jury, I feared was about to decorate the Daimler.

'Mummy, who's that man?'

'I think he may be a friend of John's.'

'What'll happen to John? Can we go to see him?'

Calmly, 'I don't know what's going to happen yet, darling.'

What I couldn't know then was that Hal, as he was being taken down to the cells, had collapsed on the stairs. He had said, desperate for breath, 'Ambulance. Tell them heart failure.' He then lost consciousness. An ambulance was called and he was whisked the 300 or so yards to Barts Hospital.

Hal

A policeman accompanied us in the ambulance. When we arrived at Barts, he was first out. I was lifted out and placed on a trolley.

I opened my eyes just enough to make out that the policeman was on my right. As they moved the trolley, I was up. I threw the blanket over the policeman's head, turned the trolley into him and pushed him over, said, 'Sorry chum,' and ran like hell. I knew the layout of Barts very well and I headed into the quadrangle. Chance had smiled on me. It was lunchtime and the sun had made a rare appearance so there were lots of people outside. The moment I had rounded the corner into the quad and was out of sight of the policeman and ambulance crew, I stopped running, took off my jacket and slowly made my way across to the King Edward Building, where I took the external flight of stairs down to the basement. There, tucked between a drainpipe and the wall, was a bandage which I wound around my head, covering my eye and down to my ear. I looked as though I had just come from Casualty. Thus disguised, and with my jacket now slung over my shoulder I climbed back up the stairs and sauntered round to the nurses' entrance, which led out into Little Britain, and turned left towards Smithfield Market. Two policemen were running towards me. If I'd been rumbled, there was no possibility of escaping them, they were too close – and too big. I stopped and looked behind me as if to look for the object of their attention. They passed. By the time I got to the front of the meat market, the area was bedecked with police uniforms. I rubbernecked with everyone else as I took refuge among the many trucks and busy meat porters.

I crossed Charterhouse Street and made my way up Eagle Lane. I rounded the bend and there it sat, the black Daimler. As I was about to cross to it, klaxons sounded. A police car hurtled into the street from the bottom end – and another from the top. I remained still at the kerbside. They almost collided on the bend but stopped, nose to nose. I waited for the doors to fly open, but no. One of them reversed at speed back to the top of the road then they both squealed away. Saved, as so often in my life, by the inseparable siblings, Crisis and Confusion.

I opened the Daimler door. Wrong car! In it were two Arab women in blue *burqas*.

'Sorry!' I said and retreated.

'No!' they yelled, 'it's us.'

And it was, in the greatest disguise ever.

The car pulled away.

Francesca dropped her veil. 'Christ! What are you doing here? What happened to your head?'

'Have you escaped?' from Claire, her face slack.

'I suppose I have. My head's fine.'

They couldn't get the questions out fast enough and didn't leave the slightest space for a single answer. The driver would not be party to any information, and I was uneasy about being overheard so promised them the story later. Francesca made a face and disappeared under her *burqa*; Claire likewise. How fortunate I was to share my life with girls who made me smile.

After a few moments, Claire spoke, 'At least tell me what happened to your head.'

'Nothing, darling girl, it's for the same reason that you're wearing bags over your heads.'

'Oh. Good. Mummy says that some women wear these things because men tell them they have to.'

'I'm afraid that's true.'

I looked at them both in their bizarre outfits. Something of an irony that they should welcome me to freedom in vestments which, to us at least, symbolised oppression.

An hour later we were at Tilbury docks. The car drew up at the gangway to a huge motor yacht. As we stepped on board I felt a tremor as the engines started. We were greeted by a young blonde gentleman who introduced himself.

'Good afternoon. Jephcott, first officer. Welcome on board. We'll be under way immediately, we've caught the tide by the skin of our teeth.'

And with that, I saw us being cast off 'for'ard'. A deep shake from the engines and we rose and dipped away from the land.

A voice from behind, 'Good afternoon, repair man.'

'Your Royal Highness, how are you?'

'Shiny like a new bike, thanks to you. Welcome aboard.'

I introduced Francesca and Claire, both bewildered. He then escorted us to our quarters, a small stateroom and two cabins. Claire was mute with excitement and wonder. Khalid offered us drinks – I had a rather large whisky – showed us how everything worked and, before leaving, invited us to dine with him at eight. The moment he left, the girls exploded.

'Where are we going?' 'Could you just—' 'What happened? I mean how did you—'

I told them all that I could with Claire present. In time, all information would be hers. She was entirely fascinated by the escape:

'Did the policeman say anything when you threw the blanket over him?' 'Do you think he hurt himself when he fell down?' 'Did he blow his whistle?' 'Did he have a truncheon?' 'Did the ambulance men try to catch you?'

Of course, since I was running like hell, I didn't know the answer to a single one of her questions. I was at pains to convey to her that what I did in escaping was wrong, not fun, not a great adventure; that no one should break the law. As I had watched her mind develop in the time I'd known her, I could see that so many of her thought processes were from me, and I so hoped that the 'Wild Hal' chromosome was not present to waste chunks of her life as it had done mine. Though of course, I now had Francesca and Claire. I wouldn't have them if my decisions had been different. Oh hell, there's no understanding any of it. The only logical proposition is chaos theory.

'Hal?' from Francesca, 'where the hell are we going?' Before I could respond, she said it again, 'Hal? Where?'

Claire was looking at me, her mouth open. My brain simply stopped. I suppose I was too tired – and now probably too old – to be able to save every point.

'Mummy, why did you call him Hal?'

'What? Did I, darling? Sorry, John. I was thinking about Hal a moment ago. I'm tired. Sorry.'

'That's all right.'

After an hour of so of chat, Claire fell into an exhausted sleep on a sofa and Francesca and I rose to go up on deck. As we went through the door, Claire's voice – 'Hal?'

'Yes?' I turned. It was an ace. Claire was looking at me, her eyebrows furrowed.

'Are you Hal?'

I looked at Francesca, who was of no help.

'Are you my father?' Another ace.

'Yes.' Claire was still serving – now to Francesca.

'Why did you tell me he was dead?'

'Because I thought he was.'

'Why did you tell Mummy you were dead?' Thank God, one I could return.

'I was dead. How could I tell her I was dead?'

Claire laughed, 'Oh, yes, sorry. I mean . . . '

We sat, one on either side of her and told her the whole story – minus the Cadell bits. Claire and I compared the elements of shock we had received from each other. My being informed, unwittingly, by her, that she was my child and she, by her own sleuthing, revealing me to be her father.

She stood up and moving to her cabin, said, 'I'm just going to sit on my own for a little while. I have rather a lot to think about.' Brave.

'Claire?' I said.

'Yes?'

'I love you more than life.'

She looked at me. 'I love you too,' and she was through the door. And her soppy old da put his arms around her ma, the other love of his life, and silently blubbed.

Eyes dried and noses blown, Francesca and I went up on deck. We were headed down the Channel. We would round the

Bay of Biscay past Marseilles, then follow the course I took all those years ago on the *San Vittore del' Lazio*. Down the Suez Canal, though not this time to Africa but through the Gulf of Aden to the Sultanate of Oman. We were now well into the Channel and beyond the median line. I was free. Having been captive for months, guarded and observed every moment, it was taking time for me to realise my liberty, to know that a small pleasure wouldn't be curtailed out of spite or stupidity, and that I was delivered from the nightly discords of rage and weeping, the incessant slamming of doors and persistent turning of locks.

Francesca was huddled into me against the wind. 'So, Hal, my Hal, how the hell did you do it? You arranged this from prison?'

'No, it was a gift. You remember me telling you about Cadell's junior, a man called Humphries?'

'Who turned out to be a queen?'

'Yes, and lucky for us all that he was. He turned up at Belmarsh one day and offered me his plan. He had sensed that Khalid would be happy to show his gratitude to me for mending rather than murdering him and guessed that he'd also be delighted to stick one to the Brits, so he made contact and put it to him. Khalid instantly agreed to supply the car, the ship and a villa in Oman. We can remain there for as long as we need. I have a job teaching surgery and the position of Unofficial Surgeon Royal.'

'Well fuck me with a bargepole.'

'Does it have to be a bargepole?'

'No. Actually, I'd rather it wasn't. But talking of which, do you now have to do something for Humphries?'

'I already have.'

'What?'

'You know what they say, "A little head never hurt." '

'Oh, you complete bugger—'

'No, just head.'

She laughed. 'God, a few weeks in jail and you've turned. So what *does* he want?'

'Nothing. I asked him that. He said, "I'm sick of it all." He said that none of the global stuff worked. That in fact it makes things worse. He also thinks that there's trouble ahead. Not tomorrow, but sometime.'

'What kind of trouble?'

'Religious, he reckons. He thinks there's going to be a Muslim equivalent of the Spanish Inquisition. Just distant rumbling at the moment, but . . . Who knows? Anyway, I asked him if he was helping me just because he was disenchanted. He said that his mother had just died after years of suffering motor neurone disease and he now wanted to do only things that he liked. Then he said. "I've always liked you Hal. That's all I can say. You know?" Then he said, "There's no one I can do anything for, but you. So . . ." '

Francesca smiled and shook her head sadly. 'He was in love with you.'

'I don't know.'

'I do. He was. That's really touching. Poor man. What if Cadell found out what he'd done? What would happen?'

'I shudder to think. But you know? I don't think Humphries cares.'

'Poor man. Poor bloody man.'

I nodded. 'I know. He does know where we are though, so I told him we'd be happy for him to visit any time.'

'Good. That's good. Do you think he'll come?'

'I think he might.'

She smiled and hugged me. After a moment, 'What do you want Hal? Do you want to stay in Oman?'

'We don't know what its like. Claire has to have school, and friends.'

'Where else can we go?'

She was worried, justifiably. So was I. Francesca and I could survive almost anywhere, but Claire couldn't, and she had to come first. 'Something'll become clear when we've had time to recover and do some thinking.'

'What about the house, Hal? Do you just lose it?'

'Actually no. It's not mine.'

'What?'

'It's yours. It's in your name. In a trust. So was the previous one. When I died it'd have gone to you.'

'I don't know what to say.'

'You'll think of something eventually.'

We'd been standing at the bow but facing east, backs to the wind. Now we turned.

'Oh, my God!' we chorused.

Ahead of us, a huge red sun was settling into the ocean. I felt a touch on my arm. 'Hello.' It was Claire.

'Hello sweetheart,' I said. 'Are you all right?'

'Yes, I think I'm very happy.'

Could one ask for more? We put her between us to keep her warm. I couldn't be sure exactly where we were but we must have been almost south of Cornwall. A picture in my mind of Parker, Lotte and Milla on the clifftop in the setting sun, young and joyful, declaring their love.

Claire asked, 'Where is it we're going? Amen?'

'Oman.'

'Oh man!' she said. 'Is it nice there?'

'Yes, it's pretty nice. You'll like the desert.'

'Then where will we go after that?'

'The exotic markets of Zanzibar, the darkest jungles of Africa, then Greenland, to visit the polar bears.'

'Oh *God*, Hal,' Francesca laughed, somewhat ruefully, 'when will this ever end with you?'

'When I die.'

'Oh bugger. You're not going to do that again, are you?'